Catherine Storr

The Complete
Polly and the Wolf

Illustrated by Marjorie Ann Watts
and Jill Bennett

THE NEW YORK REVIEW CHILDREN'S COLLECTION
New York

THIS IS A NEW YORK REVIEW BOOK
PUBLISHED BY THE NEW YORK REVIEW OF BOOKS
435 Hudson Street, New York, NY 10014
www.nyrb.com

Library of Congress Cataloging-in-Publication Data
Names: Storr, Catherine, author. | Watts, Marjorie-Ann, illustrator. | Bennett,
  Jill, 1934– illustrator.
Title: The complete Polly and the Wolf / by Catherine Storr ; illustrated by
  Marjorie Ann Watts and Jill Bennett.
Description: New York : New York Review Books, [2016] | Series: New York
  Review Books Children's Collection | Summary: "A series of adventures in
  which the clever, independent, and unstoppable Polly fools the persistent,
  hungry young Wolf time and again"— Provided by publisher.
Identifiers: LCCN 2016016264 (print) | LCCN 2016026163 (ebook) | ISBN
  9781681370019 (hardback) | ISBN 9781681370040 (ebook)
Subjects: | CYAC: Wolves—Fiction. | Deception—Fiction. | BISAC: JUVENILE
  FICTION / Animals / Wolves & Coyotes. | JUVENILE FICTION / Girls &
  Women. | JUVENILE FICTION / Humorous Stories.
Classification: LCC PZ7.S8857 Com 2016 (print) | LCC PZ7.S8857 (ebook) |
  DDC [Fic]—dc23
LC record available at https://lccn.loc.gov/2016016264

Cover design by Louise Fili, Ltd.
Cover illustration © 2015 by Lesley Barnes

ISBN 978-1-68137-001-9
Available as an electronic book; ISBN 978-1-68137-004-0

Printed in the United States of America on acid-free paper.
10 9 8 7 6 5 4 3 2 1

Contents

Clever Polly and the Stupid Wolf

Illustrated by Marjorie Ann Watts

I.

The First Story

THIS BOOK has twelve stories about Polly and how she always managed to escape from the wolf by being cleverer than he was—which wasn't very difficult because he was generally not at all clever. In fact he was rather stupid.

The very first story of all, which tells about how Polly met the wolf for the first time, has really been told already, in a book called *Clever Polly*. But because it's very annoying not to know how things started and how the people you are reading about met each other in the beginning, I'm going to put it in here. So really this book has thirteen stories about Polly and the wolf and that is all the stories there are at present about them.

This first story is a very small story because Polly was very small when it happened, so the story was just big enough to match her. And here it is.

2.

Clever Polly

ONE DAY Polly was alone downstairs. Camilla was using the Hoover upstairs, so when the front doorbell rang, Polly went to open the door. There was a great black wolf! He put his foot inside the door and said:

"Now I'm going to eat you up!"

"Oh no, please," said Polly. "I don't want to be eaten up."

"Oh, yes," said the wolf, "I am going to eat you. But first tell me, what is that delicious smell?"

"Come down to the kitchen," said Polly, "and I will show you."

She led the wolf down to the kitchen. There on the table was a delicious-looking pie.

"Have a slice?" said Polly. The wolf's mouth watered, and he said, "Yes, please!" Polly cut him a big piece. When he had eaten it, the wolf asked for another, and then for another.

"Now," said Polly, after the third helping, "what about me?"

"Sorry," said the wolf, "I'm too full of pie. I'll come back another day to deal with you."

A week later Polly was alone again, and again the bell rang. Polly ran to open the door. There was the wolf again.

"This time I'm really going to eat you up, Polly," said the wolf.

"All right," said Polly, "but first, just smell."

The wolf took a long breath. "Delicious!" he said. "What is it?"

"Come down and see," said Polly.

In the kitchen was a large chocolate cake.

"Have a slice?" said Polly.

"Yes," said the wolf greedily. He ate six big slices.

"Now, what about me?" said Polly.

"Sorry," said the wolf, "I just haven't got room. I'll come back." He slunk out of the back door.

A week later the doorbell rang again. Polly opened the door, and there was the wolf.

"Now this time you shan't escape me!" he snarled. "Get ready to be eaten up now!"

"Just smell all round first," said Polly gently.

"Marvellous!" admitted the wolf. "What is it?"

"Toffee," said Polly calmly. "But come on, eat me up."

"Couldn't I have a tiny bit of toffee first?" asked the wolf. "It's my favourite food."

"Come down and see," said Polly.

The wolf followed her downstairs. The toffee bubbled and sizzled on the stove. "I must have a taste," said the wolf.

"It's hot," said Polly.

The wolf took the spoon out of the saucepan and put it in his mouth:

OW! HOWL! OW!

It was so hot it burnt the skin off his mouth and tongue and he couldn't spit it out, it was too sticky. In terror, the wolf ran out of the house and NEVER CAME BACK!

3.

Clever Polly and the Stupid Wolf

DID I SAY that the wolf never came back? I'm wrong, he did
come back a year or two later. This time Polly was sitting at
the window of the drawing-room and she saw the wolf open
the garden gate and glance anxiously around. He looked up
and saw Polly.

"Good morning, Polly," said the wolf.

"Good morning, Wolf," said Polly. "What have you come
here for?"

"I have come to eat you up," replied the wolf. "And this
time I'm going to get you."

Polly smiled. She knew that last time she had been cleverer
than the wolf and she was not really frightened.

"I'm not going to eat you up this morning," said the wolf.
"I'm going to come back in the middle of the night and climb
in at your bedroom window and gobble you up. By the way,"
said the wolf, "which is your bedroom window?"

"That one," said Polly, pointing upwards. "Right at the top
of the house. You'll find it rather difficult, won't you, to get
right up there?"

Then the wolf smiled. "I'm cleverer than you think," he said. "I thought it would probably mean climbing and I have come prepared."

Polly saw him go to a flower bed and make a little hole in the earth. Into the hole he dropped something, she couldn't see what, and covered it carefully up again.

"Wolf," said Polly, "what were you doing then?"

"Oh," said the wolf, "this is my great cleverness. I have planted a pip of a grape. This pip will grow into a vine and the vine will climb up the house and I shall climb up the vine. I shall pop in through your bedroom window and then, Polly, I shall get you at last."

Polly laughed. "Poor Wolf," she said. "Do you know how long it will take for that pip to grow into a vine?"

"No," said the wolf. "Two or three days? I'm very hungry."

"Perhaps," said Polly, "in a week or two a little shoot might poke its way above the ground, but it would be months before the vine could start climbing and years and years before it could reach my bedroom window."

"Oh bother!" said the wolf. "I can't wait years and years and years to reach your bedroom window. I shall have to have another idea even better than this one. Goodbye, Polly, for the present," and he trotted off.

About a week later Polly was sitting at the drawing-room window again. She was sewing and did not notice the wolf come into the garden until she heard a sort of scrambling noise outside. Then she looked out of the window and saw the wolf very busy planting something in the earth again.

"Good morning, Wolf," said Polly. "What are you planting this time?"

"This time," said the wolf, "I've had a really good idea. I'm planting something which will grow up to your window in a moment."

"Oh," said Polly, interested. "What is that?"

"I have planted the rung of a ladder," said the wolf. "By tomorrow morning there'll be a long ladder stretching right up to your bedroom window. I specially chose a rung from the longest ladder I could see. A steeplejack was on the other end of it climbing a church steeple. He will be surprised when he comes down and finds the bottom rung of his ladder has gone. But in a very short time I shall be climbing in at your bedroom window, little Polly, and that will be the end of you."

Polly laughed. "Oh, poor Wolf, didn't you know that ladders don't grow from rungs or from anything else? They have to be made by men, and however many rungs you plant in this garden, even of steeplejacks' ladders, they won't grow into anything you could climb up. Go away, Wolf, and have a better idea, if you can."

The wolf looked very sad. He tucked his tail between his legs and trotted off along the road.

A week later Polly, who now knew what to expect, was sitting at the drawing-room window looking up and down the road.

"What are you waiting for?" asked her mother.

"I'm waiting for that stupid wolf," said Polly. "He's sure to come today. I wonder what silly idea he'll have got into his black head now?"

Presently the gate squeaked and the wolf came in carrying something very carefully in his mouth. He put it down on the grass and started to dig a deep hole.

Polly watched him drop the thing he had been carrying into the hole, cover it over with earth again, and stand back with a pleased expression.

"Wolf," called Polly, "what have you planted this time?"

"This time," replied the wolf, "you aren't going to escape. Have you read 'Jack and the Beanstalk,' Polly?"

"Well, I haven't exactly read it," said Polly, "but I know the story very well indeed."

"This time," said the wolf, "I've planted a bean. Now we know from the story of Jack that beans grow up to the sky in no time at all, and perhaps I shall be in your bedroom before it's light tomorrow morning, crunching up the last of your little bones."

"A bean!" said Polly, very much interested. "Where did it come from?"

"I shelled it out of its pod," said the wolf proudly.

"And the pod?" Polly asked. "Where did that come from?"

"I bought it in the vegetable shop," said the wolf, "with my own money," he added. "I bought half a pound, and it cost me a whole sixpence, but I shan't have wasted it because it will bring me a nice, juicy little girl to eat."

"You bought it?" said Polly. "Yourself, with your own money?"

"All by myself," said the wolf grandly.

"No one gave it to you?" Polly insisted.

"No one," said the wolf. He looked very proud.

"You didn't exchange it for anything?" Polly asked again.

"No," said the wolf. He was puzzled.

"Oh, poor Wolf," said Polly pityingly. "You haven't read 'Jack and the Beanstalk' at all. Don't you know that it's only a *magic* bean that grows up to the sky in a night, and you can't buy magic beans. You have to be given them by an old man in exchange for a cow or something like that. It's no good buying beans, that won't get you anywhere."

Two large tears dropped from the wolf's eyes.

"But I haven't *got* a cow," he cried.

"If you had you wouldn't need to eat me," Polly pointed out. "You could eat the cow. It's no good, Wolf, you aren't going to get me this time. Come back in a month or two, and we'll have a bean-feast off the plant you've just planted."

"I hate beans," the wolf sighed, "and I've got nearly a whole half-pound of them at home." He turned to go. "But don't be too cock-a-hoop, Miss Polly, for I'll get you yet!"

But clever Polly knew he never would.

4.

Little Polly Riding Hood

ONCE EVERY two weeks Polly went over to the other side of the town to see her grandmother. Sometimes she took a small present, and sometimes she came back with a small present for herself. Sometimes all the rest of the family went too, and sometimes Polly went alone.

One day, when she was going by herself, she had hardly got down the front doorsteps when she saw the wolf.

"Good afternoon, Polly," said the wolf. "Where are you going to, may I ask?"

"Certainly," said Polly. "I'm going to see my grandma."

"I thought so!" said the wolf, looking very much pleased. "I've been reading about a little girl who went to visit her grandmother and it's a very good story."

"Little Red Riding Hood?" suggested Polly.

"That's it!" cried the wolf. "I read it out loud to myself as a bedtime story. I did enjoy it. The wolf eats up the grand-mother *and* Little Red Riding Hood. It's almost the only story where a wolf really gets anything to eat," he added sadly.

"But in my book he doesn't get Red Riding Hood," said Polly. "Her father comes in just in time to save her."

"Oh, he doesn't in my book!" said the wolf. "I expect mine is the true story, and yours is just invented. Anyway, it seems a good idea."

"What is a good idea?" asked Polly.

"To catch little girls on their way to their grandmothers' cottages," said the wolf. "Now where had I got to?"

"I don't know what you mean," said Polly.

"Well, I'd said, 'Where are you going to?'" said the wolf. "Oh yes. Now I must say, 'Where does she live?' Where does your grandmother live, Polly Riding Hood?"

"Over the other side of the town," answered Polly.

The wolf frowned.

"It ought to be 'Through the wood,'" he said. "But perhaps town will do. How do you get there, Polly Riding Hood?"

"First I take a train and then I take a bus," said Polly.

The wolf stamped his foot.

"No, no, no!" he shouted. "That's all wrong. You can't say that. You've got to say, 'By that path winding through the trees,' or something like that. You can't go by trains and buses and things. It isn't fair."

"Well, I could say that," said Polly, "but it wouldn't be true. I do have to go by bus and train to see my grandma, so what's the good of saying I don't?"

"But then it won't work," said the wolf impatiently. "How can I get there first and gobble her up and get all dressed up to trick you into believing I am her if we've got a great train journey to do? And anyhow I haven't any money on me, so I can't even take a ticket. You just can't say that."

"All right, I won't say it," said Polly agreeably. "But it's true all the same. Now just excuse me, Wolf, I've got to get down to the station because I am going to visit my grandma even if you aren't."

The wolf slunk along behind Polly, growling to himself. He stood just behind her at the booking-office and heard her ask for her ticket, but he could not go any further. Polly got into a train and was carried away, and the wolf went sadly home.

But just two weeks later the wolf was waiting outside Polly's house again. This time he had plenty of change in his pocket. He even had a book tucked under his front leg to read in the train.

He partly hid himself behind a corner of brick wall and watched to see Polly come out on her way to her grandmother's house.

But Polly did not come out alone, as she had before. This time the whole family appeared, Polly's father and mother too. They got into the car, which was waiting in the road, and Polly's father started the engine.

The wolf ran along behind his brick wall as fast as he could, and was just in time to get out into the road ahead of the car, and to stand waving his paws as if he wanted a lift as the car came up.

Polly's father slowed down, and Polly's mother put her head out of the window.

"Where do you want to go?" she asked.

"I want to go to Polly's grandmother's house," the wolf answered. His eyes glistened as he looked at the family of plump little girls in the back of the car.

"That's where we are going," said her mother, surprised. "Do you know her then?"

"Oh no," said the wolf. "But you see, I want to get there very quickly and eat her up and then I can put on her clothes and wait for Polly, and eat her up too."

"Good heavens!" said Polly's father. "What a horrible idea! We certainly shan't give you a lift if that is what you are planning to do."

Polly's mother screwed up the window again and Polly's father drove quickly on. The wolf was left standing miserably in the road.

"Bother!" he said to himself angrily. "It's gone wrong again. I can't think why it can't be the same as the Little Red Riding Hood story. It's all these buses and cars and trains that make it go wrong."

But the wolf was determined to get Polly, and when she was due to visit her grandmother again, a fortnight later, he went down and took a ticket for the station he had heard Polly ask for. When he got out of the train, he climbed on a bus, and soon he was walking down the road where Polly's grandmother lived.

"Aha!" he said to himself, "this time I shall get them both. First the grandma, then Polly."

He unlatched the gate into the garden, and strolled up the path to Polly's grandmother's front door. He rapped sharply with the knocker.

"Who's there?" called a voice from inside the house.

The wolf was very much pleased. This was going just as it had in the story. This time there would be no mistakes.

"Little Polly Riding Hood," he said in a squeaky voice. "Come to see her dear grandmother, with a little present of butter and eggs and—er—cake!"

There was a long pause. Then the voice said doubtfully, "*Who* did you say it was?"

"Little Polly Riding Hood," said the wolf in a great hurry, quite forgetting to disguise his voice this time. "Come to eat up her dear grandmother with butter and eggs!"

There was an even longer pause. Then Polly's grandmother

put her head out of a window and looked down at the wolf.

"I beg your pardon?" she said.

"I am Polly," said the wolf firmly.

"Oh," said Polly's grandma. She appeared to be thinking hard. "Good afternoon, Polly. Do you know if anyone else happens to be coming to see me today? A wolf, for instance?"

"No. Yes," said the wolf in great confusion. "I met a Polly as I was coming here—I mean, I, Polly, met a wolf on my way here, but she can't have got here yet because I started specially early."

"That's very queer," said the grandma. "Are you quite sure you are Polly?"

"Quite sure," said the wolf.

"Well, then, I don't know who it is who is here already," said Polly's grandma. "She said she was Polly. But if you are Polly then I think this other person must be a wolf."

"No, no, I am Polly," said the wolf. "And, anyhow, you ought not to say all that. You ought to say, 'Lift the latch and come in.'"

"I don't think I'll do that," said Polly's grandma. "Because I don't want my nice little Polly eaten up by a wolf, and if you come in now the wolf who is here already might eat you up."

Another head looked out of another window. It was Polly's.

"Bad luck, Wolf," she said. "You didn't know that I was coming to lunch and tea today instead of just tea as I generally do—so I got here first. And as you are Polly, as you've just said, I must be the wolf, and you'd better run away quickly before I gobble you up, hadn't you?"

"Bother, bother, bother and *bother!*" said the wolf. "It hasn't worked out right this time either. And I did just what it said in the book. Why can't I ever get you, Polly, when that other wolf managed to get his little girl?"

"Because this isn't a fairy story," said Polly, "and I'm not Little Red Riding Hood. I am Polly and I can always escape from you, Wolf, however much you try to catch me."

"Clever Polly," said Polly's grandma. And the wolf went growling away.

5.

The Visible Wolf

POLLY was walking down the High Street one morning, when on the opposite side of the road she saw the wolf behaving in a very peculiar manner. Sometimes he put out his tongue at passers-by, sometimes he did a few dance steps in the gutter. Several times he seemed to be aiming a blow at someone's head. A few people were turning round to stare at him, but on the whole most of them were too polite to appear to take any notice.

Polly was not afraid of the wolf when there were plenty of other people about, so she crossed the road and came up to where he was standing, making faces at a baby in a perambulator.

"Wolf," she said, "you're behaving disgracefully. What on earth do you think you're doing?"

The wolf jumped about four inches in the air as Polly spoke and even after he had come down to earth again he couldn't stop shaking.

"You frightened me," he said plaintively, his teeth chattering

so that Polly could hear them. "I didn't expect you to speak to me. How do you know I am here?"

"Don't be silly," Polly said impatiently. "Of course I know you're here. I can see you, for one thing."

"You can *see* me?" the wolf said, apparently very much surprised.

"Of course I can. And from what I can see you are behaving very badly. I've never seen such an exhibition."

"But you can't see me," the wolf protested.

"I certainly can."

"But I'm invisible."

Polly was, in her turn, so much surprised that she couldn't speak for a moment. When she could, she asked, "You're *what?*"

"I'm invisible. You can't see me. No one can!"

"Tell me, Wolf," Polly asked kindly, "do you feel quite well? Have you got a headache? The sun has been rather hot this morning."

"It's not the sun. I'm invisible, I tell you. I don't know how you come to be able to see me, if you really can, but I'm invisible to everyone else."

"How do you know?" Polly asked.

"Well for one thing, she told me I would be."

"Who did?"

"The witch I bought the spell from, of course. It was very expensive, but I thought it would be worthwhile. Because now I'm invisible I can come when you aren't suspecting anything and catch you and eat you without any of this arguing. It's always argue argue with you," the wolf went on sadly. "As soon as I've got it all nice and clear in my head about when I'm going to eat you, you have to start talking and then I get muddled. Somehow you always seem to get me so that I don't know if I'm coming or going, if I'm full or I'm empty. And it always ends the same way," he finished disconsolately. "And that's with you going off scot free and me going off still hungry."

"So you went to a witch and she made you invisible," Polly prompted him. "She can't be much good at her job," she added.

"She didn't make me invisible there and then. She told me what to do to get invisible."

"What?"

"Well, I had to go out when the moon was full—that was the day before yesterday—and pick birch bark and mix it with—here!" said the wolf suddenly. "I'm not going to tell you this spell for nothing. I had to pay for it and if you want it you'll have to pay too."

"I don't want it," said Polly. "Thank you. It obviously isn't any good."

"Who said so?" said the wolf indignantly.

"I do. It's supposed to make you invisible, isn't it? Well,

you're as visible as anything. Anyone can see you. You're as thick and as black and as solid as ever you were."

"I'm not," cried the wolf. "I know I'm not. I've been doing all sorts of things to test it out and I'm sure I'm invisible. No one has taken any notice of me at all; and they would have if they'd seen me."

"What have you done? I saw you sticking your tongue out and dancing and making silly faces, but what else have you done?"

"You know how I always walk on my hind legs when I'm with people so as to look like them?" the wolf began. "Well, I walked all the way up from the butcher's to here on four legs and no one so much as turned to look at me."

"There's no reason why they should," Polly said. "They probably thought you were an outsize dog."

The wolf snorted angrily but he went on:

"I made a horrible face at a baby in a pram and it didn't take any notice at all."

"I saw you doing that," Polly agreed. "If I'd been the baby I'd have made some horrible faces back. But babies get so used to people making faces at them, they don't even look any longer. Go on."

"You see that drinking-trough for horses over there? I got into that and had a bath with a piece of soap I happened to have on me. I washed all over, right in front of everyone, and no one blinked an eyelid."

"They probably agreed that you needed that bath, and in that case they'd be too polite to stare. Is that all you did, Wolf?"

The wolf looked rather sheepish.

"It did seem as if I must be invisible by then," he said. "And I wanted to do something people couldn't help being surprised by if they could see it." He stopped.

"What did you do?" Polly asked encouragingly.

"Of course I know it's childish," the wolf said. "It's not a thing I do in the ordinary way."

"No?"

"Well, I haven't for years. It was just a test, you understand?"

"I expect I will when you tell me what it was."

"I wanted to be quite out of the ordinary."

"I daresay it was all most peculiar. But do let me into the secret."

"I just ran up and down the street a little."

"Is that all?" Polly asked, disappointed.

"Well, I believe I said 'All change,' once or twice."

"All change what?"

"And I had a whistle. Occasionally I used it."

"I see. You ran, you whistled, and you said 'All change.'"

"In between whiles I may have said 'Chuff.'"

"Just 'Chuff'?"

"No, I believe I said 'Chuff-Chuff.' More lifelike, you know. The sound an engine makes when getting up steam."

"Oh, playing trains!" Polly exclaimed. "Did you say anything else?"

"There's a peculiar noise the carriages make going over the rails. It sounds more like 'Duppidy-dee' than anything else."

"So sometimes you said 'Duppidy-dee'?"

"And then 'Duppidy-dur. Duppidy-dee, duppidy-dur, duppidy-dee, duppidy-dur.' Remarkable imitation, isn't it?"

"Remarkable," agreed Polly. "You ran, you all changed, you whistled, you chuffed, you duppidy-deed, duppidy-durred. Anything else?"

"I did have a small green flag to wave."

"Is that all?"

"Somehow or other, in the past, I seem to have acquired a porter's cap," said the wolf carefully.

"So you wore that?"

"And my sheriff's badge of course. It all adds to the effect."

"And where was this remarkable performance, Wolf?" asked Polly.

"Here," said the wolf simply. "In the High Street."

"And no one so much as looked at you?"

"Well of course there was a certain amount of sound effect," the wolf admitted. "And as I was invisible, no doubt some people were surprised to hear the—er—impressions of a train without there being anything to see."

"So some notice was taken?"

"People looked in my direction, yes, but seeing nothing they were rather at a loss to explain what they heard. Their expressions of amazement were quite amusing."

"Oh, my poor Wolf," Polly exclaimed. "You have made a fool of yourself. Of course they could see you—"

"They could not," interrupted the wolf. "I was invisible."

"Wolf," said Polly seriously, "if you are invisible, can *anyone* see you?"

"Of course not."

"Not even you yourself?"

"Naturally I couldn't."

"Wolf," said Polly gently. "Just look down at the ground where your invisible feet are."

The wolf looked down.

"Someone has left two very dirty paw marks there," he said severely.

"They are your own paws, Wolf."

"And those black things above—are they—?"

"They are your legs."

The wolf stretched out first one paw and then the other and looked at them carefully. He turned round and scrutinized his tail. Then he squinted down and saw the end of his nose.

"Am I all visible, Polly?" he asked in a very small voice.

"All of you, Wolf."

"Every single bit of me?"

"Everything, Wolf."

"Do you mean they all saw me being a train? Did they see me shunting? Did they know it was me saying 'Chuff-chuff'?"

"And 'Duppidy-dee, duppidy-dur,' Wolf."

"I'll never be able to hold up my head here again," said the wolf miserably. "Making a public spectacle of myself in the street. I'll never be able to look a baby in the face from now on. It's all your fault, Polly. I'd never have tried to become invisible if I hadn't wanted to get you to eat. Never mind. Visible or invisible, I'll get you yet and then I shall be revenged."

And Polly let him have the last word this time, as she felt rather sorry, as he went disconsolately away, for such a very, very visible wolf.

6.

Huff, Puff

IT WAS a very calm and sunny day when Polly heard a most peculiar noise outside the house. It sounded like a small storm. She could hear the wind whistling round the corner of the house, but when she looked up at the treetops they were not even swaying; everything was perfectly still.

The noise stopped. Polly went on reading.

Suddenly it began again. The clean washing hung out at the back of the house blew about violently for a short time, but the treetops and clouds took no notice. It was very odd.

Again the noise stopped as suddenly as it had begun.

Polly went to the sitting-room window which looked out in front of the house, but she could see nothing. She went to the kitchen at the back of the house and looked out.

She saw the wolf. He was leaning against the garden wall and fanning himself with a large leaf off a plane tree. He looked hot and exhausted. As Polly looked, he stopped fanning, threw away the leaf, and began some extraordinary contortions.

First he bent himself double and straightened up again.

Then he made one or two huge bites at nothing and appeared
to swallow some large mouthfuls of air. Then he threw back
his head and snorted loudly. Finally he bent double again and
started to breathe in. As he breathed in he stood up and
swelled out. He swelled and he swelled till from being a thin
black wolf he became quite a fat black wolf, and his chest was
as round as a barrel.

Then he blew.

"So that was the extraordinary noise," Polly said to herself.
She opened the kitchen window and leant out. The curtains
blew about behind her in the wolf-made wind.

"What are you doing, Wolf?" she called out to him, as his
breath gave out and the noise got less.

"Practising," the wolf said airily. "Just practising."

"What for?"

"Blowing your house down, of course."

"Blowing down this house?" Polly asked. "This house? But
you couldn't. It's much too solid."

"It looks solid I admit," the wolf said. "But I know that's all
sham. And if I go on practising I'll get plenty of push in my
blow and then one day—Heigh presto! (that's what they always say in books)," he added, "—over it will topple and I
shall eat you up."

"But this is a brick house," Polly objected.

"Well, I know it looks like brick, but it can't really be brick.
It's mud really, isn't it now?"

"You're thinking of the Three Little Pigs," said Polly. "They
built their houses of mud and sticks, the first two did, didn't
they?"

"Well, yes I am," the wolf admitted. "But there's only one
of you so I thought you'd probably build three houses. One of
mud, and the next of sticks, and then a brick one."

"This is the brick one," said Polly firmly.

"Did you build the others first?" asked the wolf.

"No, I didn't. And I didn't build this one either. I just came to live in it."

"You're sure it's not mud underneath that sort of brick pattern?" asked the wolf anxiously. "Because when I was huffing and puffing just now, it seemed to me to give a sort of wobble. As if it might fall down some time if I blew hard enough."

Polly felt a little frightened, but she was fairly sure the wolf couldn't blow down a brick house, so she said, "Try again and let me see."

The wolf doubled himself up, filled himself out and then blew with all his might. The blades of grass and the rose bushes and the clean washing waved madly in the wind, but the house never stirred at all.

"No," said Polly, very much relieved. "You aren't blowing down this house. It really is brick and I don't see why you should expect to be able to blow down a brick house. Even the wolf in the three little pigs' story couldn't do that. He had to climb down the chimney."

"I thought if I practised long enough I might be able to," the wolf said. "After all, that incident with the pigs was a long time ago. We've probably learnt a lot about blowing since then. The wonders of Science, you know, and that sort of thing. Besides I had a book."

From the grass beside him he picked up a small paper-covered volume and showed it to Polly. It was called *How to Become an Athlete*.

"An Ath what?" Polly asked, leaning even further out of the window.

"Good at games, that means," the wolf explained. "Wait a minute, there's a bit here..." He shuffled through the pages. "Ah, yes, here we are. *Deep breathing. By constant practise of the following exercises, considerable respiratory power may be attained.*"

"What sort of power?"

"You can blow very hard. I've been doing the exercises for nearly a week and I can blow much harder than before."

"But not hard enough to blow this house down," Polly said.

"Don't you think, with some more practice—?" the wolf said hopefully.

"No," said Polly. "I don't."

The wolf looked crestfallen for a moment, but then he cheered up again.

"Never mind," he said quite gaily. "If I can't blow it down with my breathing exercises I'll blow it down another way."

"How?" asked Polly.

For answer the wolf dived behind some bushes and pulled out a large shabby suitcase. From inside the suitcase he produced a pair of bellows.

"Look," he said proudly. "This will do the trick. These bellows—wait a minute."

He searched about in the suitcase and brought out a dirty piece of paper, which he unfolded and read.

"*These bellows are guaranteed to produce a wind equal to a gale of forty miles an hour if used properly.* Guaranteed, you see, Polly," said the wolf, looking at her to see if she was impressed.

"But only if you use them properly," Polly pointed out. "Anyhow, how much is a gale of forty miles an hour?"

"A great lot," the wolf assured her. "A terribly strong wind. You could hardly stand up in it. In fact I shouldn't think you could stand up in it. And now," he added, twirling the bellows round and then pointing them at Polly, "I am going to blow the house down."

"Wait a minute," said Polly, rather alarmed. "I don't want the house to fall down on my head."

She left the window and sat down on the floor under the kitchen table.

"Now I'm ready," she called out. "All right, Wolf."

She heard the wolf spit on his paws before he picked up the bellows.

"I'll Huff," he announced loudly and dramatically, "and I'll Puff and I'll Blow your house down."

There was a feeble little hiss of air, just the kind of noise a dying balloon makes. Then there was a silence.

"Perhaps you didn't use them properly," Polly called out.

"I only know one way to use bellows," the wolf said, very puzzled. "Perhaps I didn't open them far enough."

There was a cracking, tearing sound and Polly, as she came out from under the table, saw the wolf throw a pair of broken bellows over the garden wall.

"Guaranteed," he muttered crossly to himself. "I'll show them. I could make a better gale of forty miles an hour by blowing myself, with my head tied up in a bag. Bellows indeed."

"Then you won't be able to blow the house down," Polly said comfortably, seating herself on the window seat again.

"Oh, yes I shall," said the wolf, fumbling in his suitcase again. "I've got a thing here—it works by gunpowder, so it's awfully powerful. It'll blow the house down as soon as look at you."

From the suitcase he produced something the size and shape of a small vegetable marrow, in a paper bag slightly too small for it.

"What is it?" Polly asked, very much interested.

"A bomb," the wolf said casually. "Just a small one, but it's supposed to be able to blow up a small village or a large factory, so I should think it would about finish your little house, wouldn't you?"

He felt inside the paper bag and pulled out a sheet of closely printed pink paper.

"Instructions," he read out. "How to work the Wonder Bomb, and Guarantee for satisfactory results."

"Guarantee," he snarled suddenly. He screwed the paper up and threw it over the wall.

"Now then," he said. He held the paper bag upside down and shook it. "Won't come out," he said, puzzled.

"Oh, be careful," Polly implored him. "If you let that bomb drop it may go off and blow us all up."

"I've got to get it out of the bag first," the wolf complained. "I can't see how it works until I get it out."

He continued to shake the bag vigorously. Suddenly the paper tore, and the wolf just managed to catch the bomb as it fell.

"Now," he said, smelling it doubtfully all round. "Somewhere there must be something you have to do to get it to go off. The man in the shop did show me but I can't quite remember. A pin you pull out, I think, or push in, or something like that."

"Oh, do be careful," Polly said anxiously. She was terribly frightened, but it didn't seem much use to go and hide anywhere if the whole house was going to be blown up at any moment.

"Instructions," the wolf said suddenly. "There should be some instructions."

He looked inside the torn paper bag. Then he looked in his suitcase. Then he looked at Polly. A moment later he was bounding over the garden wall in the direction in which he had thrown the crumpled ball of pink paper.

"Ow," Polly heard from the other side of the wall. "Ow. Wow! Ugh! Bother these nettles! Wow!"

The wolf climbed back into the garden. He sat down on the grass and licked his paws. He had no piece of pink paper.

"You grow a lot of nettles outside your garden," he said crossly. "And I can't find the instructions anywhere. I shall have to guess."

He smelt the bomb again.

"There's a bit sticking out just here. Supposing I push it in?"

Polly summoned all her courage.

"All right," she said, as calmly as she could. "But you know the danger?"

"What?"

"If it makes the bomb go off at once—"

"It will blow your house up," interrupted the wolf triumphantly.

"Yes, but it will blow us up too."

"Us?"

"Me and you. There won't be much of me left for you to eat and there won't be any of you left to be interested in eating me."

The wolf considered this.

"You mean I might be killed?"

"If that bomb goes off while you're holding it in your hand I shouldn't think there's the slightest chance of you living any longer than me."

"Oh," said the wolf. He held out the bomb to Polly. "Here," he said generously, "you have it. I'll give it to you as a present. I haven't got the brains for this sort of thing. You have a look at it and see how it works. You're clever, you know, Polly. You'll soon find out how to make it go off."

Polly shook her head.

"No, thank you, Wolf. I don't want to be blown up any more than you do."

"Really?"

"Really. You put it back in your suitcase and take it somewhere a long way away from here and get rid of it."

"Shall I give it to a little boy who is interested in how things work?" the wolf suggested, cautiously wrapping the bomb up in the remains of the too-small paper bag.

"No, that would be very dangerous."

"Yes, I see what you mean," the wolf agreed. "He might make it go off before I was out of reach."

"I think you'd better take it back to the shop you got it from," Polly said. "Now be careful, Wolf. Don't sling that suitcase about too much, unless you want to get blown to pieces."

"I'll be very careful," the wolf promised. He picked up the suitcase, holding the handle delicately in his teeth, and trotted towards the garden gate. Just before he went out he put the suitcase gently down and tilting back his head took a long look at the roof of Polly's house.

"Polly," he called out. "Polly! When were your chimneys last swept?"

Polly couldn't help laughing, but she answered very politely, "About six months ago, I think, Wolf. Why do you want to know?"

"Oh, no particular reason," said the wolf. "I'm just interested in chimneys, that's all."

"You must come and see ours sometime," Polly said kindly. "I'm afraid they're rather narrow and some of them are very twisty. And of course none of them are quite clean. Still, you could come and look from outside. Only you'll be careful of the boiling water, won't you? We always keep a pot of boiling water underneath the only big chimney, just in case anything we don't want comes down it."

"Thank you, Polly," said the wolf rather coldly. "Most interesting. Another day, perhaps. Just at the moment I am rather busy."

And picking up the suitcase handle in his mouth again, he went out of the garden gate and trotted, very slowly and carefully, down the road.

"I'm glad," thought Polly, "he didn't blow my house down. I only hope he won't go now and blow himself up."

7.

Monday's Child

POLLY was sitting in the garden making a daisy chain. She had grown her right thumb nail especially long on purpose to be able to do this, which meant that for the last two weeks she had said to her mother, "Please don't cut the nail on that thumb, I need it long." And her mother obligingly hadn't. Now it was beautifully long and only a little black. Polly slit up fat pink stalk after fat pink stalk. The daisy chain grew longer and longer.

As she worked, Polly talked to herself. It was half talking, half singing.

"Monday's child is fair of face," she said. "Tuesday's child is full of grace. Wednesday's child—"

"Is good to fry," interrupted the wolf. He was looking hungrily over the garden wall.

"That's not right," said Polly indignantly. "It's Wednesday's child is full of woe, Thursday's child has far to go. There's nothing about frying in it at all."

"There's nothing about woe, or going far in the poem I know," protested the wolf. "What would be the use of that?"

"The use?" Polly repeated. "It isn't meant to be useful, exactly. It's just to tell you what children are like when they're born on which days."

"Which days?" the wolf asked, puzzled.

"Well, any day, then."

"But which is a Which Day?"

"Oh dear," said Polly. "Perhaps I didn't explain very well. Look, Wolf! If you're born on a Monday you'll be fair of face, because that is what the poem says. And if you're born on a Tuesday you'll be full of grace. See?"

"I'd rather be full of food," the wolf murmured, "I don't think grace sounds very satisfying."

"And if you're born on a Wednesday you'll be full of woe," said Polly, taking no notice of the interruption.

"Worse than grace," the wolf said. "But my poem's quite different. My poem says that Wednesday's child is good to fry. That's much more useful than knowing that it's full of woe. What good does it do anyone to know that? My poem is a useful poem."

"Is it all about frying?" Polly asked.

The wolf thought for a moment.

"No," he said presently. "None of the rest of it is about frying. But it's good. It tells you the sort of thing you want to know. Useful information."

"Is it all about cooking?" Polly asked severely.

"Well, yes, most of it. But it's about children too," the wolf said eagerly.

"That's disgusting," said Polly.

"It isn't, it's most interesting. And instructive. For instance, I can probably guess what day of the week you were born on, Polly."

"What day?"

The wolf looked at Polly carefully. Then he looked up at

the sky and seemed to be repeating something silently to himself.

"Either a Monday or a Friday," he said at last.

"It was a Monday," Polly admitted. "But you could have guessed that from my poem."

"What does yours say?" the wolf asked.

"Monday's child is fair of face, Tuesday's child is full of grace, and I am fair, in the hair anyway," Polly said.

"Go on. Say the whole poem."

Polly said:

> "Monday's child is fair of face,
> Tuesday's child is full of grace,
> Wednesday's child is full of woe,
> Thursday's child has far to go.
> Friday's child is loving and giving,
> Saturday's child works hard for its living.
> But the child that is born on the Sabbath day
> Is bonny and blithe and good and gay."

"Pooh," cried the wolf. "What a namby-pamby poem! There isn't a single thing I'd want to know about a child in the whole thing. And, anyway, most of it you could see with half an eye directly you met the child."

"You couldn't see that it had far to go," Polly argued.

"No," the wolf agreed. "That's the best line certainly. But it depends how far it had to go, doesn't it? I mean if it had gone a long, long way from home you might be able just to snap it up without any fuss. But then it might be tough from taking so much exercise. Not really much help."

"It isn't meant to be much help in the way you mean," said Polly.

"And it isn't what I call a poem, either," the wolf added.

"Why?" asked Polly. "It rhymes, doesn't it?"

"Oh, rhymes," said the wolf scornfully. "Yes, if that's all you want. It jingles along if that satisfies you. No, I meant it doesn't make you go all funny inside like real poetry does. It doesn't bring tears to your eyes and make you feel you understand life for the first time, like proper poetry."

"Is the poem you know proper poetry?" Polly asked suspiciously.

"Certainly it is," the wolf said indignantly. "I'll say it to you and then you'll see.

> "Monday's child is fairly tough,
> Tuesday's child is tender enough,
> Wednesday's child is good to fry,
> Thursday's child is best in pie.
> Friday's child makes good meat roll,
> Saturday's child is casserole.
> But the child that is born on the Sabbath day,
> Is delicious when eaten in any way.

"Now you can't hear that without having some pretty terrific feelings, can you?"

The wolf clasped his paws over his stomach and looked longingly at Polly.

"It gives me a queer tingling feeling in my inside," he went on. "Like a sort of beautiful, hungry pain. As if I could eat a whole lot of meals put together and not be uncomfortable afterwards. Now I'm sure your poem doesn't make you feel like that?"

"No, it doesn't," Polly admitted.

"Does it make you feel anything?" the wolf persisted.

"No-o-o. But I like it. I shall have my children born on Sunday and then they'll be like what the poem says."

"That would be nice," agreed the wolf. "But one very seldom gets a Sunday child. I believe they're delicious, even if you eat them without cooking at all!"

"I didn't mean to eat," said Polly coldly. "I meant children of my own. Bonny and blithe and all that."

"What day did you say you were born on?" the wolf enquired. "Did you say Monday or Friday?"

"Monday," said Polly. "Fair of face."

"Fairly tough," said the wolf thoughtfully to himself. "Still, there's always steaming," he added. "Or stewing in a very slow oven. Worth trying, I think."

He made a bound over the garden wall on to the lawn. But Polly had been too quick for him. She had run into the house and shut the door behind her before the wolf had recovered his balance from landing on the grass.

"Ah well," sighed the wolf, picking himself up. "These literary discussions! Very often don't get one anywhere. A tough proposition, this Polly. I'll concentrate on something tenderer and easier to get for today."

And picking up the daisy chain, which Polly had left behind her, he wound it round his ears and trotted peacefully out of the garden and away down the road.

8.

The Wolf in the Zoo

ONE DAY Polly was taken to the Zoo by her mother. She went to see the bears and the sea lions, the penguins and the camels. She saw the fishes and the monkeys and snakes and mice and tortoises. Then she saw the lions and the tigers, and she enjoyed it all very much.

"Now," she said to her mother, "I want to see the foxes and the wolves. I want to see if my Wolf is like other wolves."

Her mother showed her where the cages were, but she said she would sit down and wait for Polly, as she didn't want to go and see the foxes and wolves herself.

So Polly went over to the cages and looked at the foxes, who seemed to be asleep, and at a hyena who was awake, but cross. Then she moved on to look at the wolves.

In one cage there was a smallish wolf eating alone. In the next cage was a very large black wolf, exactly like the wolf Polly knew so well.

"But he is just like my Wolf!" Polly said in surprise.

"Hullo, Polly," said the wolf in a gloomy voice. "So you've found me at last, have you? How did you know I was here?"

"I didn't," said Polly. "It's an accident. I came over just to look at wolves. I never expected to find you here, Wolf."

"Oh, dear, oh dear," said the wolf. Two large tears dropped from his eyes on to the straw on the floor of his cage, and Polly felt rather sorry for him.

"How did you get here?" she asked. "Did you come here on purpose, or did they catch you like the other animals?"

"The Other Animals!" the wolf said bitterly. His voice was choked with tears. "Would I have come on purpose, do you think? Is it likely that I'd choose to live in this beastly little cage, where I've hardly room to turn round, when I might be outside, walking about the country and chasing you?"

"Well, I didn't know," said Polly reasonably. "You might have got tired of trying to catch little girls to eat and want to be fed for a change. They do feed you properly here, I suppose?" she added kindly.

"Bones," said the wolf, sounding very sad. "That's all. Bones. Hardly any meat on them. And raw. Think of that,

Polly, for a wolf like me, that's been used to well-cooked meals, daintily served. Just bones, thrown into the cage, without so much as a sprig of parsley or a morsel of gravy with them. I could cry when I think of the meals you've cooked me, Polly, and I look at what they give you here—"

"But how did you get here, then?" Polly asked, still curious to know.

"There was an advertisement," the wolf said. He sounded a little embarrassed. " 'Wolf wanted,' the advertisement said. 'Large black wolf welcomed by fellows of Zoo something Society. Every care taken and suitable diet provided.' So I came. It was the word Welcome that attracted me," he added sadly.

"But didn't they?" Polly asked.

"If you call this Welcoming," the wolf said, looking round his cage. "I'd hardly set foot in the grounds and spoken to one of the keepers before there was such a hullabaloo as you've never heard. Men fetching chains, and others fetching ropes, and a sort of cage thing on wheels and me pushed into it as if I was a wild animal. Welcome, indeed!" The wolf snorted. Then a tear dropped from his eye again. "If you knew how I want to be wanted," he almost wept. "I thought someone really wanted me at last. I'm large, aren't I? and black? and I'm a wolf. But if I'd been a—snake they couldn't have been less welcoming."

"Oh, poor Wolf," said Polly. She was very nearly crying herself at this pathetic story.

"And if they think raw bones are a suitable diet, they've a lot to learn about wolves," the wolf finished with a snarl.

"I've got a treacle toffee in my pocket," Polly suggested. "Would you like it?" She unwrapped it and pushed it through the bars. The wolf snapped it up so eagerly that Polly's fingers nearly disappeared too.

"No feeding the animals, Miss," a friendly keeper advised her as he passed by. "It's not safe. Treacherous beasts, wolves."

The wolf gave a growl that made the keeper more certain than ever that he was a bad-tempered, untrustworthy animal. But Polly understood that he was angry because he was miserable, and though she didn't put her hand up to the bars again, she didn't move away.

"Wolf," she whispered, when the keeper had passed out of sight. "Perhaps I could bring you something nice to eat. What would you like best in the world?"

The wolf's eyes glistened and his tongue began to drip.

"A nice fresh juicy little girl," he began. "Fried, I think, with mushrooms and onions and perhaps a little—"

"Don't be silly," Polly said sharply. "You might know I'm not going to feed you on little girls. Can't you think of something possible? Apple pie, for instance, or a Cornish pasty or fudge perhaps. Do you like fudge, Wolf?"

"I'd rather have a little g—" began the wolf, but as he caught Polly's eye he altered what he had been going to say.

"I'd like almost anything," he admitted. "Except bones. We get plenty of them here. But what I'd like best, Polly, if you could manage it, would be for you to get me out of here."

"Out of your cage?" asked Polly. She looked doubtfully at the strong bars and the lock on the door. "I don't think I could. I'm not strong enough to break the cage open, and I haven't got a key."

"Of course you couldn't break it open," said the wolf scornfully. "I can't myself, so naturally you wouldn't be able to. But you could get a key, couldn't you? After all, you are Clever Polly, you know, so you ought to be able to think of some way of getting me out."

"I'll think about it," said Polly. She felt very sorry for the wolf, and yet rather suspicious of him. "But how would I know you wouldn't start trying to eat me up again directly you came out?" she asked.

"You wouldn't know," the wolf replied candidly. "I might or I might not. It would depend on how I felt. You'd just have to wait and see."

"Then I shan't do anything about you," Polly said indignantly. "I don't know why you should expect me to help you out just to eat me up."

"Of course I should always be grateful," the wolf assured her. "I might be so grateful that I wouldn't want to eat you up. Please help me, Polly. If you don't nobody will, and I shall stay here for ever and ever until I am dead."

Polly's kind heart was touched and she promised that she would at any rate bring the wolf something to eat and if possible think of a way of getting him out.

The next day Polly was very busy baking at home and the day after she brought the wolf a large Cornish pasty full of

meat and onion and carrot and potato, nicely cooked and brown and shiny on top. She pushed it through the bars when the keeper was looking another way and watched anxiously to see what the wolf would do.

"Ah!" said the wolf. "Pasty. My favourite first course."

He swallowed the whole pasty at one gulp. Polly turned a little pale.

"Wolf," she said, after a moment or two. "Do you feel quite all right inside?"

"Better, thank you," said the wolf. "Pasty's a nice change after bones. Why?"

"I didn't mean you to eat it all in one gulp like that," Polly began.

"That's all right, thank you, Polly. You don't know what good digestions we wolves have got. Why, I could swallow down a tender little morsel like you in about three bites, I should say, and as for a little pasty like that one—why it just slipped down without any trouble."

"Yes, I daresay," said Polly sadly. "But it wasn't just an ordinary pasty."

"Excellent," declared the wolf, licking his chops.

"Yes, but it hadn't just got meat and vegetables in it."

"A touch of garlic? A suspicion of chives?"

"It had a key in it."

There was a short silence.

"Would the key have fitted the lock on the door of my cage?" the wolf asked casually.

"I think so," Polly said. "I went specially to a shop and asked for the sort of key that opens cage doors, and it looked all right."

"So I should have been able to let myself out?"

"That was what I thought," said Polly.

There was another short silence.

"Wow," said the wolf suddenly. "I've got an awful pain. In my—down here. It's hard and knobbly. It's got a sort of handle to it. I'll have to go and lie down."

"I'll try again," Polly said as she prepared to leave. "But next time, Wolf, do for goodness' sake look before you eat whatever I send."

Two days later a long thin parcel arrived for the wolf. He tore off the wrappings and inside was a stick of brightly coloured rock, with BRIGHTON written across the end. A suspicious keeper, who had come to make sure the parcel contained nothing contraband, smiled sourly as he saw the wolf studying the rock and left him with it, removing the brown paper and string.

"It's a message," said the wolf to himself. "I shall eat it very slowly and read the message as I go, and then I shall know how to escape."

He licked busily at one end of the stick. After some time he had got rid of about an inch of rock, but the writing still said BRIGHTON.

"Funny," thought the wolf. "I'd better get through some more."

But after half an hour's serious work, when there was only a piece the size of a sixpence left, the rock still said nothing but BRIGHTON.

"Maddening," the wolf snarled, crunching the remaining bit up angrily. "I was as careful as careful and it didn't make sense at all. At any rate, Polly can't tell me there was a key inside that miserable piece of rock, and if there was supposed to be a message all I can say is her spelling is very queer."

When Polly arrived a week or so later she looked sadly at the wolf through the bars.

"So it went wrong again," she said. "I'd expected you to be out by now."

"How could I get out?" the wolf asked crossly.

"I thought you'd have filed your way out. That stick of rock I sent you—"

"It didn't make sense," the wolf grumbled. "BRIGHTON it said all the way through and what use that is to me, I don't know."

"Oh, you stupid animal," Polly said, exasperated. "The stick of rock was just to throw the keepers off the scent. The important thing in the parcel was the file—that was why it had to be a long thin parcel. I meant you to file through the bars to get out. I suppose you threw the file away with the paper and string."

The wolf didn't answer this, but Polly could see that she had guessed right.

"Here's your last chance," she said, handing over a small bottle with a closely printed label. "And this time don't make any stupid mistakes, Wolf. I've got to go now, Mother's waiting for me."

When she had gone the wolf considered the bottle carefully. It had no wrappings, so there couldn't be a file concealed there. He drew out the cork with his teeth and smelt the contents. Then he stuck a long red tongue down the neck of the bottle and tasted.

"Ah," he said to himself. "Very good. Sweet and strong. I'll drink it slowly, very slowly, and then I shall find out if it's got anything hidden inside."

He drank.

When Polly saw the wolf walking quietly on a road near her home a few days later, she called out to him.

"Wolf! So you got out all right this time?"

"Yes," said the wolf rather shortly, "I got out."

"You put the sleeping medicine in the keeper's cup of tea, I suppose?"

"No," said the wolf uneasily. "I didn't exactly do that."

"In his pot of beer?"

"No."

"In his tonic water?"

"As a matter of fact," the wolf admitted, "I didn't give it to him at all. I drank it myself."

"But it said on the label—"

"I didn't read the label. Last time you sent me something with writing on it it wasn't any help, so this time I just drank the medicine to make sure there wasn't anything hidden in the bottle."

"And what happened?"

"Well, I went to sleep. And I slept and I slept and I slept. So they thought I was dead and after about a day they didn't

bother to lock the cage door. So I woke up and I came out. I just walked out, and here I am. And now," said the wolf suddenly, "I'm very, very hungry and I'm going to eat you up."

But Polly ran. She ran like the wind, and the wolf, who was stiff from being cramped in his cage at the Zoo, and sleepy from his sleeping medicine, couldn't run quickly enough to catch her. So Polly got safely home and the wolf didn't get her that time.

9.

Polly Goes for a Walk

THE WOLF, you know, was determined to get Polly somehow, by hook or by crook, and Polly was determined not to be got.

One day, when Polly was out for a walk, she saw the wolf following her carefully and looking at every step she took.

"Now what's the matter, Wolf?" Polly asked impatiently. "Why do you keep looking at my feet? I haven't got a hole in my socks, have I?"

"I'm not looking at your socks," the wolf replied. "I'm looking to see if you walk on one of the cracks in the pavement. As long as you walk on the squares you are safe, but if you walk on a line you are mine, and I shall gobble you up."

Polly took great care how she trod. She always planted her feet firmly in the middle of each square. But presently she came to a little knot of people all standing outside the post-office, and as she passed, one of them moved quickly and knocked her off her balance. One of her feet went on to a line.

48

"Got you!" growled the wolf, coming up quickly behind her, ready to snatch her away.

"Wait a moment, Wolf," said Polly. "There must be two sides to an agreement. It's all very well for you to say I belong to you if I step on a line, but what do I get when you step on a line?"

"What do you mean?" asked the wolf uncomfortably. He hadn't been looking at all where he put his paws.

"Well," said Polly, "if you are to get me to eat if I step on a line, I think it's only fair that I should be allowed to eat you if you step on a line. Don't you?"

"Well yes, I suppose it is," the wolf agreed reluctantly.

"Well, I've stepped on one line, because I was pushed, but you've stepped on lots, and all because you were careless. Now how about it, Wolf?"

"We'd better begin again," the wolf said in a great hurry. "We'll begin from when I say *now*. One, two, three...*now!*"

But Polly was careful not to step on any more lines that day, and she reached home safely.

The next day she went for a walk on the heath and presently she noticed the wolf following her again.

"Touch wood," the wolf called to her, between the trees. "As long as you are touching wood you are safe, but directly you aren't, I can come and get you."

Polly ran from tree to tree; several times the wolf made a dash at her when she was between two trees, but she managed just to reach the next tree in time. All the time she was getting nearer and nearer home, but at last she had got to the edge of the heath and to reach home she had to go down the road where there weren't any trees at all.

"Aha!" said the wolf, "now I've got you. You can't touch wood down that road so you will be mine."

Polly looked up and down the road, but she couldn't see anyone in sight. It seemed as if she might have to stand holding on to the last tree for ever.

Then she had a good idea. She broke a twig off the side of the tree and held it out to the wolf.

"Animal, Vegetable or Mineral?" she asked him.

"Vegetable, of course," said the wolf, puzzled.

"What's it made of?" asked clever Polly.

"Wood," said the wolf, "silly!"

"Well, I'm touching it," said Polly, leaving the tree and walking slowly down the road towards her home, with the twig held firmly in her hand.

For several days Polly was very cautious about going out by herself, but at last her mother asked her to go and post a letter in the pillar box at the end of the road, and Polly set off with the letter in her hand.

She was just reaching up to put the letter through the slot, when the wolf jumped out from behind the pillar box.

"Aha!" he said, his red tongue hanging out. "Now I've really got you."

Polly thought quickly. She had almost let the letter fall through the slot, but now she held on to it.

"Listen, Wolf," she said. "Why do you think I came out here?"

"For a little breath of fresh air?" suggested the wolf.

"No. Try again," said Polly.

"To meet me," said the wolf, his eyes glistening.

"Not even that," said Polly. "Look at my hand. Not that one, silly, the one at the letter box."

"To post a letter!" said the wolf in surprise.

"Right at last," said Polly. "And do you know who this letter is from and whom it's to? It's from my mother to the man who manages the Society for the Prevention of Cruelty to Children, and it's telling him to come and fetch you and take you away and put you in a cage and lock you up for ever and ever because you've eaten me up. You won't like that, will you, Wolf?"

"No," said the wolf, rather downcast. "I shan't like it at all."

Then he cheered up.

"But when I've eaten you up I'll eat up the letter too and then no one will ever know," he said.

"But the letter is almost posted," Polly said. "My hand is holding it inside the pillar box, and the moment you touch me I shall let go and it will be posted."

"Oh, please don't post it, Polly," the wolf begged. "Take it back and get your mother to alter it for me. Ask her to say that I've promised not to eat any other little girls, so I needn't be locked up for more than a week or so."

"But how can I take it back, or get her to alter it if you've already eaten me up?" asked Polly.

The wolf thought. Then he said sadly, "Perhaps I'd better not eat you this time, Polly, so that you can take the letter back and get it altered. But next time, Polly, you shan't get away so easily, so look out."

But clever Polly smiled to herself, as she posted her mother's letter to an aunt in the country in a different pillar box that afternoon. For she had beaten the wolf again.

10.

The Seventh Little Kid

POLLY was alone in the house, not for the first time, when the front doorbell rang. Being, after her earlier experiences, rather cautious, she did not open the door straight away, but lifted the letter-box lid and tried to peep through.

"Who is there?" she called out.

"Your mother, my dear," said a harsh and familiar voice. "Come back from shopping, with a present for you."

"You don't sound at all like my mother," Polly said suspiciously. She couldn't see much through the letter box, and what she could see didn't help. "Say that again."

"Your mother, my dear," said the voice again, "with something nice for you."

"Why?" asked Polly, interested in spite of herself.

"Why, what?" said the voice impatiently.

"Why with something nice for me. I mean, specially? It isn't my birthday."

"Oh bother," said the voice very cross and harsher than ever. "Why do you want to say all that? I don't know. Just to get you to open the door, of course."

"Oh, go away, Wolf," said Polly. "I know it's you. Your voice is all wrong for my mother. She's got a nice soft voice and you sound like a—well, like a wolf. Of course I shan't open the door, you'd only eat me up."

The wolf padded away down the front doorsteps without any difficulties. But a week or so later, when Polly was again alone in the house, the front doorbell rang again.

"Who is it, please?" called Polly through the letter box.

"Yourmothermydearcomebackfromshoppingwithsome-thingniceforeachofyou," said the wolf very quickly, in a high sweet voice quite unlike his own.

"Oh," said Polly. She knew quite well it wasn't her mother, who had in fact gone out to tea with a friend.

"It's early closing day," she said. "How did you manage to do any shopping?"

There was a silence. Then the wolf said, "I went some-where else where it wasn't early closing day."

"What have you brought for me?" Polly asked, laughing to herself.

"Don't ask silly questions," the wolf said angrily, but still in his false voice. "I told you it was something nice."

"Why don't you use your own front-door key and let yourself in?" Polly asked.

"I—I—I left it at home," said the wolf. "Don't keep on talking so much, I can't keep this plum stone in my mouth all the time without making my tongue sore."

"What is the plum stone doing in your mouth?" Polly asked with interest.

"Making my voice higher and sweeter of course. I should have thought you could hear that. Go on, Polly, you haven't asked to see my hand."

"Let me see your hand, Wolf?" said Polly obligingly. The wolf put up to the letter box a long black paw and at once started off down the front doorsteps.

"Hi!" said Polly. "Why are you going? Don't you want me to open the door any more?"

"Oh yes, I want you to," the wolf said, turning back. "But of course you won't this time. First you know me because of my voice, and the next time you know me because of my black hand, but the third time you let me in and I gobble you up. Haven't you read about the Seven Little Kids, Polly?"

"I think I have," Polly said. "It's about a wolf, isn't it?"

"Yes, and he eats them all up but one," said the wolf gloatingly. "Just think! Five little kids, all to himself! No one to share with! All for him!"

"Six," said Polly. "One away from seven leaves six, not five, Wolf."

"Better and better," sighed the wolf. "Anyway, I'll be back some time, Polly, in full disguise, and then it will all come right, you'll see."

When he had gone Polly found the fairytales book with the story of the wolf and the seven little kids in it, and read it carefully. It seemed that if a wolf ever did come into the house, the clock case was the only safe place to hide in.

But a day or two later, when Polly's mother really had gone shopping and really had also forgotten her keys, a voice called from outside the door, "Polly! I've forgotten my key, and I've got a very heavy basket. Come and open the door for me will you please!"

"Oh no!" said clever Polly, very much pleased with herself. "No you don't. I know who you are and I won't open the door on any account."

"Hurry up," urged the voice, "I'm nearly dropping a bag full of eggs and the basket handle is cutting my arm."

"Go away, Wolf," said Polly. "I'm busy and I don't want to play this morning."

"Polly!" said the voice angrily. "Open the door for goodness' sake or..."

There was a loud smashing noise. Polly ran upstairs and looked out of a window. On the doorstep stood her mother, looking very cross, and at her feet was the remains of a dozen large eggs.

Polly ran down again and let her in.

"I've got to go out again," her mother said, when she had unloaded her shopping basket. "I still haven't finished my shopping. And if I ask you to let me in again, don't keep me waiting so long," she added as she left.

So next time the front door bell rang, without waiting to ask any questions or even to look out, Polly ran to open the door. And in stepped the wolf, wearing two pairs of white gloves.

Polly did not stop to admire the gloves. She ran as quickly as she could into the sitting-room and climbed into the clock case.

The wolf came in a leisurely way after her, straight to the clock case, opened the little door and stood looking at Polly cowering inside.

"Come out," he said, in the high sweet voice. "Bother this plum stone!" He spat it out and added in his ordinary voice, "That's better. Come out."

Polly was frightened, but she was not going to give in so easily.

"Are you going to eat me up, Wolf?" she asked.

"I certainly am."

"Like the seventh little kid?"

"Just like the seventh little kid, only I shall enjoy you more because I haven't had six to eat already."

"Wolf," said Polly. "Did you read the rest of that story?"

"I read up to where he ate the six little kids," said the wolf. "I wasn't interested in what happened after that."

"So you don't know what happened to that wolf? And what will happen to you if you eat me?"

"No," the wolf said uneasily. "Must you tell me now? Make it short, I'm terribly hungry."

"I'll be as quick as I can," Polly promised. "But I think you ought to know what you're letting yourself in for. The mother goat knew, of course, what had happened to her kids, so she found the wolf when he was asleep and she cut him open with her big scissors and got the kids out of his stomach and sewed him up again with six big stones inside."

"Wow," the wolf exclaimed.

"Of course she gave him an anaesthetic?" he suggested a moment later. "Something so that he didn't feel anything?"

"I don't believe so," Polly answered.

"I wonder if the wound hurt afterwards," the wolf pondered.

"I expect it did like anything," Polly agreed.

"Has your mother any big scissors?" the wolf asked casually.

"Enormous ones. She uses them for cutting out our frocks generally."

"And needles and thread?"

"Very big needles for sewing carpets and that tough thread —all hairy and hard."

"And I can't be sure never to go to sleep," the wolf said under his breath. "Well, goodbye, Polly," he went on aloud. "It's been so nice seeing you. Remember me to your mother. I'm afraid I can't stay till she gets back. And you can come out of that clock case," he called back as he reached the front door. It slammed behind him.

From the other side of it came the sound of someone licking the doorstep.

"Eggs," Polly heard the wolf say to himself. "Not very well cooked. Funny place to fry eggs, a doorstep. Still it's better than nothing. Thoughtful of them to have left them there, as I can't have Polly herself."

II.

In the Wolf's Kitchen

POLLY had been very careful for a long time not to give the wolf a chance of catching her. But perhaps she got a little careless, for one day she had hardly got outside the house before the wolf had caught her up in his mouth and run away with her. He took her into his house, locked the door behind them, and said:

"Now, Polly, I've really got you at last, and this time all your cleverness won't help you, for I am going to gobble you up."

"Oh very well," said Polly obligingly. She looked round. "Where is the kitchen?" she asked.

"The kitchen?" said the wolf.

"But of course, the kitchen," Polly said. "You are going to cook me, aren't you? Oh, Wolf," she said, as she looked at his surprised face, "you can't mean that you were going to eat me raw?"

"No, no, of course not," said the wolf, hastily. "I shouldn't think of it. Of course I'm going to cook you. The kitchen is here, along this passage. But I'm afraid it's rather dark and rather—well, not quite as clean as it might be."

60

"Never mind," said Polly, following him, "I daresay that won't bother me."

The kitchen was very dark and very dirty. The windows were covered with soot and cobwebs, the floor had not been swept for days, and all the cups and plates needed washing. It was a terrible sight.

"Oh, dear," said Polly, as she looked round. "You certainly need someone to do a little housework here, Wolf. Now let's think what we are going to eat for lunch today, and then while you go out and do the shopping, I'll see if I can make this look a little better."

"We needn't think about what we are going to eat," snarled the wolf, "because I am going to eat *you!*"

"Oh, Wolf," said Polly sadly, "how terribly impatient you are. Just feel my arm and see if I'm ready to be eaten yet." She stuck out her elbow.

The wolf felt Polly's elbow and shook his head.

"Bony," he said. "Very disappointing. And you always looked such a nice solid little girl."

"I'd make a much better meal for you if you fattened me up a bit first," Polly assured him.

"If you expect me to go out catching little boys and girls for you to get fat on, you're very much mistaken," the wolf said indignantly.

"No, no," said Polly, "I don't. All I suggest is that I should stay here for a little and try to get fat on my own cooking. Of course I should cook for you as well," she added. "And you know I cook quite nicely."

"I remember," said the wolf drily.

"Well then, won't you go out and get some carrots and potatoes, and some rashers of bacon, and perhaps tomatoes and mushrooms? And I'll make a stew for today," said Polly.

The wolf grumbled a little, but at last he went out with a large market basket, locking the front door behind him. While he was gone Polly scrubbed the kitchen table and the floor. She lit the fire, and swept the hearth, she washed all the dishes and polished the saucepans till they winked. The only thing she couldn't do was to get the windows quite clean, because as she was locked in she couldn't wash the outsides. When the wolf came back he found the kitchen still rather dark, but spotless and shining. Polly peeled the potatoes, while the wolf sliced up onions and carrots, and presently a pot was simmering over the fire, sending out the most delicious smells.

"Mm-mm-mm," said the wolf greedily a little later. "Very good, this stew. This ought to fatten you up, Polly. Have some more, and mop up your gravy with a big hunk of bread."

"I couldn't eat any more, thank you," said Polly politely. "But there is a little more for you, Wolf, if you can manage it."

The wolf held out his plate and gobbled up his third helping. It was too dark for him to see how very little Polly had really eaten, and he felt full and comfortable and certain that on this sort of food Polly would soon be plump enough to eat.

After the meal the wolf fell asleep and slept soundly till the next morning. Then he felt Polly's arm again to see if she was ready to be eaten yet.

"Still disgustingly bony," he said snappishly.

"Never mind," said Polly. "There's no hurry. Today, Wolf, we'll have cheese pudding and sultana roll. Here is a list of what you'll have to buy and while you are out, I'll go on cleaning the house."

"Are cheese pudding and sultana roll fattening?" asked the wolf suspiciously.

"Very," said Polly. "Why, my grandma never eats them because she is trying to get thinner, but people who want to get fat eat almost nothing but sultana roll."

So the wolf went out and did the shopping—but he remembered to lock the door behind him. And when he came back Polly made cheese pudding and sultana roll, and again at dinner Polly ate very little and the wolf ate a great deal, and went to sleep afterwards, and dreamt of Polly pudding and Polly roll, in happy, greedy dreams.

The next day the wolf felt Polly's arm and it was still very bony.

"Today," he said, "you had better cook something really solid. I can't wait much longer, and I don't believe you are getting fatter at all. I believe you cheated me when you said yesterday's meal was fattening."

"All right," said Polly. "We'll have toad-in-the-hole and pancakes."

"Pancakes!" said the wolf joyously. Then he added, in a suspicious voice, "I don't like toads. They don't taste at all nice."

"No, no," said Polly. "Not real toad. Sausages. In batter. Very good, and very filling."

So for lunch they had toad-in-the-hole and pancakes. Polly ate two mouthfuls of toad-in-the-hole, and one small pancake, but the wolf ate a meat tin full of toad, and eleven pancakes, thick with sugar. Afterwards he was too full to go up to bed, but slept in the kitchen, with his feet on the mantelpiece.

The next morning he was very cross. He felt Polly's elbow and growled at her.

"You're only skin and bone still," he said. "You're not worth the trouble I've been to to catch you. Why aren't you getting fat? I'm getting fatter since you've been here. Why aren't you?"

"I don't know," said Polly, pretending to look very sad. "I was much fatter than this at home."

"Are you cooking properly?" asked the wolf. "Just like your mother cooks?"

"I thought I was," said Polly. "But there must be something wrong about what I do. Perhaps I've left something out, or put in something wrong."

"Think," the wolf urged her. "Think hard. I can't wait much longer, and you don't seem to be getting any fatter."

Polly thought. Then she shook her head.

"It's no good," she said. "Whatever it is I can't think of it."

"Wouldn't your mother know?" asked the wolf.

"Now that's really a good idea," said Polly, "Clever Wolf to think of that. I'll go home and ask my mother what I've been doing wrong, and then when she has told me, I can cook so as to make me fat enough for you to eat."

"Go home quickly, then," said the wolf, unlocking the front door, "and ask your mother from me to tell you how to cook good fattening meals. Don't let her forget anything and don't you forget this time. Hurry up, Polly, I can't wait till you come back."

And Polly did hurry up, and perhaps the wolf is still waiting, for she ran home and never went back to the wolf's kitchen again.

12.

The Wolf in Disguise

"Now," SAID the wolf to himself one day just before Christmas, "I really must catch that Polly. I've tried This and I've tried That, and I've never managed to get her yet. What can I do to make sure of her this time, and get my Christmas dinner?"

He thought and thought and then he had a good idea.

"I know!" he exclaimed. "I'll disguise myself. Of course the trouble before has always been that Polly could see I was a wolf. Now I'll dress up as a human being and Polly won't have any idea that I am a wolf until I have gobbled her up."

So the next day the wolf disguised himself as a milkman and came round to Polly's house with a float full of milk bottles.

"Milk-oh!" he called out. But the door did not open.

"Milk-OH!" said the wolf louder.

"Just leave the bottles on the doorstep, please," said Polly's voice from the window.

"I don't know how much milk you want today," said the wolf. "You'd better come and tell me."

"Sorry, I can't," said Polly. "I'm on top of a ladder, hanging

up Christmas decorations, and I can't come down just now.
I've left a note saying how much milk I want in one of the
empty bottles."

Sure enough, there was the note. The wolf looked at it and
left two pints, as it said, and then went off, very cross. Being
a milkman was no good, he could see. Polly wouldn't open
the door just for a milkman.

A day or two later there was a knock on the door of Polly's
house, and there on the doorstep stood a large, dark butcher,
with a blue stripy apron and a wooden tray of meat over his
shoulder. He rang the bell.

A window over the front door was opened, and a head all
white with soap-suds looked out.

"Who is that?" asked Polly's voice. "I can't open my eyes or
the soap will get into them."

"It's the butcher," replied the wolf. "With a large juicy
piece of meat for you."

He had decided that Polly certainly wouldn't be able to resist a piece of meat.

"Thank you," said Polly. "I'll be down in a minute or two.
I've just got to finish having my hair washed and then I'll
come down and open the door."

The wolf was delighted. In a minute or two Polly would
open the door and he would really get her at last. He could
hardly wait. His mouth began to water as he thought about it,
and he felt terribly hungry.

"She is being a long time," he thought. "I'm getting hungrier and hungrier. I wonder how long hair-washing takes?"

He had put his meat tray down on the doorstep while he
waited, and now he looked longingly at the piece of meat on
the tray. It was juicy, and very tempting.

"She doesn't know how large it is," he said to himself. "She
would never miss one bite off it."

So he took one bite. It was delicious, but it made him hungrier still.

"I'm sure more than two minutes have gone," he thought. "I'll have to have another bite to keep myself going."

His second bite was larger than his first.

"Really, it isn't worth leaving just that little bit," he said, as he swallowed down the last bit of meat. "Polly will never know whether I've got the meat or not. I'll keep the tray up where she can't see it and she'll think the meat is still there."

He hoisted the tray on to his shoulder. Just at that moment Polly looked out of the window again.

"Sorry to be so long," she called out. "Mother would give me a second soaping. And please, Butcher, she says, is it frying steak or stewing steak?"

"Oh—both!" said the wolf quickly. "Either," he added.

"But where is it?" asked Polly. "Just now when I looked out I saw a great piece of meat on your tray, but now it isn't there!"

"Not there! Good heavens!" said the wolf. "Some great animal must have eaten it while I was looking the other way."

"Oh dear," said Polly, "so you haven't any meat for us, then?"

"No, I suppose I haven't," said the wolf sadly.

"Well, I shan't come to the door, then," said Polly, "and anyhow I've got to have my hair dried now. Next time you come you'd better make sure no one eats the meat before you deliver it to us, Butcher."

When he got home again the wolf thought and thought what he could take to the door of Polly's house that she wouldn't be able to resist and that he could.

Suddenly he knew. He would be a postman with a parcel. Polly couldn't possibly refuse to open the door to a postman with a parcel for her, and as long as the parcel did not contain meat, he himself would not be tempted.

So a few days later a Wolf postman rang the bell at Polly's door. In his hand he held a large brown paper parcel, addressed to Polly.

For a long time no one answered the door. Then the flap of the letter box lifted up from inside and Polly's voice said, "Who is it?"

"The postman," said the wolf, as carelessly as he could, "with a parcel for someone called Polly."

"Oh! Will you leave it on the doorstep, please," said Polly.

"No, I can't do that," said the wolf. "You must open the door and take it in. Post-office regulations."

"But I'm not allowed to open the door," said Polly. "My mother thinks that a wolf has been calling here lately, and she has told me not to open the door to anyone unless she is there too, and she's not here, so I can't."

"Oh, what a pity," said the wolf. "Then I shall have to take this lovely parcel away again."

"Won't you bring it another day?" asked Polly.

"No, there won't be time before Christmas," said the wolf, very much pleased with himself.

"Well, perhaps it isn't anything I want anyway," said Polly, comforting herself.

"Oh but it is," said the wolf quickly. "It's something very exciting, that you'd like very much."

"What is it?" asked Polly.

"I don't think I ought to tell you," said the wolf primly.

"How do you know what it is?" asked Polly. "If you're really a postman you ought not to know what's inside the parcels you carry."

"Oh—but it's—it's—a talking bird," said the wolf. "I heard it talking to itself inside the parcel."

"What did it say?" asked Polly.

"Oh—'tweet, tweet,' and things like that," replied the wolf.

"Oh, just bird talk. Then I don't think I want it," said Polly. She was beginning to be a little suspicious.

"Oh no," said the wolf hastily. "It can say words too. It says 'Mum' and 'Dad', and 'Pretty Polly'," he added.

"It sounds lovely," said Polly. "But can it talk to you? I only want a bird who can carry on a conversation."

"Oh yes, we had ever such a long talk coming up the hill," the wolf assured her.

"What did you talk about?" asked Polly.

"Well, the weather," said the wolf, "and how hungry it makes us. And about Christmas dinner. And—and—the weather—and being very hungry."

"What did the bird say it ate?" asked Polly.

The wolf was beginning to enjoy himself. Obviously Polly was interested now, and at any moment she would open the door to be given the parcel, and then he would be able to gobble her up.

"The bird said it ate gooseberries and chocolate creams," he said, inventing wildly. "So then I said I wouldn't like that at all. Not solid enough for me, I said. Give me a juicy little g–" he stopped himself just in time.

"A juicy little what?" asked Polly.

"A juicy little grilled steak," said the wolf hastily.

"And what did the bird say then?"

"He said, 'Well, that may be all very well for a wolf'–"

"Oho!" said Polly. "So that's what you are! Not a postman at all, nothing but a wolf. Now listen, Wolf. Go away, and take your parcel, which I don't want, because it isn't a bird in a cage or anything like it, and don't come back either in your own skin or dressed up as anyone else, because whatever you do, I shan't let you catch me, now or ever. Happy Christmas, Wolf." She shut the letter-box lid.

So the wolf did not get his Christmas dinner after all.

13.

A Short Story

OUTSIDE Polly's house the lawn was white with daisies in the spring, and one day Polly, looking out of the window, saw the wolf, sitting on the grass busily taking the petals one by one, off a daisy. He was muttering to himself.

Polly leaned a little further, and rather dangerously, out of the window to listen. He wasn't saying, "She loves me, she loves me not," as you or I might, but, "I get her, I don't get her, I get her, I don't get her."

"Bother," he ended suddenly, throwing away a stalk with no petals left on it. Obviously he had not got the answer he wanted. He picked another flower and started again.

"I get her," he announced loudly, looking up at the house triumphantly, as he came to the end of his daisy.

"Oh no you don't," said Polly. "I saw you take off two petals together and count them as one. Cheating, Wolf, that is, and very unfair."

"I didn't think anyone was looking," the wolf said. "You must have terribly good eyesight to be able to see from there."

"I have," said Polly. "But even if I hadn't you ought not to cheat. You don't deserve to get anyone or anything if you cheat because no one is looking."

"So you don't think I shall get you then?" the wolf asked, disappointed.

"Not on that daisy," Polly answered.

"On the others?" the wolf asked hopefully.

"If you do them all," Polly answered decidedly.

"Do you mean I've got to do the whole lot?" the wolf said in despair. He looked round the lawn. "Why, there are hundreds here," he protested. "It would take me years to take the petals off all of them."

"But you'll never know if you're going to get me or not unless you do," Polly insisted.

"But by the time I've finished these daisies there'll probably be some more coming up."

"It will keep you rather busy," Polly admitted. "But I expect you'll get through quite a lot if you stick to it. Besides you'll get quicker in time. Practice, you know," she said encouragingly.

"But my paws are so clumsy," the wolf protested. "It isn't as if I had neat little hands like you."

"You've quite nice paws, for a wolf," Polly said kindly.

"You wouldn't like to help me, I suppose?" the wolf asked hopefully.

"No thank you," said Polly. "I've got quite a lot of other things I want to do."

"If I get through all these daisies," said the wolf, "and it ends up that I'm going to get you at last, will you agree to come along quietly, without any fuss?"

Polly looked round the lawn. There were hundreds, probably thousands of daisies. But then the wolf might get really quick at taking the petals off. Or he might cheat.

"This isn't all the daisies in the world, Wolf," Polly pointed out.

"Oh but surely there are enough here?" the wolf almost wailed.

"Quite enough," Polly said. "But, of course, you'll never know if it's the truth until you've got to the last daisy. And of course I couldn't agree to be eaten quietly, without any fuss, if I didn't know it was the truth."

"You mean, I've got to unpick all the daisies there are, any-where, everywhere?" cried the wolf.

"And when you get to the very last, if it says you are going to get me, I'll come," said clever Polly. "You can start here," she added. "There are a nice lot here to begin with."

So the wolf spends his time picking daisies on Polly's lawn, and as there are plenty of daisies in the world, Polly thinks it will be a long time before he finds out whether or not he will ever get her. A Very Long Time.

Polly and the Wolf
Again

Illustrated by Marjorie Ann Watts

I.

The Clever Wolf and Poor
Stupid Little Polly (1)

THE WOLF sat at home in his kitchen, where he usually enjoyed himself so much; his elbows were on the table, and he was chewing, but there was no feeling of peace, of comfortable fullness, of not being likely to be hungry again for several hours, which was how the wolf liked to feel in his own house.

The table was covered with sheets of paper. Some of them had only a word or two written on them, some had a whole sentence. Most of them were blank.

Presently the wolf sighed, spat out the object he had been chewing—it was a pencil—and tried again. On a large, clean sheet of paper he wrote, laboriously:

"One day the Clever Wolf caught Polly and ate her all up!"

He stopped. He read what he had written. Then he read it again. He put the pencil back between his teeth and began to search among the sheets of paper for something. When he found it, he opened it flat on the table and leant over it, spelling out the longer words as he read. It was a book.

But reading did not seem much more satisfactory than writing. Every now and then the wolf snarled, and at last he

shut the book up with a snap and pushed it away from him; but as he did so, his eyes fell on the cover, and the name of the book, printed there in large black letters:

CLEVER POLLY AND THE STUPID WOLF

"It's so unfair!" he muttered angrily to himself. "Clever Polly, indeed! Just because she's managed to escape me for a time. And calling me stupid! Me! Why, I always used to win when we played Hide the Piglet as wolf cubs. 'Stupid Wolf!' I'll show them. I'll write a book full of stories which will show how clever I am—far cleverer than that silly little Polly. I'll start the story of my life now, and then everyone will be able to see that it's not me that is stupid."

He pulled another sheet of paper towards him.

"I was born," he began writing in his untidy sprawling hand, "in a large and comfortable hole, in the year—"

He stopped.

"Well, I know I'm about eleven," he said to himself. "So if I take eleven away from now, I shall know when I was born. Eleven away from...eleven away from...What am I taking eleven away from?"

"I'll do it with beans!" he thought, encouraging himself. "It's always easier with beans."

Leaving his pencil on the table, he got up and fetched a large canister of dried beans from a shelf over the stove. He shook a small shower out on the table; one or two fell on the floor.

"Nine, ten, eleven," counted the wolf. He tipped the spare beans back into the canister.

"But I'm taking eleven away from something," he remembered. He looked doubtfully into the tin and tipped it a little to see how full it was. The beans made an agreeable rattling sound as they slid about inside, and the wolf shook the canister gently several times to hear it again.

"There seem to be an awful lot of beans in there," he said aloud. "I wonder just what I've got to take eleven away from?"

He sat down to consider the point. Could it be eleven? He spread the eleven beans out on the table and looked at them. Then he took eleven beans off the table, counting them one by one.

"Eleven away leaves none. So eleven years ago was nothing. The year nothing. It seems a very long time ago."

The wolf was puzzled. It did certainly seem a very long time ago, but it still didn't sound quite right. He could not remember ever having seen a book which gave as a date the year nothing.

"It can't be right," he decided. "It must be eleven away from something else. I wonder what it is? Who could I ask to tell me?"

There was, of course, only one answer to this, and five

minutes later the wolf had walked down the path through the garden to Polly's front door and was ringing her bell.

"I'll talk to you from up here if you don't mind," said Polly's voice from the first-floor window. "Yes, Wolf, what can I do for you today?"

"You can tell me what I have to take eleven away from."

"Eleven? Why eleven?"

"Because that is how old I am."

"Why do you want to take how old you are away from anything?"

"Because I want to know what year it was."

"What year what was?"

"The year I was born in, of course. Silly!" said the wolf triumphantly. "I said it was Silly Polly and you are! What do I take it away from?"

"Nineteen fifty-seven."

"And what do I have to do with it?" the wolf asked, now thoroughly muddled.

"You take that away from it."

"What's That?"

"Eleven. Well, that's what you said," Polly answered, a little confused herself.

"Don't go away," pleaded the wolf. "Let me get it straight in my head. I take eleven away from nineteen and then from fifty-seven and then—"

"No, stupid. Not from nineteen, from nineteen hundred and fifty-seven; and then the answer is the year you were born in!"

"Nineteen hundred!" said the wolf, appalled.

"And fifty-seven."

"Nineteen hundred and fifty-seven. I don't think I've got enough beans," said the wolf gloomily.

"I don't see how beans come into it," Polly said. "It's years you're counting in, not beans."

"It's beans while I'm actually counting," the wolf said firmly. "And you're sure the answer is the year I was born?"

"Certain."

"Thank you. Good morning," the wolf called over his shoulder, as he trotted away down the garden path. He went home, sat down at his kitchen table and began to count out beans.

"A hundred and thirty-three, a hundred and thirty-four, a hundred and thirty-five...Bother."

The hundred and thirty-sixth bean was a very highly polished one. It slipped out of the wolf's paw, leapt nimbly into the air, fell on the floor, and rolled under the cooking stove.

"Bother, bother, BOTHER!" the wolf said out loud. He looked into the canister. There were only seven or eight beans left: he could not afford to lose one. He got down from his chair and lay flat on his front on the floor to look for the missing bean. It lay out of reach, right at the back of the cooker, against the wall, in company with a burnt chestnut and a very dirty toasting fork.

"My toasting fork!" the wolf exclaimed, delighted to see it again; it had been missing for several months. He retrieved the fork, dusted it with his tail, and used it to poke out the bean.

The wolf dusted the bean, said solemnly out loud, "One hundred and thirty-six," and put it on the table.

He gave a triumphant wave of his useful tail. Several beans were swept off the table and disappeared under various pieces of furniture.

"Oh—!" cried the wolf, enraged. He sat down at the table, staring angrily at the remaining beans. He tipped up the canister and added the rest of the beans to the pile he had already counted.

"A hundred and thirty-seven, a hundred and thirty-eight, a hundred and...What's the use when I want nineteen hundred and something? I'll never be able to count the whole lot!"

He absent-mindedly put the last bean in his mouth. It wasn't too bad. He ate another.

"Easier with a spoon," he murmured a minute or two later, and going to the dresser fetched a battered tablespoon. With its help he ate another two dozen beans fairly quickly.

"That's funny!" he thought after the second spoonful. "I believe I generally eat these cooked. Very absent-minded I seem to be getting."

He fetched a saucepan, filled it with water, and put it on the fire. When the water was boiling he tossed in the remaining beans, salt, pepper and herbs. He fried some rashers of bacon, an onion and a few mushrooms in a pan, and when everything was cooked he mixed it into a glorious mess together, added a tomato and, in a very few mouthfuls, swallowed the lot.

"Ah," he said, wiping his mouth on the back of his paw, "that's better. Now, let me see—What was I doing?"

He looked round the kitchen and his eye fell on the empty canister.

"Oh!" he said aloud. "Bother!"

"Never mind," he said. "They tasted much better than they counted. Besides it would have taken me ages to get up to nineteen hundred and fifty-seven. I'd never have had time to write anything. After all what does it matter what year it was I was born? I'm here now, that's the important thing."

He picked up the last sheet of paper he had written on and tore it across several times. Then, sitting down, he pulled another towards him and wrote in a bolder hand:

THE CLEVER WOLF AND POOR STUPID POLLY

"Fortunately," (the wolf wrote), "I was born."

2.

The Clever Wolf and Poor
Stupid Little Polly (2)

A FEW DAYS later Polly was looking longingly in at the window of her nearest bookshop, rehearsing to herself what she would buy if she had enough money, when she realized that someone large and dark was standing by her side. The wolf was gazing through the glass and was murmuring the titles aloud to himself.

"*Fairy Tales.* Hmm. *Well-Known Fairy Tales.* If they're well known already, who wants another book about them? *Grimm Fairy Tales*—that sounds more interesting. I like grim stories as long as they're really frightening and full of crunching bones and blood and things!"

"Don't be beastly, Wolf," Polly said, rather sharply.

The wolf jumped.

"You frightened me," he said reproachfully. "I didn't know you were there."

"I was here first," Polly reminded him.

"I daresay. I was looking at the books and I stopped noticing you. When I get my nose into a good book," the wolf went on dreamily, "I get carried away."

"Don't show off, Wolf," Polly said. "I know you can read, but I don't believe you ever get lost in a book unless it's a cookery book. When I was in your house there wasn't a book to be seen."

"I get them all out of the library," the wolf said hastily. "And anyhow now I'm not just reading, I'm writing a book."

"Oh, Wolf!" cried Polly, very much impressed. "How wonderful. What's it about?"

"Us," the wolf said. "Well, me really. Mostly me, but a little you. Only you don't last very long, of course."

"Why of course?"

"Because I eat you up. Very soon. Because in my book I am Clever and you are Stupid. It's quite different from that silly book that was written about us before."

"It must be."

"This," said the wolf, puffing out his chest, "is terrific. It's a Guide to Wolves on how to catch conceited little girls who pretend to be clever."

"I'd like to read it, please," Polly said.

"Well—" the wolf said, shifting uneasily from one leg to another. "It's not as easy as it sounds. Have you ever written a book, Polly?"

"No. I've written letters."

"So have I. Dozens. Hundreds. If I added up all the letters I'd written there'd be plenty of whole words among them, too. But still, have you ever tried to write a book?"

"I wrote the beginning of a story once," Polly said.

"Pooh!" cried the wolf, "the beginning! That's the easy part. Anyone can begin a story—you just say, 'Once upon a time there was a nice juicy little girl,' and there you are."

"Is it the ending you can't do?" Polly asked.

The wolf looked thoughtful. "Not exactly," he said, "I think it's the middle. I always seem to get to the end quicker than I meant to, and then the story seems too short. How long would you think a book ought to be, Polly?"

Polly thought hard. "About a hundred pages," she suggested.

"Oh NO!" the wolf said, horrified. "Not a hundred pages of writing. A short book, Polly."

"Oh, I see," Polly said. "Well—twenty pages?"

"That's an awful lot," the wolf said sadly.

"It couldn't be less than ten," Polly said, "or it wouldn't count as a book at all. Have you written any of it at all yet, Wolf?"

"Of course I have. Lots of it."

"I wish I could read it," Polly said.

"Well, I might have a copy on me. Wait a minute and let me look."

The wolf opened a dilapidated string bag and searched inside it among a sheaf of dog-eared sheets of paper. At last he extracted a small school exercise book with grey paper covers and handed it modestly to Polly.

On the outside front cover was printed:

STUDENTS' EXERCISE BOOK

Below this was a space for the name and class of the student. This was filled in: NAME—Wolf. CLASS—Upper.

Polly opened the book and looked inside.

"Once upon a time," she read, "there was a very clever Wolf. He knew a stupid girl called Polly. One day he ate her all up."

A line or two farther down the page, the author had tried again.

"Fortunately I was born. My mother and father were wolves, so naturally I was one too. I am clever, though some people call me stupid which I am not, only they are so stupid themselves they can't see I am the Clever one. One day I caught Polly and ate her up."

Over the page was a third attempt.

"It was a lovely day," the wolf had written, "and the Clever Wolf went out for a walk. Suddenly he saw poor stupid little Polly, so he jumped on her and ate . . ."

Here the masterpiece abruptly ended. The rest of the book was empty.

"What do you think of it?" the wolf asked eagerly.

"Well," Polly said kindly, "I think it's very good as far as you've got. But it's not very far, is it? I mean there's got to be a bit more than that to make a proper book, hasn't there?"

"You mean the stories aren't long enough?"

"No, I don't think they are. They seem somehow—well, like you said, they haven't any middles."

"I know," the wolf said in despair, "but what can I do about it? You see my wolf is so clever, he catches Polly at once and eats her up. There's none of this TALK that goes on in that other book," the wolf said scornfully. "Why, talk is all they ever do. Quite different from me. So when I'm writing about it they don't talk, they just do things, and what I do, in my book, is I eat you up."

"Yes, I see," Polly agreed. "Only it doesn't make such a good story."

"It's a wonderful story!"

"All right, it's a wonderful story—for you, at any rate. But it isn't long enough."

"It will be if I write some more of them."

"You can't."

"Yes I can, easily. I wrote those three without any difficulty—"

"But you can't put all those three into your book."

"Why not?"

"Oh, you Stupid Wolf!" Polly cried, exasperated. "How can you have three stories, one after another, about us, if you've eaten me up in the first one? Where am I supposed to come from in the second and the third, if I'm inside you before they ever begin?"

"Oh," the wolf said. "Funny, I never thought of that. And they were such good stories, too," he added sadly. "Never mind," he said suddenly, "I always said all this talk won't get us anywhere."

He looked hastily up and down the street. There was no one about. The wolf turned and pounced on Polly.

But it wasn't on Polly. She had opened the door of the bookshop and slipped inside. Just in time. Through the window, the infuriated wolf saw her speak to the proprietor, who went away to the back of the shop and came back with a heavy-looking volume.

With hardly a glance at the window, Polly propped the book up on a shelf so that the wolf could see its title as she began to read.

How to Deal, the title read, *with Dumb Animals*.

3.

Father Christmas

ONE DAY Polly was in the kitchen, washing currants and sultanas to put in a birthday cake, when the front door bell rang.

"Oh dear," said Polly's mother, "my hands are all floury. Be a kind girl, Polly, and go and open the door for me, will you?"

Polly was a kind girl, and she dried her hands and went to the front door. As she left the kitchen, her mother called after her. "But don't open the door if it's a wolf!"

This reminded Polly of some of her earlier adventures, and before she opened the door she said cautiously through the letter box, "Who are you?"

"A friend," said a familiar voice.

"Which one?" Polly asked. "Mary?"

"No, not Mary."

"Jennifer?"

"No, not Jennifer."

"Penelope?"

"No. At least I don't think so. No," said the wolf decidedly, "not Penelope."

"Well, I don't know who you are then," Polly said. "I can't guess. You tell me."

"Father Christmas."

"*Father Christmas?*" said Polly. She was so much surprised that she nearly opened the front door by mistake.

"Father Christmas," said the person on the doorstep. "With a sack full of toys. Now be a good little girl, Polly, and open the door and I'll give you a present out of my sack."

Polly didn't answer at once.

"Did you say Father Christmas?" she asked at last.

"Yes of course I did," said the wolf loudly. "Surely you've heard of Father Christmas before, haven't you? Comes to good children and gives them presents and all that. But not, of course, to naughty little girls who don't open doors when they're told to."

"Yes," Polly said.

"Well, then, what's wrong with that? You know all about Father Christmas and I'm pretending to be—I mean, here

he is. I don't see what's bothering you and making you so slow."

"I've heard of Father Christmas, of course," Polly agreed. "But not in the middle of the summer."

"Middle of the what?" the wolf shouted through the door.

"Middle of the summer."

There was a short silence.

"How do you know it's the summer?" the wolf asked argumentatively.

"We're making Mother's birthday cake."

"Well? I don't see what that has to do with it."

"Mother's birthday is in July."

"Perhaps she's rather late in making her cake?" the wolf suggested.

"No, she isn't. She's a few days early, as a matter of fact."

"You mean it's going to be her birthday in a day or two?"

"You've got it, Wolf," Polly agreed.

"So we're in July now?"

"Yes."

"It's not Christmas?"

"No."

"Not even if we happened to be in Australia? They have Christmas in the summer there, you know," the wolf said persuasively.

"But not here. It's nearly half a year till Christmas," Polly said firmly.

"A pity," the wolf said. "I really thought I'd got you that time. I must have muddled up my calendar again—it's so confusing, all the weeks starting with Mondays."

Polly heard the would-be Father Christmas clumping down the path from the front door; she went back to the currants.

The weeks went by; Mother's birthday was over and forgotten, holidays by the sea marked the end of summer and the beginning of autumn, and it was not until the end of September, when the leaves were turning yellow and brown, and the days were getting shorter and colder, that Polly heard from the wolf again. She was in the sitting room when the telephone rang; Polly lifted the receiver.

"I ont oo thpeak oo Folly," a very muffled voice said.

"I'm sorry," Polly said politely, "I really can't hear."

"Thpeak oo FOlly."

"I still can't quite hear," Polly said.

"I ont oo—oh BOTHER these beastly whiskers," said quite a different voice. "There, now can you hear? I've taken bits of them off."

"Yes, I can hear all right," Polly said puzzled. "But how can you take off your whiskers?"

"They weren't really mine. I mean they're mine, of course, but not in the usual way. I didn't grow them, I bought them."

"Well," Polly asked, "how did you keep them on before you took them off?"

"Stuck them on with gum," the voice replied cheerfully. "But I haven't taken that bit off yet. The bit I took off was the bit that goes all round your mouth. You know, a moustache. It got awfully in the way of talking, though. The hair kept on getting into my mouth."

"It sounded rather funny," Polly agreed. "But why did you have to put it on?"

"So as to look like the real one."

"The real what?"

"Father Christmas, of course, silly. How would I be able to make you think I was Father Christmas if I didn't wear a white beard and all that cotton-woolly sort of stuff round my face, and a red coat and hood and all that?"

"Wolf," said Polly solemnly—for of course it couldn't be

anyone else—"do you mean to say you were pretending to be Father Christmas?"

"Yes."

"And then what?"

"I was going to say if you'd meet me at some lonely spot—say the crossroads at midnight—I'd give you a present out of my sack."

"And you thought I'd come?"

"Well," said the wolf persuasively, "after all I look exactly like Santa Claus now."

"Yes, but I can't see you."

"Can't see me?" said the wolf, in surprise.

"We can't either of us see each other. You try, Wolf."

There was a long silence. Polly rattled the receiver.

"Wolf!" she called. "Wolf, are you there?"

"Yes," said the wolf's voice, at last.

"What are you doing?"

"Well, I was having a look. I tried with a small telescope I happened to have by me, but I must admit I can't see much. The trouble is that it's so terribly dark in there. Hold on for a minute, Polly. I'm just going to fetch a candle."

Polly held on. Presently, she heard a fizz and a splutter as the match was struck to light the candle. There was a long pause, broken by the wolf's heavy breathing. Polly heard him muttering: "Not down there...Try the other end then...Perhaps if I unscrew this bit...Let's see this bit of wire properly..."

There was a deafening explosion, which made poor Polly jump. Her ear felt as if it would never hear properly again. Obviously the wolf had held his candle too near to the wires and something had exploded.

"I do hope he hasn't hurt himself," Polly thought, as she

hung up her own receiver. "It sounded like an awfully loud explosion."

She saw the wolf a day or two later in the street. His face and head were covered with bandages, from amongst which one eye looked sadly out.

"Oh, Wolf, I am so sorry," said kind Polly, stopping as he was just going to pass her. "Does it hurt very much? It must have been an awfully big explosion."

"Explosion? Where?" said the wolf, looking eagerly up and down the street.

"Not here. At your home. When you rang me up the other day."

"Oh that!" said the wolf airily. "That wasn't really an explosion. Just a spark or two and a sort of bang, that's all. I just got the candle in the way of the wires and they melted together, or something. Nothing to get alarmed about, thank you, Polly."

"But your face," Polly said, "the bandages. Didn't you get hurt in that explosion?"

"No. But that gum! Whee-e-e-w! I'll tell you what, Polly," the wolf said impressively, "don't ever try and stick a beard or whiskers on top of where your fur grows with spirit gum. It goes on all right, but getting it off is—well! If it had been my own hair it wouldn't have been more painful getting it off. Next time I'm going to have one of those beards on sort of spectacle things you just hook over your ears. Don't you think that would be better?"

"Much better."

"Not so painful to take off?"

"I should think not," Polly agreed.

"Well you just wait till I've got these bandages off," the wolf said gaily, "and then you'll see! My own mother wouldn't know me."

Perhaps it took longer than Polly expected to grow wolf fur again: at any rate it was a month or two before Polly heard from the wolf again, and she had nearly forgotten his promise, or threat, of coming to find her. It was just before Christmas, and Polly was out with her mother doing Christmas shopping. The streets were crowded and the shop windows were gay with silver balls and frosted snow. Everything sparkled and shone and glowed, and Polly held on to Mother's hand and danced along the pavements.

"Polly," said her mother. "Would you like to go to the toy department of Jarold's? I've got to get one or two small things there, and you could look around. I think they've got some displays of model railways and puppets, and they generally have a sort of Christmas fair with Father Christmas to talk to."

Polly said yes, she would very much, and they turned in at the doors of the enormous shop and took a luxuriant gilded lift up to the third floor, to the toy department. It really was fascinating. While her mother was buying coloured glass balls for the Christmas tree, and a snowstorm for Lucy, Polly wandered about and looked at everything. She saw trains and dolls and bears; she saw puzzles and puppets and paperweights. She saw bicycles, tricycles, swings and slides, boats and boomerangs and cars and carriages. At last she saw an archway, above which was written "Christmas Tree Land." Polly walked in.

There was a sort of scene arranged in the shop itself, and it was very pretty. There were lots of Christmas trees, all covered with sparkling white snow, and the rest of the place was rather dark so that all the light seemed to come from the trees. In the distance you could see reindeer grazing, or running, and high snowy mountains and forests of more Christmas trees. At the end of the part where Polly was, sat Father Christmas on a sort of throne. There was a crowd of children round him and a man in ordinary clothes, a shop manager, was encouraging their mothers to bring them up to Father Christmas so that they could tell him what they hoped to find in their stockings or under the tree on Christmas Day.

Polly drew near. She thought she would tell Father Christmas that what she wanted more than anything else in the world was a clown's suit. She joined a line of children waiting to get up to the throne.

The child in front of Polly was frightened. She kept on running out of line back to her mother, and her mother kept on putting her back in her place again.

"I don't want to go and talk to that Father Christmas," the little girl said, "he isn't a proper Father Christmas."

"Nonsense," her mother said sharply. "Don't be so silly. Stand in that line and go up and tell him what you want in your stocking like a nice little girl."

The little girl began to cry. Polly, looking sharply at Father

Christmas, couldn't help rather agreeing with her. Father Christmas had the usual red coat and hood and a lot of bushy white hair all over his face. But somehow his manner wasn't quite right. He certainly asked the children questions, but not in the pleasantest tone of voice, and his reply to some of their answers was more of a snarl than a promise.

The little girl in front of Polly was finally persuaded to go up and say something in a breathy, awestruck whisper. Polly, just behind her, was near enough to hear the answer.

"Box of sweets," said Father Christmas in a distinctly un-pleasant tone. "What do you want a box of sweets for? You're quite fat enough already to satisfy any ordinary person, I should think."

The child clutched her mother's hand tightly, and the man-ager, who was standing near, looked displeased. "Come, come," Polly heard him say sharply in Father Christmas's ear, "you can do better than that, surely."

Father Christmas jumped, threw a sharp glance over his shoulder at the manager and leant forward to the little girl. "Yes, of course you shall have a box of sweets," he said. "Only wouldn't you like something more interesting? For instance a big juicy steak, with plenty of fried potatoes? Or what about pork chops? I always think myself there's nothing like..."

"Next please," the manager called out loudly. "And a happy Christmas to you, dear," he added to the surprised little girl who was being led away by her mother, unable to make head or tail of this extraordinary Father Christmas.

Polly moved up. The Father Christmas inclined his ear to-wards her to hear what she wanted in her stocking, but Polly had something else to say.

"Wolf, how could you!" she hissed in a horrified whisper. "Pretending to be Father Christmas to all these poor little children—and you're not doing it at all well, either."

"It wasn't my fault," the wolf said gloomily. "I never meant to let myself in for this terrible affair. I just put on my costume—and I did the beard rather well this time, don't you think?—and I went out to see if I could find you, and this wretched man"—and he threw a glance of black hate at the shop manager—"nobbled me in the street, and pulled me in here, and set me to asking the same stupid question of all these beastly children. And they all want the same things," he added venomously. "If it's boys they want space guns, and if it's girls they want party frocks and television sets. Not one of them's asked for anything sensible to eat. One of them did ask for a baby sister," he said thoughtfully, "but did she really want her to eat, I ask myself?"

"I should hope not," Polly said firmly.

"And I'm much too hot and my whiskers tickle my ears horribly," the wolf complained. "And there's not a chance of snatching a bite with this man standing over me all the time."

"Wolf, you wouldn't eat the children!" Polly said in protest.

"Not all of them," the wolf answered. "Some of them aren't very—"

"Next please," said the manager loudly. A deliciously plump, juicy little boy was pushed to stand just behind Polly. He was reciting to himself and his mother, "I want a gun, an' I want soldiers, an' I want a rocking 'orse, an' I want a steam engine, an' I want…"

"I think you're going to be busy today," Polly said. "I probably shan't be seeing you for a time. Happy Christmas," she added politely, as she made way for the juicy little boy. "I hope you enjoy yourself with all these friendly little girls and boys."

"Grrrrrr," replied Father Christmas. "I'll enjoy myself still more when I've unhooked my beard and got my teeth into one unfriendly little girl. Just you wait, Polly: Christmas or no Christmas, I'll get you yet."

4.

The Hypnotist

POLLY was sitting on a bench on the Heath near one of the ponds, looking at the boys sailing boats. There were a good many people sitting, standing, and talking to each other, so Polly was not really frightened, though she was a little surprised, to find the wolf sitting at the other end of the bench from her. When she saw him he was gazing at her fixedly.

"Good morning, Wolf," Polly said politely.

"Good morning, Polly," the wolf said, in a deeper voice than usual.

"It's a lovely day."

"Yes," said the wolf, without taking his eyes off Polly's face.

"Don't you like seeing the ships sailing on the pond?"

"Yes," said the wolf, without taking his eyes off Polly's face.

"Especially the sailing ships—the ones with sails."

"Especially the ones with tails... Oh do be quiet, Polly," the wolf said impatiently in his ordinary voice. "How can I concentrate when you keep on talking about things that don't matter?"

"I'm sorry," said Polly, a little hurt in her feelings. "I was only trying to be polite. I didn't know you were concentrating."

She turned back to look at the pond again, leaving the wolf to his concentration. But this time he interrupted her.

"Polly," said the wolf in his new deep voice, "look at me."

Polly turned and looked at him.

"Look at me," the wolf said again.

"I am looking," Polly said impatiently. "What is it? I can't see anything different."

"Look at me," said the wolf for the third time.

Polly looked very carefully. Then she clapped her hands.

"I see! How silly of me not to notice before. You've painted a white moustache over your mouth like a funny man in a pantomime. It's very good, Wolf."

"I haven't," said the wolf crossly. "Bother those ice-cream cornets! They always get all over you." He put out a long wet red tongue and licked the moustache off. "Better?"

"A little more to the left."

"Thanks," said the wolf, and then, going back to his deep voice, he began again. "Look at me, Polly."

"I'm looking," said Polly.

"Look at me, Polly."

"I'm still looking."

"Look at me, Polly."

"I know!" Polly said, suddenly enlightened. She continued to stare at the wolf, without saying any more. Presently she winked, then she made a face, then she wiggled her scalp. At almost the same moment a fly, who had been buzzing round for some time, alighted on one of the wolf's ears. Immediately both ears stood upright, twitched violently, and the wolf shook his head with something between a sneeze and a hiccup.

Polly burst out laughing.

"You win," she said as soon as she could. "I can only wiggle the top of my head, but your ears are splendid. Let's try again. Why what's the matter, Wolf?"

For the wolf, not looking at all pleased with his triumph, was tapping the ground angrily with his paw and scowling in her direction.

"What do you think we're doing, may I ask?" he demanded.

"Playing who can laugh last. Aren't we?" Polly asked, puzzled. "Why did you keep on telling me to look at you, like that, if we aren't? And I laughed first, so you've won, and you needn't look so annoyed about it."

"I wasn't playing anything so childish," the wolf said angrily. "I shouldn't dream of partaking in such an infantile pastime. You don't seem to realize, Polly, I'm giving you a chance of sharing a very interesting scientific experiment."

"What's that?"

"Trying out something new. Scientific. Science. You know." The wolf waved his arms about to demonstrate science.

"Steam engines, and wheels go round, and bombs, and what makes guinea pigs have no tails and that sort of thing."

"Oh," said Polly, "but what has that to do with me?"

"Well, I want you to do an experiment with me."

"But I don't know anything about steam engines," Polly said, "or bombs. And not much about guinea pigs," she added.

"It's not about any of those, silly. It's something much newer. It's very fashionable, in fact. Have you never heard of Hypnosis?"

"Is it a horse?" asked Polly. Her sister was interested in horses and Polly had heard many of their names.

"It's certainly not a horse. It's a—well it's a sort of a thing. I'll explain. Some doctors can do what's called hypnotize other people—it's like putting them to sleep, so they don't know what they're doing, and then the other person, the doctor who is doing the hypnotizing, can tell the person who's asleep what to do, and she has to do it."

"It's rather muddling," Polly remarked.

"No it isn't," the wolf said angrily. "It's perfectly simple. Look, I hypnotize you and you sort of go to sleep and I tell you to go and walk into the pond and you have to."

"I should say 'no'," Polly protested.

"You can't. You're asleep."

"But if I'm asleep why do I hear what you say?"

"Because you're hypnotized. And when you're hypnotized you have to do whatever the hypnotist tells you, whether you like it or not. And now I'm going to hypnotize you," the wolf said abruptly, and then in his deep voice, "Look at me, Polly."

"I'd rather look at the pond. I don't think I want to be hypnotized, Wolf."

"Look at me, Polly."

"There's a ship with red sails. I do like red sails. I like them much better than white."

"Look at me, Polly."

"Oh all right," Polly said impatiently, "I'll look if you want me to. Only do hurry up, and tell me when it's over."

"Look at me, Polly—and don't talk," the wolf added in his natural voice.

For several moments the wolf and Polly sat staring at each other from opposite ends of the bench. Neither of them moved and neither spoke.

"You are feeling very sleepy, Polly!" said the wolf.

"Yes, I am, rather," Polly agreed. "I think it's the sun. It's really warm today—I expect it's almost spring."

"You are feeling very sleepy, Polly," said the wolf again.

Polly did not answer.

"You are asleep, Polly," the wolf said, his voice deeper than ever.

"Almost," Polly said comfortably. She shut her eyes.

"Now you are asleep," the wolf said, leaning forward towards her. "You have to do everything I tell you. You won't wake up till I tell you to. Now, listen carefully. Are you listening?"

There was a short silence.

"Are you listening?" the wolf said impatiently.

Polly nodded sleepily.

"Good. Now, Polly, after I've woken you up out of your hypnotic sleep, you are going to get up and walk down the road on the right, across the next little bit of heath until you come to the house on the corner where the two big elm trees have grown through the old wall. You turn along there and you go on till you come to the house with the green door and the shiny brass knocker, and you go in. That's my house, Polly. The door won't be locked and you just walk in, straight through the hall and into the kitchen at the end and—well I'll meet you there."

The wolf's voice died away into a loving whisper. Polly opened one eye.

"And then what happens, Wolf?"

"And then I eat you all up. Oh yes—I forgot to mention one thing—there won't be any talk."

"No talk at all?"

"Not a word. You just come in and I cook you and eat you up and there's no argument. None of this 'Wouldn't you rather have this, Wolf?' or 'Do you think we'd better wait for a day or two?' or anything like that. Do you understand, Polly?"

"I understand, Wolf."

"Very well. Now, Polly," said the wolf, in an artificially cheerful voice, "in a minute's time from now you are going to wake up. You will feel very much refreshed, as if you had had eight hours of sound sleep. And after you've woken up you're going to do what I told you."

"I'm awfully sleepy," Polly said, stretching her arms and blinking at the sun.

"But refreshed?"

"I don't notice it much yet," Polly admitted. She stood up and started walking away from the pond.

"Hi!" the wolf called after her. "That's not the right direction. I said down the road on the right."

"I know," said Polly. "But I think something must have gone wrong with the experiment. I heard everything you said, but I just don't want to do it. I don't feel any more like walking into your house and getting eaten up than I ever do."

"Didn't you fall into a trance? Weren't you properly asleep?"

"I'm afraid not," Polly said apologetically.

"Bother, bother, bother, BOTHER," said the wolf, "nothing ever goes right. And I'm sure I did all the things it said in the book! Wait a minute, let me think."

He sank his head between his paws and shut his eyes, concentrating. Polly began to move further away.

"Don't go," the wolf pleaded, "wait just a second, Polly, I've remembered something. You have to look at a bright light till your eyes get tired and then we can start all the suggesting part of it."

Polly looked quickly around her. As lunchtime approached the crowd had thinned out, and there were now only a few people left round the pond. It would not be very funny, Polly reflected, to be left quite alone with a hungry wolf, whether he succeeded in hypnotizing her or not.

"Please, Polly," pleaded the wolf. "Just look at the sun for a minute or two and see if you don't begin to feel sleepy and hypnotized."

"It's very bad for you to look at the sun," Polly protested. "My father says you can hurt your eyes very badly if you look straight at the sun for even a short time."

"Pooh," said the wolf, "that may be true of poor weak human eyes, but we wolves can look at the sun for hours without it hurting us."

To prove his point he gazed straight into the sun.

"Be careful, Wolf," said Polly kindly after a short time, "don't go and blind yourself just to prove that your eyes are stronger than mine."

"Your eyes are stronger than mine," the wolf repeated in a far away sing-song voice.

"Wolf! Do listen properly! I said, don't be silly, stop looking at the sun and go home before you hurt yourself."

"Don't be silly," the wolf said, still in his faraway voice. "Stop looking at the sun." He withdrew his eyes from the sky and fixed them on Polly, but obviously without seeing her at all. "Go home before I hurt myself."

He got up off the seat and began to walk in the direction

of his house, but without taking any notice of where he was going. In another minute he would have walked straight into the pond, if Polly hadn't caught him and guided him away from it.

"Wolf! What is the matter with you? Are you asleep or something?"

"Asleep or something," the wolf said, nodding his head drowsily.

"Oh, Wolf!" Polly cried, "I see! You're the one who got hypnotized, because you would insist on looking at the sun. All right, now I'll tell you what to do. Go home, Wolf, and have a nice vegetarian lunch—some biscuits and cheese and a lightly boiled egg. And then go to bed and have a long, long sleep and when you wake up you'll feel very much refreshed and very obliging and not at all hungry. And don't ever come and try to eat me all up again, do you understand? Never, never, never."

"Never," repeated the wolf, and he sounded so sad that

Polly, who really quite enjoyed having a wolf around to get the better of, said relentingly:

"Well, not for a long time. And I'm clever, and you're stupid, remember that!"

"I'm clever and you're stupid," repeated the wolf dreamily as he took his way off, leaving Clever Polly wondering what sort of a wolf she would meet next time.

5.

The Deaf Wolf

"It's a good idea," the wolf said to himself, putting down the book of English fairy stories he had just been reading. "It's very difficult getting Polly within snapping distance. It's worth trying, anyway."

He looked again at the illustration of a fox with one paw behind his ear, pretending to be so deaf that the incautious gingerbread man talking to him would come nearer in order to make him hear.

"I could do that easily," the wolf thought. "I'll put cotton wool in my ears. Then I really shan't be able to hear anything Polly says, and she'll come right up to shout in my ear and I'll just give one spring, like it says in the book and—"

He lost himself in a happy dream.

Polly was in the garden, playing with Lucy. First Lucy wanted to swing; then she wanted to play ball; then she wanted to pick all her mother's precious roses, and Polly could only divert her attention from this scheme by offering to give her rides on her back. She was on all fours, getting her knees and the skirt of her frock very green on the grass, and being half throttled by Lucy's plump arms round her neck, when she heard a curious noise on the other side of the hedge.

"A-harrup—a-harrup—a-harrup," the noise said.

"Horse!" said Lucy delightedly. She slid off Polly's back and went to look through a special hole in the hedge, just the right height for her, which she had discovered a week or so ago.

"It didn't sound like a horse," Polly said, getting up and stretching her cramped legs deliciously.

"Not horse," Lucy agreed. "No horse," she added, rather disappointed as she still saw nothing in the road outside. "Polly horse again?" she asked persuasively.

"No, Lucy, I really can't," Polly said. "I'm too tired."

"Lucy tired," said Lucy, lying down full length on the grass to make sure she was understood.

"All right. Let's both be tired," said Polly, thankfully lying down beside her.

"I not tired," Lucy said indignantly, getting up again immediately. "Sing 'Oranges and Lemons'."

"A-harrack!" said a persistent voice beyond the hedge. A familiar black head rose above it and looked over into the garden.

"Dog! Big dog!" said Lucy, delighted.

"Good morning, Wolf," said Polly politely.

"Not as much as yesterday," the wolf said in a gloomy voice.

"I don't quite understand," Polly said. "I didn't ask you about yesterday."

"But a bit more than the day before. It was one of those chops with nothing but gristle and bone," the wolf explained.

"I don't know what you thought I said," Polly shouted across the hedge, "but I wasn't talking about chops. I just said good morning."

"And I'm warning you, if you're talking about warning,"

the wolf said, suddenly disagreeable. "I'll get you sooner or later as sure as eggs is eggs."

"Are eggs. Not is eggs; it's not grammar. Are eggs."

"However many legs you have," the wolf said nastily.

There was a pause. It seemed a difficult conversation to keep up, and Polly was not sure where they had got to. Lucy, who had stopped trying to be the chopper as well as the chorus in 'Oranges and Lemons,' had come to stand beside her to stare up at the wolf, her hands behind her back, stomach well out. It seemed a good moment to introduce her.

"This is Lucy, my smallest sister," she said.

"I'm sorry," the wolf said, more politely. "I hope it doesn't hurt."

"What doesn't hurt? Lucy doesn't, only when she rides on my back for too long at a time."

"It's a funny place to have a blister." The wolf looked puzzled. "I always get them on my paws. Perhaps it's the way you walk."

"What's wrong with the way I walk? I can't walk any other way."

"Oh well," the wolf said huffily, "don't talk then if you don't want to."

"Oh dear," Polly sighed. "You are being difficult today, Wolf. You don't seem to like anything I say, you keep on misunderstanding. You seem to think I'm trying to be rude."

"I don't," the wolf said. "I only wish you'd try a bit harder."

"Try to be rude?"

"Yes. If you'd try to be food I could easily pretend you were, and then—well you would be," the wolf said simply.

"Oh you're hopeless!" Polly said angrily. "Why don't you listen properly? I said *rude*, RUDE, not *food*."

"Very impolite of you," the wolf replied. "I never have cared for rude children!"

"Big, big, BIG dog!" Lucy said admiringly.

"I am not!" the wolf said hotly. "Many names I've been called before now, but Pig Hog never. You've taught this horrid little girl, whoever she is, to be as rude as you are, Polly, and you ought to be ashamed of yourself."

Lucy, not liking to be looked at so angrily, turned round and ran back into the house to find her mother and ask if lunch wasn't nearly ready. The wolf looked after her thoughtfully, noticing the twinkling of her plump legs, and a pleasanter expression came over his face.

"She seems quite at home in your house, Polly. Staying with you for a time, perhaps? A relation? Cousin or something? Never mind," he added hastily, as Polly opened her mouth to answer, "I don't really want to know. She might be your sister for all I care. What is important now we are alone at last, is to get on with our conversation."

"We hadn't got very far," Polly said. "You didn't seem to hear anything I said."

"Instead of what?"

"I SAID!" Polly shouted, "NOT INSTEAD! I SAID!"

"What did you say?"

"I said you didn't seem to hear what I said."

"Oh," the wolf said, looking interested. "And what did you say?"

Polly found this difficult to answer. "A lot of things," she said at last, unable to remember any one of them. Her throat was quite dry with talking so loudly across the hedge, but it was only when she really shouted that the wolf seemed to hear properly.

"I see," she said suddenly, in her ordinary voice again, "you're deaf! How awful for you. I am sorry!"

"I know you're Polly," the wolf said. "You don't have to tell me that at this time of day."

"I said I was SORRY."

"It's all right," the wolf said amiably, "you can't help it. Anyhow as Pollies go you're quite all right."

"You're DEAF, Wolf!" Polly shouted.

"Yes!" said the wolf looking really delighted, "you're quite right, I am. Clever of you to notice. Now let's get started."

The wolf trotted down the road till he was opposite the garden gate, lay down and turned his eyes on her in a rather theatrical way. Then he panted slightly with his tongue out, and waited.

Polly waited too.

Presently the wolf got up, shook himself, came a yard or two nearer the gate and lay down again in almost exactly the same position. He again turned his eyes towards Polly, and waited.

Polly waited too.

The wolf switched his tail angrily about, raising a good deal of dust out of the road; then he shook his head violently and scratched at his ears. Two small objects fell out of them, which he covered with his paw. Then he looked even more intently at Polly.

Polly looked back at the wolf.

"Well, go on," the wolf said at last, impatiently. "Aren't you ever going to begin?"

"Begin what?"

"Talking to me, of course. Telling me things I can't hear properly."

"But if you can't hear properly, what's the good—" Polly began, but the wolf cut her short.

"Go on, go on! It doesn't matter what it's about, only do, for goodness' sake, talk!"

"About anything? Doesn't it matter at all?"

"Anything," the wolf said eagerly, "absolutely anything. Just go on talking, Polly, and I promise I won't complain. I just want to hear your voice, and I'll be quite content—or rather I just want not to hear your voice."

"I don't understand," Polly said.

"Never mind. You don't have to understand. You only have to talk."

"And you're not deaf now. You can hear everything I say."

"Of course!" cried the wolf, delighted, "that's what's wrong! How stu– I mean that wasn't as clever of me as usual. I quite forgot I was *hearing* you. That won't do at all."

He picked up from the road the two objects which had fallen when he scratched his ears, and tucked them back, one in each ear.

"Earplugs," he explained to the wondering Polly. "Now I'm all right. Shan't be able to hear a word you say. Now, talk."

Still without understanding, Polly began.

"Hoddley, poddley, puddle and frogs,
Cats are to marry the poodle dogs."

She stopped and looked at the wolf to see how he was taking it. He nodded at her agreeably.

"Delightful. I couldn't catch every word, but do go on."

"Cats in blue jackets," continued Polly, "and dogs in red hats, what will become of the mice and the rats?"

The wolf looked puzzled.

"I don't think I can have heard every word correctly," he said. "It seems an unusual situation. But do go on."

"There isn't any more," said Polly.

"If I'd heard it before I shouldn't ask you to repeat it to me," said the wolf, with a flash of temper.

"THERE ISN'T ANY MORE!" shouted Polly.

The wolf propped himself up elaborately on three legs and put the fourth behind his ear.

"I can't quite catch what you said."

"THERE-ISN'T-ANY-MORE."

"Come a little nearer, my dear," said the wolf, in an unnaturally sweet voice, "and let me hear what you say."

Polly looked. There was a reasonable distance between the wolf and herself, but she didn't feel inclined to get very much nearer. She also had a strong feeling that the wolf had in fact heard her last shout, which had been a remarkably loud noise.

"WAIT A MOMENT," she called, "I'LL BE BACK AT ONCE."

She ran into the house. It really was lunchtime now, and Polly was hungry, and the smell coming up from the kitchen was almost more than she could bear. However she ran upstairs to the dressing-up chest on the landing, which contained, among a great many other things, an ear trumpet which belonged to Mother's great-aunt Anna, and had never been used since she died years and years and years ago.

It was only a moment before Polly was back in the garden: from well on her side of the gate she offered the ear trumpet to the astonished wolf.

"Just put that to your ear and you'll be able to hear quite well," she said.

"?" said the wolf.

"JUST TAKE THIS AND YOU'LL BE ABLE TO HEAR."

"What is it?" the wolf asked suspiciously. "Will it go off bang?"

"No, silly. It's for you. It's an ear trumpet."

"I don't like junket," the wolf said sulkily.

"AN EAR TRUMPET! TRY IT."

The wolf put out his paw and took it gingerly. He looked down the big end of the trumpet, and shook his head. Then he squinted through the small end up at the sky. He looked across at Polly.

"PUT YOUR EAR TO IT," she shouted.

"What for?" asked the wolf, shaking the ear trumpet as if he expected something to fall out of it.

"SO THAT YOU CAN HEAR ME TALK."

"But you stupid little girl," the wolf said, throwing the trumpet back into the garden. "Can't you understand, I don't want to hear you talk? I want *not* to be able to hear you talk. I just want you to come closer and closer, until you're so close that I just jump on you and gobble you all up. Now do you understand?"

Polly put the ear trumpet to her mouth and shouted at the wolf, "TAKE OUT THOSE EARPLUGS FOR A MINUTE, WOLF."

The wolf looked very angry, but he did as Polly asked.

"Thank goodness for that," Polly said, in her ordinary voice. "I couldn't go on shouting any longer. Look, Wolf, if that's how you'd planned to catch me this time you'd got something quite wrong. Of course I wasn't going to come any nearer."

"Why not?" said the wolf in an aggrieved tone.

"You'd forgotten something. In those stories where the animal—it's usually a fox, isn't it?—pretends to be deaf, the creature he is going to catch comes right up to tell him something. But you got that wrong, Wolf. The creature in the stories always wants to show off. He really wants the fox to hear. But I don't care tuppence if you hear what I'm saying or not. So of course I shan't come any nearer. As a matter of fact there's only one thing I want at the moment and it's nothing to do with your hearing me or not."

"What is it?"

"Lunch," said Polly, tucking the ear trumpet under her arm and turning towards the house. "And I'm going to have it."

"So do I want mine," said the wolf sadly, turning in the opposite direction, "but it looks as if I wasn't going to have it, today at any rate."

6.

Cherry Stones

IT WAS the middle of the summer, and Polly was having a delicious time one hot, lazy afternoon, sitting in the garden with a bowl of cherries beside her. Beside the patch of grass where she was sitting was a big flat flagstone, which was part of a path, and on this Polly arranged her nicely sucked-clean cherry stones. She arranged them in different patterns; squares and triangles and a big circle and a star; she rearranged them to write letters with. There were quite a lot of them, and more every minute.

Presently Polly arranged the stones in neat rows of eights. There were several rows. She seemed to be playing some sort of game with them, counting them perhaps; but she didn't look very much pleased with the result. Several times she went through them, a finger hovering for a moment over each stone, and each time she ended by frowning and shaking her head and hastily eating another cherry and adding the stone to her collection. But still she didn't seem satisfied.

The wolf, who had been watching this ritual going on for some time, from the other side of the garden wall, was completely puzzled. He stood it for as long as he could, and then his curiosity got the better of him.

"Hi, Polly!" he said.

Polly jumped. Then she saw the wolf, waved to him, shook her head with her finger to her lips, and went on counting.

"What are you doing, Polly?" the wolf asked.

"Wait a minute," Polly said, "I'm just finishing...cotton, rags, silk, satin—oh bother!"

"Why 'Oh bother'?"

"Because it's come wrong again."

"What has?"

"Who I'm going to marry."

The wolf peered a little further over the hedge but saw nothing more than the rows of stones on the path which Polly had been counting before he interrupted her.

"Who you're going to marry?" repeated the wolf.

"And what in. And what I'm going to wear."

"What are you going to wear? And what in?"

"What I go to be married in. Oh you know, Wolf. Coach, carriage, wheelbarrow, dustcart, and I keep on getting wheelbarrow. It's so undignified."

"Where's the wheelbarrow?" said the wolf, looking round the garden. "And anyhow aren't you a bit young to be married, Polly? We shall miss you," he added politely.

"Oh dear," Polly sighed. "You are stupid sometimes, Wolf. I'm not going to be married yet, not for ages, but I'm finding out what it will be like by telling on cherry stones. You know, you lay out all your cherry stones and you say a sort of rhyme to yourself and you count the cherry stones as you go, and whatever one you end on is what you're going to get. Like this:

"Tinker, tailor,
Soldier, sailor,
Rich man, poor man,
Beggarman, thief."

"Are they all about marriage and weddings?" the wolf enquired.

"All the ones I know are," Polly said firmly.

"Pooh!" cried the wolf. "We have much more interesting rhymes than that."

"Oh, do you have them too?" Polly said, interested.

"Of course we do. Only we don't generally do them on cherry stones."

"Oh! What do you do them on?"

"Bones," said the wolf simply.

"Ugh! How horrible!" Polly said, and shivered.

"Not at all. There's nothing so comforting as a nice clean bone, well licked by all the members of the family."

"And the rhymes?" asked Polly quickly. "I'd awfully like to

hear them, and I'm sure you could think of them if you tried very hard. Have some cherries to help."

She threw him a double handful of cherries. The wolf caught them dextrously in his mouth and ate them, arranging the stones on the road outside the garden out of Polly's sight. Polly heard him murmuring to himself over them and soon his head reappeared over the hedge.

"I've got one of them," he announced.

"Oh, do tell me."

The wolf shut his eyes and recited:

> "Thinny, Fatty,
> In a meat patty;
> Tender, tough,
> It cuts up rough."

"I don't think I'd like my husband to be in a meat patty," Polly said, rather puzzled.

"There's another version of that one which some people prefer," the wolf went on, not taking any notice of her remark. "It says:

> "Juicy,
> Tender,
> Stringy, tough,
> Leathery,
> Hairy,
> I've had enough.

"or some people say, 'You've had enough,' but I think that's rather rude."

"I think it's disgusting either way," Polly said. "Who wants a juicy husband? Or a leathery one? And I'm not sure how hairy," she added thoughtfully.

"Oh you are *stupid!*" the wolf cried angrily. "Can't you ever stop thinking about husbands and weddings? Our rhymes aren't silly little jingles about useless things like that, they're proper poetry, about the real things in life. About FOOD," he finished, seeing that Polly still looked bewildered.

"Oh, food," Polly said, understanding at last.

"Give me a few more cherries, Polly," the wolf begged, "and I'll tell you some more."

Polly threw the wolf another handful of cherries and he disappeared behind the hedge once again.

"Bother!" she heard him say to himself. "I must have swallowed one. It isn't coming out right."

"Polly," he said, suddenly reappearing, "could you spare me just one more—? Thank you! Now I shall get it right."

Through the thick dark green leaves of the hedge, Polly heard him mutter:

"Young,
Old,
Hot,
Cold.
Nasty,
Nice,
Served up twice."

"What did you say, Wolf?" she called out.

"Served up twice. And I don't like the same dish twice running. It puts me off my food. I shall have to have another cherry, please, Polly."

"You haven't told me the rhyme yet, Wolf."

"Fought,
Caught,
Stolen,
Bought,"

gabbled the wolf in a great hurry. "My cherry, please."

Polly threw it. She ate another handful herself and began to count the stones on the path again.

"Church,
Bar,
Sword,
Squire,
Artist,
Lord."

"Now this," the wolf announced, leaning cosily over the hedge, "is a really useful one. It's so difficult, isn't it, to know straight off whether a joint of meat is going to be enough for everyone?

"Plenty for all,
Will just feed four,
Three get a meal,
For two, no more.
Enough for one,
My story's done."

"And if it's only enough for one, and there's a whole family of you, what do you do?" Polly enquired.

"Don't tell them, of course." The wolf looked amazed. "After all if there's only enough for one, it's very hard on them, isn't it, to know that you had it and they didn't?"

"You might give it to one of them," Polly suggested.

"I should never do anything so silly," the wolf replied roundly.

Polly and the wolf considered each other for a minute or two over the hedge.

"But this time," the wolf said triumphantly, "it all comes out right. It's young, a meal for three (which means a good hearty meal), it's in a meat patty, or soon will be, it's stringy, that's bad, but one can't have everything. And it's stolen, which is just what it's going to be, so NOW, Polly, I'VE GOT YOU," and he jumped over the hedge right into the garden.

"Wait a moment," Polly said, thinking very hard and very quickly, "I must count my cherry stones too."

"Nonsense," the wolf said, "I'm in a hurry. I'm not going to wait even half a moment. I'm going to carry you off and eat you up NOW."

"Oh, Wolf," said Polly reproachfully, "I don't think you're being very kind. After all I did give you the cherries whose stones you've been counting, and I could have eaten them all myself, you know. It's only fair that I should be allowed to count my stones and see what they say about the situation."

"All that stuff about marriage," the wolf sneered, "I don't see how that is going to help you."

"They aren't all about marriage," Polly said, as firmly as she could. "This one's about food too, like yours, but in a different way. It's about oneself as food—how one tastes. It's very important for a Polly," she said desperately.

"Sounds interesting," the wolf admitted. "What is it?"

"Well I'll tell you," Polly said, "if you'll let me do it on my cherry stones."

"And it will really tell us how you'll taste?"

"It should," Polly answered, hoping fervently that she had worked it out right in her mind.

"We'll do it together," the wolf promised. "Now say it."

"I'm delightful," began Polly.

> "I'm delicious.
> I'm ten times better than Jane."

"Excellent," said the wolf heartily. "I see we shan't go far wrong on that. Let's begin counting."

"I haven't finished," Polly said quickly. "That's only the first half."

"Oh, is there more? Go on, then."

"I'm as tough as old shoe," Polly went on.

> "Even steamed, I won't do.
> I'll give you a terrible pain."

The wolf snarled angrily.

"That's all," said Polly.

"I don't believe a word of it," the wolf said, "you look tender enough. Not a bit like an old shoe."

"It's only the rhyme," Polly reminded him. "I wasn't actually saying it about myself."

The wolf looked more cheerful.

"There are the stones," Polly said, pointing to the flagstone and hoping desperately that she had counted right while she made up her rhyme.

The wolf lay down on the grass, beside the flagstone.

"You count them out," he said anxiously to Polly. "The suspense is almost too much for me. I can't wait to know what you're going to be like."

Polly obediently squatted down beside the wolf and pointed to each stone in turn, as she recited her verse.

> "I'm delightful,
> I'm delicious,
> I'm ten times better than Jane.
> I'm as tough as old shoe,
> Even steamed I won't do,
> I'll give you a horrible pain."

There were a good many cherry stones and Polly went through the rhyme several times. She was getting very nervous and the wolf was getting very impatient before she reached the final count.

"I'm delicious," said Polly, trying to see out of the corner of her eye whether there were four or five stones left.

> "I'm ten times better than Jane,
> I'm as tough as old shoe (there are two more, I hope it isn't three).
> Even steamed I won't do,
> I'll give you a horrible pain (thank goodness it really is the last one)."

"Go on," said the wolf, who had shut his eyes during the last round.

"That's all," said Polly.

"It can't be. There must be some more. Begin again, then."

"There aren't any more stones," Polly explained.

"You mean to stand there, and tell me you'll give me a pain?"

"That's what the cherry stones say," Polly said.

"But when I counted mine they said you'd be young, and in a meat patty and—"

"It doesn't matter how you'd cook me, I'd still give you a pain."

"Enough for three," the wolf moaned.

"That just makes it a worse pain."

"I might do it on my cherry stones. It might come out different," the wolf suggested, suddenly hopeful.

"It wouldn't show you how I'd taste," Polly warned him, but the wolf was already over the further side of the hedge, counting busily. A triumphant roar came from him and his head appeared over the bushes.

"Ten times better than Jane!" he cried. "It's all right, Polly, I can have you."

"Oh, Wolf," Polly sighed, "don't be so stupid. What your cherry stones say is just about you, not about me. How you'll taste when someone eats you."

"I hadn't thought of that." The wolf hesitated. "Are you sure, Polly?"

"Quite sure. After all it says 'I' all the way through, doesn't it? Not 'You're ten times better than Jane', but I. Meaning you, Wolf, if you're counting. See?"

"I see."

"And," said Polly, following up her advantage, "do your cherry stones really say you're ten times better than Jane?"

"They certainly do," the wolf said proudly.

"Then look out!" said Polly, taking a step towards him. "Because I don't think, this time, I can resist trying to see if it's true, and I know just what Jane is like."

"Oh!" said the wolf. He didn't look to see if Polly was coming any further after him. He ran as fast as he could down the road in case fierce Polly caught up with him and began to eat him. When at last he dared to slow down and finally to stop, he sat by the roadside, congratulating himself on his narrow escape, and licking the dust off his tail.

"At any rate," he thought. "It was lucky for me I didn't eat Polly today. Nice of her to warn me, because I don't want to have a pain. Especially not a horrible one, of course."

He got up and wandered along in the direction of his own house.

"Ten times better than Jane!" he ruminated. "I wonder! I bet I'm good to eat then. Jane looks tasty enough; I must be delicious! It's a pity—"

But not even the wolf was stupid enough to consider for very long the possibility of eating himself.

7.

Wolf into Fox

ONE MORNING Polly was shopping in Woolworths. She bought a packet of seeds for her garden, a red hair slide, a quarter of a pound of fruit jellies and a pencil. Finally she went to the counter where they sell soap and sponges and shampoos and scent to buy a shampoo for Jane who was having her hair washed that evening.

There was one other customer at the counter, and the salesgirl was having a little difficulty with him.

"Well, I don't know about dyeing fur," she was saying doubtfully. "I should think you'd better ask at the household counter."

"Household?" said the customer.

"Down the other end of the store," the salesgirl said, and she pointed. "They've got the dyes there for household articles like carpets and fur rugs."

"It's not for carpets or rugs, you stupid girl," the customer said angrily. "It's for me."

"Well, I'm sorry, I'm sure," the girl said, "but I distinctly

heard you say fur, so if it isn't a rug or a coat I don't know what you want with fur."

Polly caught the wolf by the elbow just as he opened his mouth to protest and led him towards the household counter.

"It's no good getting angry," she said soothingly. "She'll never understand that it's real fur and that you really are a wolf; and if she did she'd be so frightened she'd scream and then people would come and catch you and lock you up and all that, and then where should we be? You'd much better let her go on thinking it's a fancy dress and come and buy your dye quietly. What colour do you want, Wolf?"

The wolf allowed himself to be led towards the dyes. They were set out on the household counter in a series of attractive little bottles, each cork tied up with a rag of a different bright colour.

"Aren't they pretty?" said Polly, admiring them. "What sort

of colour, Wolf? Look, the bright red is lovely—and so is the jade green. Or, look, Wolf! Do have the purple."

"Don't be so silly," the wolf said sharply. "How could I possibly go about with purple fur?"

"Oh," said Polly. "I'd forgotten it was for you. I'm sorry. No, I suppose you couldn't. Only it is such a gorgeous colour."

"Not purple," said the wolf firmly. "You've never seen a purple fox, have you?"

"No. I've hardly ever seen a fox at all," Polly admitted.

"Well, then."

"But why a fox? I mean, you're a wolf. Why does it matter if foxes aren't purple? You aren't one."

"Not yet," said the wolf. He screwed up his eyes and looked hard at Polly.

"Why are you making a face like that?"

"It's a mysterious face," the wolf said, undoing it again. "It means I'm not going to tell you any more. At present," he added, and made the face again.

Polly knew very well that if you want to get a secret out of someone who doesn't mean to tell it to you, the best way of getting what you want is to pretend to be quite uninterested. Because anyone with a secret worth anything is almost as anxious to tell you about it as you are to hear. So she turned away and looked fixedly at the tins of biscuits on the next counter, and hummed a tune to herself.

"I'm not going to tell you any more," the wolf said rather more loudly.

"Good! More about what?"

"About my turning into a fox."

"Oh, are you? I hadn't noticed," Polly said, in what she hoped sounded a very casual way.

"No, you stupid little thing, I haven't started it yet. When

I've got the dye, I shall be the right colour for a fox and then you'll see I'll look exactly like one!"

"Why a fox?" Polly couldn't help asking.

"Because they always win. Haven't you noticed in fairy stories and all that sort of thing, the fox is always the clever one? I don't know why," the wolf said thoughtfully, "but whenever there's any trouble between a wolf and a fox in those old stories, the fox always somehow turns out to be cleverer than the wolf."

"Perhaps foxes are really cleverer than wolves," Polly suggested.

"They're certainly not," the wolf said angrily.

"Then why try to be a fox?"

"I'm not exactly going to be one," the wolf said. "I'm just going to look like one. Then when I'm in a story with you—I mean with anyone I might want to get the better of—I shall look right for being the cleverest of us. And if I look right, I'll feel right. And if I feel right, I shall feel cleverer than you and then I shall eat you up."

"It sounds easy," Polly agreed.

"It is!" the wolf said simply. He turned to the counter and picked out a bottle of reddish-brown dye. "I'll have this, please," he said to the salesgirl, handing over a sixpenny bit. Then he dropped on to his four feet and ran quickly out of the shop.

For the next day or two Polly looked anxiously about to see the new Fox-Wolf. But as the days passed and there was no sign of him, she began to wonder if perhaps his plans hadn't gone right, if he had had some sort of accident, or was ill. Every large dog of a black or brownish colour that she met, Polly scrutinized carefully, but they all turned out to be nothing but dogs, with no particular interest in Polly.

Ten days or so after her first encounter with the would-be-Fox, Polly was again in Woolworths. This time she was at the ribbon counter, buying two penn'orth of red ribbon, when she heard a well-known voice further down the shop. A shaggy-looking person, muffled in a mackintosh, was at the household counter, buying five little bottles of reddish-brown dye. When he had paid for them and was tucking the bottles into his pockets, Polly stepped up behind him.

"Wolf!" she said.

He gave a great jump, and looked round.

"You shouldn't startle me so," he said reproachfully. "I nearly dropped one of the bottles and there aren't any more. These are the last five they've got. If I broke one of these I might have to wait ages to get any more!"

"But what do you need so many for?" Polly asked. "Wasn't one enough?"

"No," the wolf said. "One wasn't enough. I had to come back the next week and buy two more!"

"Why a week?" Polly asked.

"I was waiting to see what happened."

"What happened to what?"

"What happened to me after I'd taken it."

"But you don't have to wait. You just mix it with water and put the whatever it is you want to dye in, and then you hang it up to dry and then you see. It couldn't take more than about a day."

The wolf looked a little embarrassed.

"I didn't do it quite like that," he said.

"Didn't you mix it with water?"

"Y-yes."

"Perhaps you put in too much. Didn't you read the instructions, Wolf?"

"No, as a matter of fact, I didn't. You see, I sort of forgot to read what it said, and as it was in a bottle it seemed as if it ought to be—as if it was meant—well, in fact, Polly, I did mix it with water and then I drank it all up."

"Oh, Wolf, how awful!" Polly said. "Didn't it make you feel ill?"

"Yes, very ill."

"You might have died, Wolf."

"Yes," said the wolf, looking more cheerful. "You're quite right. But I didn't. And the funny thing is, it didn't turn me reddish-brown at all!"

"Not at all?"

"Not so much as a hair of me. So then I read the instructions and I saw I'd made a little mistake."

"A very stupid mistake, Wolf!"

"Not at all. A very understandable mistake. Everyone knows that bottles have drinks in them. Well, anyhow!" he went on in a hurry. "Then I read the instructions and I saw I ought to have put myself into it, not it into me. So when I felt better I came to get some more. I got two bottles, but that wasn't nearly enough, so I bought two more. And now if I have all these," he jingled his pockets, "I shall have enough I should think."

"Enough for what?" Polly asked.

"To finish me off."

"Why do you need finishing off?"

They were out of Woolworths by this time and the wolf suddenly threw off his mackintosh and said, "Look, Stupid!"

Polly looked. Her once sleek black wolf was now a rather horrid sight. His head and front legs were a fine chestnut brown—they had taken the dye very well indeed—his back legs and tail were the old original black wolf colour, but round his waist he was a disagreeable mixture of both colours.

"You see?" the wolf said. "Even you can't pretend it's exactly a finished job, can you? Now do you understand why I need a few more bottles of dye?"

"You've done your front end awfully well," Polly said consolingly.

"But what's the good of being a fox one end when I'm still a wolf the other?" the wolf said reasonably. "And it's so embarrassing looking like this. I can't go out without a mackintosh and it's just my luck that all this week the sun has gone on shining so I look almost as silly wearing a mackintosh as I would look if I didn't wear it."

"You might look as if you thought it was just going to rain," Polly said comfortingly. "It often does, in England."

"But it hasn't lately. That's just what's so annoying," the wolf said.

"Never mind," Polly said quickly. "Now you can go and finish your back half with the rest of the bottles, and then you'll be able to come out without your mackintosh, and looking like a fox!"

"And then you'd just better watch out, Polly," said the wolf, quite cheered up. "Because I'll be so clever then I'll get you before you can say Wolf Robinson!"

Polly went home and tied up her hair with her red ribbon. She wondered how the wolf was getting on with his dyeing, and she wondered if being fox colour and feeling cleverer would really make any difference to the wolf, or to Polly. She didn't think he'd be much better at catching her, but she thought she had better be careful, and, if possible, clever. She also wondered, as she saw the sun shining brightly every day, whether the poor wolf was still having to wear his mackintosh. He certainly was not in luck: people said the spell of fine weather seemed as if it would go on for ever, and those

who had gardens began to complain of drought and to wish
for rain.

It was hot and thundery and still dry when Polly, out for a
walk by herself, not far from home, suddenly saw a reddish-
brown shape slink through the bushes at the side of the road,
and a moment later a triumphant Fox stood before her: rather
larger than life and full of cunning.

"Now, Polly," said the fox-wolf, "this time I really have got
you."

Polly looked around. There was no one within call, and the
fox-wolf really did look rather convincing. For almost the first
time in history, her heart sank.

"You've done it awfully well," she said, as admiringly as
she could. "It's beautifully even all over. Sometimes dyeing
comes out a bit patchy."

"I haven't any patches at all," the fox-wolf agreed, turning
round so that Polly could see the whole of him. "But don't try

to take the chance to run away," he added, turning back very quickly.

Polly, to whom the idea had occurred, stood very still. It seemed that this animal was really cleverer than he had been.

"So, you've been able to leave off your mackintosh," she said, hoping to delay until she saw some chance of escape.

"Of course. I have nothing to hide," the fox-wolf said in an insufferably self-satisfied tone. He looked down at himself approvingly. "And now, Polly—"

Polly took a step back. The fox-wolf came nearer. Polly opened her mouth to go on with the conversation, which she hoped still to keep on a polite level, when she felt a wet splash on her nose. She looked suspiciously at the fox-wolf and saw a splash arrive on his nose too. Drops as big as half crowns fell rapidly in the dusty path between and all around them. In the distance they heard a faint roll of thunder.

"It's going to rain," Polly said.

"It is raining," the fox-wolf said.

"Hard."

"Very hard."

"You might need your mackintosh."

"I'm not going to bother about that till I've dealt with you," the fox-wolf replied threateningly. He stepped forward again, through what was now a drenching downpour, but hesitated when he saw Polly's face. She was looking first at him and then at the rain and then at the ground round his feet as if she couldn't believe her eyes.

"What is it?" he asked impatiently.

"Oh, Fox-Wolf—Oh, Wolf—oh, whatever you are, do look!"

"Look at what?"

"The puddle and your fur—oh, Wolf you aren't fast dyed! Your colour's all coming off in the rain. You're only half a fox now, Wolf, and in a minute or two you're going to be just Wolf again and as stupid as ever."

The animal looked down at the reddish-brown puddle round his feet, getting bigger and more reddish-brown all the time: and then down at his streaked, spiky brown-black fur, getting blacker as quickly as the water on the ground got red.

"It's coming off!" he muttered stupidly. "But it was supposed to be a fast dye!"

"Did you get right into the bath of dye?" Polly asked.

"Right in," said the wolf dejectedly.

"And stayed there for twenty minutes?"

"An hour and a half to make sure!" said the wolf.

"Did you remember to put in a tablespoonful of salt?"

"I used pepper and mustard as well," the wolf said. "The mustard stung my eyes!"

"And did you bring it to the boil!"

"Of course I did."

"And keep it boiling?"

"Of course. I'm not such a fool," the wolf said, "as to think you can get results if you don't do what the instructions tell you to."

"It must have hurt," Polly said. "You must be awfully brave, Wolf."

"Why?"

"To stay all that time in a bath of boiling dye!"

"Oh, I didn't stay in it when it got too hot," the wolf said cheerfully. "Naturally I got out before I boiled it. You don't expect me to stay in boiling dye, Polly, surely? Not even a wolf—not even you," he harshly corrected himself, "could be as stupid as that."

"Well," said Polly (she was soaked, but no longer at all frightened). "Now I understand what's happening. Just look at yourself, Wolf."

"Fox," the wolf corrected her.

"Wolf," said Polly firmly. "You're as black as you ever were; the dye's all gone. And I expect all the cleverness has gone too, hasn't it?"

The wolf looked unhappily down at his dripping black fur. If a tear or two fell at the same time it was unnoticeable in so much rain. There was another roll of thunder, closer this time.

"I don't feel my best," he admitted.

"You're very wet and cold, aren't you, Wolf?" Polly urged.

The wolf shivered violently for an answer.

"You feel pretty stupid, don't you, Wolf?"

"I don't understand. Fast dye," the wolf murmured to himself.

"I should get home and have a warm bath and a nice drink of hot cocoa and go straight to bed," Polly said kindly.

"I will," the wolf said gratefully, turning to trot away.

"And next time you want to be a different colour, try boiling in it," Polly called after him, as she began to run home herself.

"I may be stupid," she heard the wolf say before the next peal of thunder overtook them; and as it died away, "but not as stupid as all that."

8.

The Riddlemaster

SITTING on one of the public benches in the High Street one warm Saturday morning, Polly licked all round the top of an ice-cream horn.

A large person sat down suddenly beside her. The bench swayed and creaked, and Polly looked round.

"Good morning, Wolf!"

"Good morning, Polly."

"Nice day, Wolf."

"Going to be hot, Polly."

"Mmm," Polly said. She was engaged in trying to save a useful bit of ice cream with her tongue before it dripped on to the pavement and was wasted.

"In fact it is hot now, Polly."

"I'm not too hot," Polly said.

"Perhaps that delicious looking ice is cooling you down," the wolf said enviously.

"Perhaps it is," Polly agreed.

"I'm absolutely boiling," the wolf said.

Polly fished in the pocket of her cotton dress and pulled

out a threepenny bit. It was more than half what she had left, but she was a kind girl, and in a way she was fond of the wolf, tiresome as he sometimes was.

"Here you are, Wolf," she said, holding it out to him. "Go into Woolworths and get one for yourself."

There was a scurry of feet, a flash of black fur, and a little cloud of white summer dust rose off the pavement near Polly's feet. The wolf had gone.

Two minutes later he came back, a good deal more slowly. He was licking his ice-cream horn with a very long red tongue and it was disappearing extremely quickly. He sat down again beside Polly with a satisfied grunt.

"Mm! Just what I needed. Thank you very much, Polly."

"Not at all, Wolf," said Polly, who had thought that he might have said this before.

She went on licking her ice in a happy dream-like state, while the wolf did the same, but twice as fast.

Presently, in a slightly aggrieved voice, the wolf said, "Haven't you nearly finished?"

"Well no, not nearly," Polly said. She always enjoyed spinning out ices as long as possible. "Have you?"

"Ages ago."

"I wish you wouldn't look at me so hard, Wolf," Polly said, wriggling. "It makes me feel uncomfortable when I'm eating."

"I was only thinking," the wolf said.

"You look sad, then, when you think," Polly remarked.

"I generally am. It's a very sad world, Polly."

"Is it?" said Polly, in surprise.

"Yes. A lot of sad things happen."

"What things?" asked Polly.

"Well, I finish up all my ice cream."

"That's fairly sad. But at any rate you did have it," Polly said.

"I haven't got it Now," the wolf said. "And it's Now that I want it. Now is the only time to eat ice cream."

"When you are eating it, it is Now," Polly remarked.

"But when I'm not, it isn't. I wish it was always Now," the wolf sighed.

"It sounds like a riddle," Polly said.

"What does?"

"What you were saying. When is Now not Now or something like that. You know the sort I mean, when is a door not a door?"

"I love riddles," said the wolf in a much more cheerful voice. "I know lots. Let's ask each other riddles."

"Yes, let's," said Polly.

"And I tell you what would make it really amusing. Let's say that whoever wins can eat the other person up."

"Wins how?" Polly asked cautiously.

"By asking three riddles the other person can't answer."

"Three in a row," Polly insisted.

"Very well. Three in a row."

"And I can stop whenever I want to."

"All right," the wolf agreed unwillingly. "And I'll start," he added quickly. "What made the penny stamp?"

Polly knew it was because the threepenny bit, and said so. Then she asked the wolf what made the apple turnover, and he knew the answer to that. Polly knew what was the longest word in the dictionary, and the wolf knew what has an eye but cannot see. This reminded him of the question of what has hands, but no fingers and a face, but no nose, to which Polly was able to reply that it was a clock.

"My turn," she said, with relief. "Wolf, what gets bigger, the more you take away from it?"

The wolf looked puzzled.

"Are you sure you've got it right, Polly?" he asked at length. "You don't mean it gets smaller the more you take away from it?"

"No, I don't."

"It gets bigger?"

"Yes."

"No cake I ever saw did that," the wolf said, thinking aloud. "Some special kind of pudding, perhaps?"

"It's not a pudding," Polly said.

"I know!" the wolf said triumphantly. "It's the sort of pain you get when you're hungry. And the more you don't eat the worse the pain gets. That's getting bigger the less you do about it."

"No, you're wrong," Polly said. "It isn't a pain or anything to eat, either. It's a hole. The more you take away, the bigger it gets, don't you see, Wolf?"

"Being hungry is a sort of hole in your inside," the wolf said. "But anyhow it's my turn now. I'm going to ask you a new riddle, so you won't know the answer already, and I don't suppose you'll be able to guess it, either. What gets filled up three or four times a day, and yet can always hold more?"

"Do you mean it can hold more after it's been filled?" Polly asked.

The wolf thought, and then said, "Yes."

"But it couldn't, Wolf! If it was really properly filled up it couldn't hold any more."

"It does though," the wolf said triumphantly. "It seems to be quite bursting full and then you try very hard and it still holds a little more."

Polly had her suspicions of what this might be, but she didn't want to say in case she was wrong.

"I can't guess."

"It's me!" the wolf cried in delight. "Got you, that time, Polly! However full up I am, I can always manage a little bit more. Your turn next, Polly."

"What," Polly said, "is the difference between an elephant and a pillar box?"

The wolf thought for some time.

"The elephant is bigger," he said, at last.

"Yes. But that isn't the right answer."

"The pillar box is red. Bright red. And the elephant isn't."

"Ye-es. But that isn't the right answer either."

The wolf looked puzzled. He stared hard at the old-fashioned Victorian pillar box in the High Street. It had a crimped lid with a knob on top like a silver teapot. But it didn't help him. After some time he said crossly, "I don't know."

"You mean you can't tell the difference between an elephant and a pillar box?"

"No."

"Then I shan't send you to post my letters," Polly said triumphantly. She thought this was a very funny riddle.

The wolf, however, didn't.

"You don't see the joke, Wolf?" Polly asked, a little disappointed that he was so unmoved.

"I see it, yes. But I don't think it's funny. It's not a proper riddle at all. It's just silly."

"Now you ask me something," Polly suggested. After a minute or two's thought, the wolf said, "What is the difference between pea soup and a clean pocket handkerchief?"

"Pea soup is hot and a pocket handkerchief is cold," said Polly.

"No. Anyhow you could have cold pea soup."

"Pea soup is green," said Polly.

"I expect a clean pocket handkerchief could be green too, if it tried," said the wolf. "Do you give it up?"

"Well," said Polly, "of course I do know the difference, but I don't know what you want me to say."

"I want you to say you don't know the difference between them," said the wolf crossly.

"But I do," said Polly.

"But then I can't say what I was going to say!" the wolf cried.

He looked so much disappointed that Polly relented.

"All right, then, you say it."

"You don't know the difference between pea soup and a clean pocket handkerchief?"

"I'll pretend I don't. No, then," said Polly.

"You ought to be more careful what you keep in your pockets," the wolf said. He laughed so much at this that he choked, and Polly had to beat him hard on the back before he recovered and could sit back comfortably on the seat again.

"Your turn," he said, as soon as he could speak.

Polly thought carefully. She thought of a riddle about a man going to St Ives; of one about the man who showed a portrait to another man; of one about a candle; but she was not satisfied with any of them. With so many riddles it isn't really so much a question of guessing the answers, as of knowing them or not knowing them already, and if the wolf were to invent a completely new riddle out of his head, he would be able to eat her, Polly, in no time at all.

"Hurry up," said the wolf.

Perhaps it was seeing his long red tongue at such very close quarters, or it may have been the feeling that she had no time to lose, that made Polly say, before she had considered what she was going to say, "What is it that has teeth, but no mouth?"

"Grrrr," said the wolf, showing all his teeth for a moment. "Are you quite sure he hasn't a mouth, Polly?"

"Quite sure. And I'm supposed to be asking the questions, not you, Wolf."

The wolf did not appear to hear this. He had now turned his back on Polly and was going through some sort of rapid repetition in a subdued gabble, through which Polly could hear only occasional words.

"...Grandma, so I said the better to see you with, gabble, gabble, gabble, Ears you've got, gabble gabble better to hear gabble gabble gabble gabble gabble TEETH gabble eat you all up."

He turned round with a satisfied air.

"I've guessed it, Polly. It's a GRANDMOTHER."

"No," said Polly, astonished.

"Well then, Red Riding Hood's grandmother if you are so particular. The story mentions her eyes and her ears and her teeth, so I expect she hadn't got anything else. No mouth anyhow."

"It's not anyone's grandmother."

"Not a grandmother," said the wolf slowly. He shook his

head. "It's difficult. Tell me some more about it. Are they sharp teeth, Polly?"

"They can be," Polly said.

"As sharp as mine?" asked the wolf, showing his for comparison.

"No," said Polly, drawing back a little. "But more tidily arranged," she added.

The wolf shut his jaws with a snap.

"I give up," he said in a disagreeable tone. "There isn't anything I know of that has teeth and no mouth. What use would the teeth be to anyone without a mouth? I mean, what is the point of taking a nice juicy bite out of something if you've got to find someone else's mouth to swallow it for you? It doesn't make sense."

"It's a comb," said Polly, when she got a chance to speak.

"A what?" cried the wolf in disgust.

"A COMB. What you do your hair with. It's got teeth, hasn't it? But no mouth. A comb, Wolf."

The wolf looked sulky. Then he said in a bright voice, "My turn now, and I'll begin straight away. What is the difference between a nice fat young pink pig and a plate of sausages and bacon? You don't know, of course, so I'll tell you. It's—"

"Wolf!" Polly interrupted.

"It's a very good riddle, this one, and I can't blame you for not having guessed it. The answer is—"

"WOLF!" Polly said, "I want to tell you something."

"Not the answer?"

"No. Not the answer. Something else."

"Well, go on."

"Look, Wolf, we made a bargain, didn't we, that whoever lost three lives running by not being able to answer riddles, might be eaten up by the other person?"

"Yes," the wolf agreed. "And you've lost two already, and

now you're not going to be able to answer the third and then I shall eat you up. Now I'll tell you what the difference is between a nice fat little pink—"

"NO!" Polly shouted. "Listen, Wolf! I may have lost two lives already, but you have lost three!"

"I haven't!"

"Yes, you have! You couldn't answer the riddle about the hole, you didn't know the difference between an elephant and a pillar box—"

"I do!" said the wolf indignantly.

"Well, you may now, but you didn't when I asked you the riddle; and you didn't know about the comb having teeth and no mouth. That was three you couldn't answer in a row, so it isn't you that is going to eat me up."

"What is it then?" the wolf asked, shaken.

"It's me that is going to eat you up!" said Polly.

The wolf moved rather further away.

"Are you really going to eat me up, Polly?"

"In a moment, Wolf. I'm just considering how I'll have you cooked," said Polly.

"I'm very tough, Polly."

"That's all right, Wolf. I can simmer you gently over a low flame until you are tender."

"I don't suppose I'd fit very nicely into any of your saucepans, Polly."

"I can use the big one Mother has for making jam. That's an enormous saucepan," said Polly thoughtfully, measuring the wolf with her eyes.

The wolf began visibly to shake where he sat.

"Oh please, Polly, don't eat me. Don't eat me up this time," he urged. "Let me off this once. I promise I'll never do it again."

"Never do what again?" Polly asked.

"I don't know. What was I doing?" the wolf asked himself in despair.

"Trying to get me to eat," Polly suggested.

"Well, of course, I'm always doing that," the wolf agreed.

"And you would have eaten me?" Polly asked.

"Not if you'd asked very nicely, I wouldn't," the wolf said. "Like I'm asking now."

"And if I didn't eat you up, you'd stop trying to get me?"

The wolf considered.

"Look," he said, "I can't say I'll stop for ever, because after all a wolf is a wolf, and if I promised to stop for ever I wouldn't be a wolf any more. But I promise to stop for a long time. I won't try any more today."

"And what about after today?" Polly insisted.

"The first time I catch you," the wolf said dreamily, "if you ask very nicely I'll let you go because you've let me off today. But after that, no mercy! It'll be just Snap! Crunch! Swallow!"

"All right," Polly said, recollecting that so far the wolf had not ever got as far as catching her successfully even once. "You can go."

The wolf ducked his head gratefully and trotted off. Polly saw him threading his way between the busy shoppers in the High Street.

But she sat contentedly in the hot sun and wondered what was the difference between a fat pink pig and a plate of sausages and bacon. Not much, if she knew her wolf!

9.

The Kidnapping

ONE DAY Polly was in the kitchen, washing up dreamily at the sink. Outside the sun was shining hot and bright, and a delicious smell of newly cut grass came in through the open window. Bert, the odd-job man, was piling up the grass cuttings in a corner of the garden to make a compost heap; Lucy, Polly's little sister, was helping him, or thought she was helping, by carrying small piles of grass to and fro, sometimes in the right direction, but more often in the wrong one.

"Bert," said a voice from the other side of the house. "Bert! Come here a minute, will you?"

"Wharris'it?" Bert called back, but he went on piling up his compost heap.

"See you about something very important!" the voice said urgently.

Polly could see Bert say *bother*; she couldn't hear it, but the way he put down the rake showed exactly how he was feeling. Then he went off along the path in the direction of the voice. Lucy, alone in the back garden, filled a small tin pail with gravel and wandered over the lawn, sprinkling it with little stones.

Suddenly a large black Something jumped over the garden wall, snatched up Lucy and was off again before Polly had quite realized what was happening. But she knew directly who it had been. Only the wolf would come into the garden like that and steal small fat Lucy. For what? It was a horrible thought.

For the first time in all her dealings with the wolf, Polly was frightened. But she knew she must do something quickly, so she ran out of the kitchen, without even waiting to dry her hands, out through the garden and into the hot dusty road outside.

She looked up and down, but there was no one in sight. A scatter of small pebbles led off to the right.

"He must have gone home," Polly thought. "He wouldn't take Lucy anywhere she'd be recognized, it wouldn't be safe for him."

The pebbles led in the direction of the wolf's house. Polly had never gone that way alone before, and she didn't much like doing it now, but the thought of Lucy in the wolf's power drove her on.

Outside the wolf's door she stopped. She wasn't sure how she was going to get Lucy out; she had no plans and she didn't want to have to go into the house herself. She put up her hand to ring the door bell; then she took it down again. She actually lifted the knocker, but let it fall back silently. Polly, for once, was at a loss.

She was just summoning her courage to let the wolf know she had arrived, when something went hurtling past her head. Someone inside the house had thrown a stick out of the window just beside the porch, and it had only just missed hitting her in the face. A moment later a large black body followed the stick out of the window. The wolf retrieved the stick and jumped neatly back through the window again.

"Good dog," Polly heard Lucy's voice saying, "fetch stick."

"I'm not a dog, you silly little girl," the wolf's voice said crossly. "I'm a wolf, and I'm going to—"

"More," said Lucy. She always said more for something she had enjoyed the first time—more cake, more dance, more Red Riding Hood. The stick flew out of the window again, this time further from Polly's head.

"Fetch stick! Good dog!"

The wolf came, rather more slowly, out of the window and went back again with the stick in his mouth.

"Clever dog," Lucy said approvingly.

"You're stupid," the wolf said, really annoyed. "You're almost as stupid as Polly. Listen, stupid little Lucy, I'm NOT a dog, I'm a wolf, and I'm going to eat you all up."

"Good wolf," said Lucy contentedly. "Fetch stick."

For the third time the stick came out and was fetched by a reluctant and now definitely sulky wolf. As he landed inside the room again, he turned and slammed the bottom of the window down hard.

"Now you can't throw the stick out again," he said. "You can't reach up to the top opening. Now do listen properly, Lucy. I am not a dog, do you understand?"

"Not dog," said Lucy agreeably.

Polly moved up to the window and peered in. It was not a very comfortable-looking room, a sort of parlour, furnished stiffly and scantily, with hard knobbly-looking chairs and a shiny horsehair sofa. A large dog basket containing a piece of striped blanket near the fireplace seemed to indicate that the wolf sometimes slept here; there was a round table in the middle of the room, partly covered by a red woollen crochet mat.

Lucy was sitting comfortably in the dog basket. She had

discovered a hole in the stripy blanket and she was picking at the edges and enlarging it with apparent satisfaction. The wolf was sitting at the table, looking annoyed, tapping on the table, biting his nails, and showing every sign of being anxious and jumpy.

"I am NOT a dog, Lucy," he said again, impressively.

Lucy took no notice of this remark.

"I am a wolf."

"Wolf," Lucy agreed. She stuck her thumb through the hole in the blanket and said, "Look! Thumb!"

"I am a wolf and I'm going to eat you all up."

This was a game with which Lucy was quite familiar. She climbed out of the basket and approached the wolf with her mouth wide open.

"Eat you all up," she repeated, and, reaching the wolf, sank her small sharp teeth into his front left leg.

"Ow! Wow!" the wolf said indignantly, pulling away from her sharply. "Don't do that! It hurts, you horrible little creature!" He nursed his wounded limb tenderly with the other paw and looked at Lucy in hurt surprise.

But Lucy was delighted. She had seldom had a playfellow who acted pain and surprise so well, and she was encouraged to improve on her efforts. She walked round behind the wolf, saw his irresistible feathery tail hanging out between the bars of the chair, and gave it a sharp pull.

The wolf turned round with a yelp of astonishment and pain.

"Eat you all up," said Lucy, opening her mouth at him again and laughing heartily. She made another successful snap at his other front paw.

"You beastly little girl," the wolf said, now nearly in tears. "You don't understand the simplest remark. I didn't bring you here to bite me and pull my tail and make me do stupid, use-

less things like jumping in and out of windows to fetch your
horrid stick as if I were a tame dog. Can't you see it isn't you
that's going to eat me up, it's me that is going to eat you up.
Now. For my lunch. No," he added, looking at the marble-pillared
clock on the mantelpiece, which permanently told the time of
a quarter past four. "For my tea."

"Tea," said Lucy. She was rather like an echo sometimes,
picking on the one familiar word out of a long speech. "Lucy's
tea."

"Not for you," the wolf said firmly.

"TEA," said Lucy, equally firmly and a good deal louder.

"No tea for you. For me," the wolf explained.

"TEA," said Lucy at the top of her voice. Her face suddenly
grew brick red and her mouth went square. An enormous
tear rolled down her cheek and made a considerable pool on
the oilcloth floor.

"Don't cry!" the wolf said, alarmed. "For goodness' sake
don't cry. And don't shriek. Someone might hear, and anyhow
I can't bear children who cry, it makes me go funny all over."

"Tea," Lucy said in a quieter voice, but the wolf recognized
the dangers of delay.

"Yes, yes," he said soothingly, "tea for Lucy."

"Lucy's chair," said Lucy, climbing up and sitting on it ex-
pectantly. No more tears appeared, and her colour was miraculously restored to normal.

"That's the chair I always sit on," the wolf complained.

"LUCY'S CHAIR," Lucy said. Her colour began to rise
alarmingly, and her mouth began to set into corners.

"Yes, yes, Lucy's chair." The wolf pulled a sort of
cross-legged stool up to the table and sat on it, trying to look
as if he were enjoying himself.

"Butter," Lucy demanded.

The wolf slipped off his stool and disappeared out of the

door. When he came back a minute or two later, he was carrying a tray on which he seemed to have loaded everything he could think of that Lucy could possibly want for tea. There was a large brown steaming teapot, a rusty battered kettle, a sugar bowl, a chipped mug with a picture of an engine on it, a cocoa tin with no lid, half full of biscuits, a plastic plate, the end of a brown loaf, and a sizeable piece of butter in a green soap dish. He put the tray on the table and looked at Lucy nervously.

"Tea," said Lucy approvingly. She leant forward and seized the mug, looked into it, found it empty, and held it out to the wolf.

"Tea," she said again. "Lucy's tea. Butter."

The wolf hastily picked up the teapot in a paw that trembled slightly and tipped it to pour into the mug. But when Lucy saw the colour of the liquid that came out of the spout, her face changed.

"Tea!" she said in disgust. "No tea. Milk!"

She took the mug away just before the wolf removed the teapot. A stream of nearly boiling tea cascaded down to the floor and splashed on his foot.

"Ow! That hurts! You've made me hurt my foot," he cried reproachfully. But Lucy was not interested in the wolf's troubles.

"MILK," was all she said, but the wolf knew better now than to delay. He left the room and was back again with a jug of milk quicker than Polly would have believed possible. He filled Lucy's mug, and she drank thirstily, and then held out the mug again for more.

"But this is all I've got," the wolf pleaded. "The milkman doesn't call again until tomorrow, and I meant to make a milk pudding for supper."

"MORE MILK," Lucy said.

"I'll just keep enough to put in my tea," the wolf said, apologetically, pouring out about half the mugful.

"MORE," said Lucy. "Lucy thirsty," she explained in a friendly way, as she drained the last remnants of the unfortunate wolf's milk supply. She looked round the table for further replenishment. "Butter."

The wolf, obviously at the end of his resources, pushed the soap dish towards her. Lucy frowned.

"Bread 'n' butter," she said, clearly pitying anyone who did not understand the simplest rules of behaviour.

The wolf cut a large slice of bread and spread it with a moderate supply of butter. Lucy took it, and began to lick the butter. The wolf stared at her in horror. He sat in a stupefied silence till Lucy, having licked the bread quite dry of its butter, held it out to him and said emphatically, "More."

"More?" said the wolf. He could hardly believe his ears.

"More butter," said Lucy impatiently.

"But you haven't eaten the bread. I mean to say, people don't just go on having more butter on the same piece of bread. That isn't what bread and butter means," the wolf protested.

"MORE BUTTER."

"Oh, very well. Have it your own way." The wolf spread a generous layer of butter on the slice of bread and handed it back to Lucy.

He poured himself out a cup of bitter black tea. There was no milk left, so he sweetened it liberally with sugar, and began to drink, making a face as he tasted how nasty it was. But Lucy had noticed his last action and had had a new idea.

"Sugar," she said, dropping her bread, now licked nearly clean again, on the floor. She held out her hand for the sugar basin.

"No," said the wolf, with unusual firmness. "I'm not going to let you polish off all my sugar." He hid the sugar basin

behind him, on his stool. "Have a biscuit?" He held the cocoa
tin out towards Lucy.

Lucy looked doubtfully into the tin.

"Choc bikkit?" she enquired.

"No-o—but there's a very nice one here. Look!" and the
wolf held up a crumbling Oval Osborne.

"No bikkit," said Lucy.

"Nice biscuit," said the wolf.

"No bikkit."

"No, no. Certainly. It's a repellent biscuit," the wolf said,
putting it back in the cocoa tin. "You don't want a nasty biscuit like that. I'll find you a really good biscuit this time."

He scrabbled busily about at the bottom of the tin, then
produced the same biscuit and held it out to Lucy invitingly.

"Sugar," said Lucy.

"No," said the wolf.

"SUGAR."

"No."

Lucy abandoned this unprofitable conversation and looked
round the room for inspiration.

"Lucy have a apple?" she asked politely.

"I haven't got any apples," the wolf replied.

"Banana?"

"I haven't any bananas."

"Then I have bun," Lucy said decisively. She was sure there
could be no one who couldn't produce at least bun, even if
they were so unfortunate as not to have apples and bananas.

"I haven't got—" the wolf began, but he changed his mind.
He was reluctantly learning a little cunning too. He looked
into the biscuit tin for the third time and gave a start of
well-acted surprise.

"Why, what's this?" he cried. "I was just going to say I

hadn't got any buns, but there's one left at the bottom of the tin."

He held the Oval Osborne biscuit out to Lucy in a trembling paw. She gave him an enchanting smile and took it.

"Gank you."

It seemed to Polly that this was the moment to ring the front door bell. She pressed it firmly, and kept her finger there for some time.

The door was opened abruptly. An exhausted, frayed wolf, visibly at his last resources, stood before her.

"Polly!" he said. "You've come in the nick of time. Another five minutes and I don't know what I should have done. For goodness' sake come in and take her away before she eats up everything I've got in the house. Do you know," he went on, trembling with rage, as he led the way from the front door to the room where Lucy was finishing her biscuit, "that she even tried to eat me?"

Lucy was sitting comfortably and crumbily on the wolf's special chair when Polly came into the room. She looked at Polly without any special surprise and said agreeably, "Good morning, Polly." She always said "Good morning," whatever the time of the day, finding it easier to pronounce than "Good afternoon."

"I've come to take you home," Polly said. She had decided to pretend that the whole affair had been carried on under the politest circumstances. "Get down from your chair, Lucy, and thank the kind wolf for asking you to tea."

Lucy obediently struggled off the chair and made for the door as fast as she could.

"Say thank you," Polly reminded her as they reached the front door again.

"Gank you, Wolf," Lucy said. "Lucy come back soon."

"Not too soon," the wolf pleaded. He looked very limp as he held the door open for them to go out.

"And now," Lucy said, as, holding Polly's hand, she trotted down the short garden path, "Lucy go home and have TEA."

Behind her Polly heard the wolf groan. He had at last met his match.

Tales of Polly and the Hungry Wolf

Illustrated by Jill Bennett

I.

The Enchanted Polly

THE WOLF sat gloomily in his kitchen. Once, in happier days, he had actually had Polly there for a short time. Now all he had to comfort him was a nearly empty larder and his small library of well pawed-over books. It was one of these he was reading now.

He read about clever animals who caught beautiful little girls and kept them, sometimes as servants, sometimes as wives. Sometimes they meant to eat them. But it was disappointing that though all the tigers, lions, dragons, foxes, wolves and other animals seemed to have very little difficulty in catching their prey, most of them somehow or other failed to keep them. The beautiful little girls generally managed to escape at the last minute, often by tricks which the wolf considered very unsportsmanlike.

The story he was reading just now was about a dragon chasing a princess, who had once been in his cave, but had then run away. She couldn't run as fast as the dragon could move, but she turned herself first into a fly, then into an old woman, and lastly into a bridge over a river. The dragon never managed to recognize her in any of her disguises, and in the end he was drowned in the river under the princess-bridge.

"Terrible the things these girls get up to! No wonder I've never been able to catch that Polly. Here am I, a simple wolf, while she can turn into almost anything she chooses. It's all so unfair!" the wolf exclaimed. Then he remembered that even if he couldn't take on different shapes, he at least had brains. "I'll show her! She shan't deceive me. Whatever she pretends to be, I shall know it's really her. I'm not stupid like that dragon. I am clever," the wolf thought. He had heard that fish was good for the brains, so he opened a tin of tuna and gobbled it down for supper. In case that didn't do the trick, he slept with another tin of tuna under his pillow that night. He very cleverly decided not to open it first, in case the oil made a mess on the bedclothes. "Wow! I am brilliant this evening," he said to himself.

The next day, Polly, coming home from school, saw the wolf standing outside a shop and staring fixedly in at the window. She had hoped that he wouldn't notice her, but just as she was behind him, he turned round. She was preparing to run, when he spoke.

"Little girl!"

Polly looked around. There were plenty of people walking up and down near by, but there was no other little girl in sight.

"Little girl! Little girl!" the wolf said again.

"Are you talking to me?" Polly asked.

"Of course I am talking to you. You don't think that when I talk to myself I call myself 'little girl', do you? I'm not little, for one thing, and I'm not a girl, for another. I don't make stupid mistakes like that," the wolf said irritably.

"If you mean me, why don't you say my name?" Polly asked.

"Because I don't know it, of course. You look remarkably like a girl called Polly, but I know you aren't her because she is somewhere else, in disguise. That's why I have to call you 'little girl'. Now stop asking silly questions and give me a sensible answer for a change," the wolf said.

"A sensible answer to what?"

The wolf pointed to the window he had been gazing at.

"Do you see those two flies inside the window?"

Polly looked. Sure enough, two flies were climbing up on the other side of the glass. As soon as one reached nearly to the top, it buzzed angrily down to the bottom again. The wolf was following their movements with great interest, his long tongue lolling out and sometimes twitching slightly.

"Those flies. I daresay they look just the same to you, little girl? You can't tell which is which? Can you?"

Polly looked carefully and then said, "No, I can't."

"You see no difference between them?"

"Perhaps that one that's crawling up now is a little bigger," Polly said, pointing.

"Nonsense. They are exactly the same. But I'll tell you something that will surprise you. Although they look alike to you, I know which is which," the wolf said.

"Which is which, then? I mean, if they look exactly the same, what's the difference between them?"

"You're trying to muddle me. What I mean is, I know which of them really is a proper fly and which isn't."

"Which is the proper fly?" Polly asked.

The wolf looked closely at both flies. Then he pointed. "That one."

"If that's the real fly, what is the other one?" Polly asked.

"Aha! Now, little girl, you are going to be surprised. That other fly—is a girl."

"A girl fly?"

"Don't be so stupid. Not a girl fly, a girl. A real girl, like you. A human girl. Young, plump. Well, plumpish. Delicious."

Polly looked at the two flies again. The real fly was doing the angry buzzing act down from the top of the window to the bottom. The fly who was really a girl was skipping up the glass. At this moment she stopped and began twiddling her front pair of legs.

"You see? She knows that I know who she is. She is wringing her hands because she sees that I have penetrated her disguise and that in a moment I shall claim her as my own," the wolf said, triumphant.

"Flies often do that with their front legs. My mother says it looks like knitting," Polly said.

"Nonsense. Only flies that are really girls would do it. Look at the other fly. The real one."

As the wolf said this, the other fly also stopped on its path up the window and also knitted with its front legs.

"You see?" Polly said.

"He's copying the Polly fly," the wolf said quickly.

"Polly?" said Polly.

"That...Fly...Is...Only...Pretending to be a fly. She... Is...Really...A...Girl," the wolf said in the loud slow tones used for speaking to fools or foreigners.

"Why?" Polly asked.

"I can't go back to the beginning. All I can tell you is that there is a maddening child who lives round here, the one who looks rather like you, called Polly. She thinks she is clever. She believes that if she disguises herself as a fly, I shan't know who she is, so she will escape from my clutches. But she's not all that clever. I don't suppose she's any cleverer than you are. And I am much too clever for her. It didn't take me any time to see that that was no ordinary fly."

"What happens next?" Polly asked, interested.

"I catch her and eat her all up," the wolf replied.

"I wouldn't think she'll taste very good. Not if she's still a fly."

"She won't remain a fly. Directly I lay my paw on her and say her real name, she will be compelled to resume her ordinary shape. She'll be a girl again, like you. And then…Yum!" the wolf said with gusto.

"How are you going to lay your paw on her? Both those flies are inside the window and we're outside," Polly said.

"I am now going into the shop to claim my prize," the wolf said. He disappeared. Polly took the opportunity to get herself safely home to tea.

A day or two later, Polly, walking down the High Street, caught sight of the wolf standing very close to a group of three stout, elderly ladies, who were talking to each other as they waited for the bus. They were so busy gossiping that they didn't notice the wolf edging nearer and nearer, until he was within touching distance of the stoutest of the ladies. His paw was raised to touch the stoutest lady on the shoulder, when she turned her head and saw a very large, dark person standing uncomfortably close.

"Here! Move off, can't you? No one asked you to join the party," she said, taking a surprised step backwards.

"Aha!" the wolf said.

"Pardon? What's that supposed to mean?" the stoutest lady asked.

"I said, Aha. You can't deceive me…"

"Here! Who do you think you're talking to? You be careful, me lad, or I'll get the police on to you."

"It's no good. I know you," the wolf said.

"I don't know you. And I don't want to, so take yourself off," the stoutest lady said, raising her umbrella threateningly. The two women behind her pressed closer and one of them seized a handful of the wolf's fur.

"You are Polly, and I claim you as my own," the wolf said, trying to lay a paw on the stoutest lady's shoulder.

There was a scuffle. There were cries of "Keep your dirty paws off me!" and "Who do you think you are?" and "Never been so insulted in my life." Someone was calling for the police. Others were trying to beat the wolf with sticks or umbrellas. One of the stout ladies was having hysterics. The wolf was howling with rage and pain. It was lucky for him that just then the huge red bus lumbered up, and since it was already late and the next one probably wouldn't be there for nearly an hour, the stout ladies had to leave him on the pavement, and climb into the bus, murmuring angrily as they went.

Polly felt almost sorry for the wolf. This did not prevent her from keeping a safe distance the next day, when she saw him standing disconsolately on a bridge that ran over a motorway not far from her home. He looked bedraggled. One ear had been torn, and there were small bare patches on his neck as if handfuls of fur had been pulled out. He was peering down at the motorway beneath the bridge, and Polly was wondering whether to go home and hope that he hadn't seen her, when he called out to her.

"Little girl! Little girl!"

"If he doesn't recognize me, perhaps it's safe to stay," Polly thought, and she moved a little nearer.

"Little girl! Come and look at this bridge," the wolf said.

"I'm looking," Polly said.

"Have you noticed anything funny about it?" the wolf asked.

"No, I haven't. What's funny about it?" Polly called back.

"Ssssh. Don't shout like that. She might hear."

"Who might hear?"

"Polly."

"Where is Polly?" Polly asked. She wanted to see just how stupid the wolf could be.

"She has turned herself into a bridge this time," the wolf said.

"A bridge? Why?"

"You must be the same little girl who was so stupid last time I tried to explain about Polly. She turns herself into different shapes so that I shan't recognize her. Don't you remember? Last time she was disguised as an old lady. The time before that she was a fly. This time it's a bridge. In the stories it's a bridge over a river, but there doesn't seem to be a river round here, so I suppose she thought a motorway would do instead. She's made one mistake, though."

"What's that?" Polly asked.

"This bridge hasn't got a road going over it. And it's got steps each end. That's stupid. How can cars climb up steps?"

"This bridge isn't meant for cars. It's meant for people," Polly said.

"Nonsense. Bridges are meant for cars. And horses and carts. Why should there be a bridge just for people? They can walk across a bridge for cars, but cars can't climb stairs and get across a silly bridge like this. That's how I know it isn't a real bridge. It's that stupid little Polly," the wolf said.

"So what are you going to do?" Polly asked.

"I shall seize her and tell her that I know that it's her. Then she has to go back to her real shape. Then I shall eat her," the wolf said.

"That's what you said before," Polly said.

"When? What did I say before? Something very intelligent, I'm sure."

"When you were watching those flies. What happened to them?"

"The flies. Oh, that," the wolf said.

"Yes, that. Wasn't one of the flies Polly after all?"

"Of course it was. I told you so at the time," the wolf said.

"Then why didn't you catch her and eat her up?" Polly asked.

"It was very confusing. They buzzed so. And rushed up and down the window. You saw for yourself. They were very much alike, you must agree."

"I couldn't tell which was which," Polly said.

"Exactly. That was the difficulty," the wolf said.

"So you got the wrong one?"

"I laid my paw on the Polly fly and said her name. Nothing happened. I had got the real fly by mistake. Meanwhile the other fly, the Polly fly, had gone. Flown. It was most disappointing."

"What went wrong with the old ladies?" Polly asked.

The wolf looked surprised and pained.

"It was a disgraceful affair. I should prefer not to talk about it. I was treated abominably."

"And now you've discovered that Polly is disguised as this bridge?" Polly asked.

"That's right."

"What are you waiting for? When are you going to lay your hand on this bridge and say that you know who it really is?" Polly asked. She was ready to run if she thought the wolf might come to his senses and make a grab for the real Polly.

"I'm just making sure in my mind that I remember how to swim," the wolf said.

"What has swimming got to do with it?" Polly asked, surprised.

The wolf groaned loudly.

"I must say that for sheer stupidity you beat even that stupid little Polly I was telling you about. Don't you ever read a good book? Don't you know that the princess turns herself into a bridge, and the dragon or the giant or the wolf who is after her stands on the bridge and says her real name and then she turns back into a princess again? And then the dragon, or whoever it is, falls into the river below and is drowned. That's because dragons are stupid. But I am not stupid. I have very cleverly had swimming lessons in the public baths. I just have to remember how to work my front and back legs, and I shan't drown. Instead I shall quickly swim to the river bank, climb out and eat up the princess. I mean, I shall eat up the Polly."

"But there isn't a river under this bridge," Polly pointed out.

The wolf looked down at the endless procession of lorries, cars and coaches passing beneath the bridge.

"No. I had forgotten. In that case there's no need to wait. I don't have to remember how to swim and I needn't get my fur wet. So much the better." He turned towards the middle of the bridge.

"Wolf!" Polly called after him.

"What is it now?"

"When you say Polly's name and the bridge disappears, you won't be in a river, but you will be down there," Polly said, pointing down to the motorway.

"What about it?" the wolf said.

"The traffic won't stop for you. All the cars and coaches and things are going much too fast. Their brakes couldn't work quickly enough. You'll get run over. Squashed. Flat as a pancake," Polly said.

The wolf stopped. He looked over the railing to the stream of traffic below.

"Are you quite sure they won't stop?" he asked.

"Quite sure."

"You wouldn't like to do a small scientific experiment? You jump down there and we shall see how many cars stop and what happens to you?"

"No, thank you, Wolf. I wouldn't like to do that at all," said clever Polly.

The wolf returned from the middle of the bridge and stood carefully to one side.

"Do you think I should be safe if I fell from here?" he asked.

"It's still quite a long way to fall on to the ground," Polly said.

"What would you suggest then?"

"I think you should go over to the other side. Then you should go down the steps to the bottom, so that you don't fall anywhere. Then you can lay your paw on that end of the bridge and tell it that you know it's Polly," Polly said.

"You are really quite a kind little girl. And not as much stupider than Polly as I thought," the wolf said, preparing to do as Polly had advised. Halfway across the bridge he turned and looked back.

"Wait there and see the great transformation! See a bridge turn into a Polly and get snapped up by the clever wolf," he shouted.

But Polly knew better than that. Before the wolf had got down the steps on the further side of the motorway, Polly had run home. She didn't want to risk being chased and caught, when the wolf discovered that the bridge was only a bridge after all.

2.

The Great Eating Competition

"I DARE you!" the wolf said loudly. He had to speak loudly, because he and Polly had met in the High Street on a Saturday morning, and there were plenty of other noises, over which he wanted to make himself heard. Cars were grinding up the hill, horns were blowing, motorbikes were revving, children were calling, babies were yelling and people were shouting so that their friends could hear what they were saying.

"What do you dare me to do?" Polly shouted back.

"A trial of strength. A trial of something or other. You know the sort of thing. We could try which of us could lift the heaviest stone."

"There aren't any heavy stones around here," Polly said, looking up and down the High Street.

"We could try that lady. I'm sure she weighs as much as a really large stone." The wolf pointed a paw towards a very large lady, just about to go over a zebra crossing.

"I wouldn't try to lift her, if I were you. If you did, she'd probably call the police and have you put in prison." Polly wasn't sure whether or not the wolf might have been able to lift the lady, but she was quite sure that she herself would not be able to.

"Oh, all right. You suggest something, then," the wolf said, sulkily.

"Shall we see who can talk the fastest?" Polly asked.

"That's mean! You know you'd win that. Not because I haven't got plenty to say, and very well worth saying too. But because I like to think before I speak."

"I've read a story where the people tried to see who could tell the biggest lie," Polly said.

"I am shocked. I am horrified. I thought you were a good, truth-telling girl," the wolf said primly. He spoiled the effect by asking quickly, "What did they say? What was the biggest lie?"

"I meant a made-up story. Like someone saying he'd taken a bite out of the moon," Polly said.

"Really? That would explain a lot. I have often wondered why the moon so often seems to have suffered from some sort of attack. Sometimes from one side, sometimes from the other. Often you can see just where someone has taken a bite out of her. I never knew that before," the wolf said, considering the matter.

"But I didn't mean that that was true. I meant, that was the sort of story someone might make up."

"But why should he say so if it isn't true?"

"To see if anyone else could think of a bigger lie," Polly said.

"Easy! Anything would be a bigger lie than saying that there is someone taking bites out of the moon. You can see that it's true every now and then, by just looking at her."

Polly felt unable to go on with the subject. It was obviously not going to be possible to convince the wolf that someone was not regularly taking mouthfuls of moon. She waited for his next remark.

"I'll tell you what. Suppose we have a competition to see which of us could eat up the other one fastest," the wolf said.

Polly thought about this. She was puzzled. "How would that work?" she asked.

"Simple. Simple to anyone with any brains, that is. Suppose I start eating you at, say, ten o'clock this morning..."

Polly looked at the clock tower. The clock showed that it was now a quarter to ten.

"We have an umpire, with a watch. I eat as fast as I can, and when I have finished, snap, gobble-you-up, crackle, crunch, I tell him so. He looks around to make sure that there's nothing left that could reasonably be considered eatable. I shouldn't be eating your clothes, you know, Polly. I should kindly leave them for you or another little girl to use again."

"But they wouldn't be much use to me if you'd eaten me all up," Polly pointed out.

The wolf took no notice of this and hurried on. "So, I tell the umpire. He looks at his watch and he sees that I have taken exactly forty minutes. Fifty perhaps. It would depend on how tough you had turned out to be, and on other details which I won't mention just now. Then the umpire announces that I have won. Easy!" The wolf sounded very much pleased with himself.

"What happens when it's my turn to eat you up?" Polly asked.

"It would take you far longer than forty or fifty minutes to eat me. It might take you hours. Possibly even a whole day. I am larger than you. I am exceedingly tough. And then there's the hair," the wolf said.

"What about hair?"

"Hair is a great slower-down of fast eating. Hair in the wrong places can make a quick snap almost impossible. I mean in the wrong places for a mouthful, of course. Naturally for a wolf it is right and proper to have hair all over. A great deal of hair, covering most of his body. While you are very nearly quite bald. Your hair all grows in one place, on top of your face. It would be easy to get rid of it in five minutes or so, while it would take you several hours to get rid of mine, I reckon," the wolf said with pride.

"But if it had been me that started, you wouldn't have had a chance to try. I would have eaten you first."

"That's why I should start. After all, as we know that I could eat you faster than you could eat me, there wouldn't be any point in your trying."

"But that wouldn't be fair!" Polly exclaimed.

"Life is not fair. Some people are born as wolves, others are only feeble little girls. Some people are born with brains. Others are stupid from the beginning. There's nothing you can do about that."

"You can do something about trying to make a competition fair," Polly said.

"What do you mean? You couldn't make yourself eat twice as fast, could you? Only it would have to be more like a hundred times as fast."

"I don't think anyone could make me eat that much faster. But they could make you eat more slowly. That's what they do when there is a horse-race," Polly said.

"Do you have races where horses eat each other? I never knew. I'd like to see that."

"Don't be disgusting, Wolf. They don't eat each other. They gallop. The horse that gallops fastest wins the race. If one horse is much faster than the others, it has to carry a heavier weight than the others. They fasten pieces of lead to its saddle, to slow it down," Polly said.

"How monstrous! Poor horse. Terribly unfair."

"No, it isn't. It makes the race fairer for the other horses. The slower ones have a chance to win."

"Now, let's stop thinking about boring things like galloping horses. Let's talk about us," the wolf suggested.

"Don't you see? If we are going to have an eating race, we have to make it as fair as we can, by making you eat more slowly."

"I can assure you, Polly, that no amount of heavy weights on my saddle would make any difference to my eating habits. And anyway, I don't have a saddle. So you will find it all very difficult. Probably quite impossible," the wolf said. He moved a little nearer to Polly and a long red tongue came out and licked his wicked lips.

"Of course it wouldn't be any good putting weights on you. No one wants to stop you from running fast," Polly said.

"Right! So what are we waiting for?"

"We have to think of something that stops you eating so fast."

"I should like to see what could do that," the wolf said.

"We could put a sort of clamp into your mouth so that you couldn't open it very wide."

"Not wide enough to take a large bite out of a juicy little Polly?" the wolf asked.

"That's right. You'd only be able to take a tiny bite at a time."

"That wouldn't be any fun. If you can't take a really large, refreshing bite out of something you fancy, half the pleasure of eating goes," the wolf complained.

"Perhaps a muzzle would be better. You see dogs wearing them over their noses sometimes."

"Then I wouldn't be able to eat at all."

"You'd probably be able to drink," Polly said kindly.

"While you were crunching away at me? That would be terrible."

"Or perhaps...? Yes. I think probably that's what they'd do. That would be much the best way," Polly said, looking at the wolf's large mouth full of teeth.

"What?" the wolf asked, trembling slightly.

"We could fix your teeth."

"What do you mean by fix?"

"Make them blunt. File them, so that they aren't sharp enough to bite quickly," Polly said.

"File my beautiful, long, sharp teeth!"

"No. Now I think about it, that would take too long. It would be easier to take most of them out," Polly said.

"Take them out!" the wolf repeated. He seemed dazed.

"We wouldn't take out the front ones. We don't want to spoil your looks. Just the back teeth," Polly explained.

"But it's the teeth at the back that do half the work. The grinding up of the meat, the crunching of the bones..."

"That's why they'd have to come out. I daresay they'd try to do it without hurting you too much. Sometimes they make people go to sleep before they pull out a really big tooth," Polly said kindly.

"All my teeth are big," the wolf said.

"I can see that. So you could ask the dentist to give you gas and air, and then you'd go to sleep and he could take them all out at once."

The wolf shivered.

"It would be a long time before they grew again," he said.

"I don't think they would grow again. You're too old. It's only very young creatures who grow a second set of teeth when the first ones come out."

The wolf ran his tongue over his teeth, counting them fondly.

"I could promise to eat very slowly," he said.

"You might forget in the excitement of getting me to eat at last."

"I could drink a glass of water between each mouthful."

"Very bad for the digestion. You don't want to ruin your stomach so that you'd never enjoy another meal," Polly said.

"Would they be taking out your teeth too?" the wolf asked.

Polly shook her head. "They wouldn't need to. Even with all my teeth, I wouldn't be able to eat faster than you," she said.

The wolf considered this.

"Polly!"

"Yes, Wolf?"

"It was a good idea of yours that we should try which of us could eat the other fastest, but now that I have thought the matter over carefully I think it might not work very well. I feel that the end result might not be quite what we expected. I think we had better forget the whole plan."

"I understand," Polly said.

"I am sorry to have to disappoint you. The fact is that today I happen to be very busy. I have a great many things to attend to at home. Also I happen not to be particularly hungry this morning. I believe that all I shall be able to manage for my dinner will be a lightly boiled egg. Perhaps also a small piece of dry toast. I don't really feel equal to tackling a whole Polly just now."

"That's quite all right. I don't really want to eat you today, Wolf," Polly said politely.

"Another time," the wolf called as he turned down the High Street towards his home. As he trotted off he was congratulating himself on his great cleverness. He had quickly seen the dangers into which Polly had tried to entrap him. The horror of having his jaws clamped together! The shame of wearing a muzzle like a dog! Worse still, the loss of any of his useful, long, sharp (and rather yellow) teeth!

"Foiled again! Who says I am not the cleverest? As well, of course, as much the quickest eater," the wolf murmured to himself. It was only a pity, he thought, that he hadn't had the chance to prove it this time.

3.

The Spell

THE WOLF shut his large book with a loud bang.

"Of course! What I need is a spell! A spell which would make that stupid little Polly come to see me, asking me to be kind enough to eat her up," he said.

He was amazed that the idea hadn't occurred to him before. In the book he had just been reading there was no shortage of spells. Beautiful princesses got turned into frogs, frogs turned into handsome princes, kings were trapped and enchanted by witches, several small juicy children were forced, by magic, to work for giants and ogres or other unpleasant characters and were often in the gravest danger of being eaten. If all this could happen to princesses and princes, why shouldn't a perfectly ordinary little Polly be made, by a spell, to come and look for a very respectable wolf? And even made to ask him to eat her? Without any fuss, and without any of this endless argument. The wolf was bored with argument. All he wanted was a good meal, and to know that at last he had got the better of Polly, clever as she was supposed to be.

He thought carefully. He had to find a really reliable spell. He didn't want one which was going to run out at an awkward moment. Or one which never got going. The wolf put some money into a small leather bag which he tied securely round his neck, and trotted off to see what the High Street shops had to offer.

A shop window piled with saucepans, pails, baskets, cat litter and bottles of different-coloured mixtures first attracted him. A solid-looking stool was labelled "Built to last." This sounded promising. The wolf didn't want a long-lasting stool, of course, but if this shop sold reliable stools, why not surefire spells? He was encouraged by seeing that a bottle of purplish liquid was apparently called MAGICLEAN. He went boldly into the shop.

"I want a spell," the wolf said to a stupid-looking girl who was leaning against a white kitchen cupboard and reading a newspaper.

"A what?"

"A spell."

"Don't keep them. No one asks for them nowadays," the girl said, without taking her eyes from the page in front of her.

"Yes, you do. I saw one in the window."

"Must have made a mistake. Told you, we don't keep them. They're out of date," the girl said, still not looking at the wolf.

"I tell you, I saw it. Here. Look!" the wolf said, seeing more bottles of the same purplish stuff on a shelf near by.

"What, that? Why didn't you say so?" the girl said. She snatched a bottle from the shelf, and began searching in a drawer for a paper bag.

"That'll be seventy-nine pence," she said.

"Wait a moment. What does it do?" the wolf asked.

"What do you mean, what does it do?"

"What I say. What does the magic do? It might not be what

I need. What I want is a simple spell which will make a small girl…"

"I don't know what you're on about. Can't you read? This is for cleaning out ovens. Says so on the label," the girl said. She put the bottle within an inch or two of the wolf's nose. The printing on the label was very small and the wolf was unable to read a word.

"Is that all? Just cleans ovens? Nothing else?" he said, disappointed.

"What d'you expect for seventy-nine p? A beauty cream? Though it would take more than that to make you fit to look at," the girl said unpleasantly. She put the bottle back on its shelf and returned to her newspaper. The wolf, insulted, went quickly out of the shop.

"What a very disagreeable girl. And stupid! Even stupider than Polly," he thought. He stopped in front of another shop window to examine his own reflection.

"I don't know what she can have meant by that remark

about a beauty cream. I am a remarkably good-looking wolf," he decided, and, slightly comforted by what he had seen, went on his way.

He stopped next to visit a food store. He found it difficult to pass by the containers of frozen meat, though he knew from past experience that you had to wait for hours before you could get your teeth properly into those tempting-looking hunks. He passed the shelves of bread and biscuits. At last he found what he was looking for. A small packet. On the outside was printed "TENDERIZER. FOR ANY KIND OF MEAT."

He carried three packets to the check-out desk.

"Does it really work?" he asked the girl who rang up the cost on the cash register.

"Like magic," she said.

"Have you got any more magic spells?" the wolf asked, interested. But by this time the girl was attending to the customer behind the wolf, and she took no notice of his question, only pushed his three packets of tenderizer towards him.

Outside the shop, the wolf looked carefully at the instructions on the packets. "SPRINKLE A FEW DROPS ON THE MEAT BEFORE COOKING. LEAVE FOR TEN TO FIFTEEN MINUTES BEFORE PUTTING IN THE OVEN," he read. He opened the packet. Inside was a small bottle.

Very carefully the wolf sprinkled three or four drops on to his own front leg.

"If it makes me tender, it really is magic," he thought.

He stood still on the pavement, watching the clock on the clock tower. At the end of ten minutes, he opened his mouth and brought his front leg towards it.

"Wow! That hurt!" he said in surprise as his teeth met his own skin. He looked quickly round. He would not have liked Polly to see him testing his own tenderness in this way. She might have thought it was stu ... not a very clever thing to do.

He continued to walk down the street, looking in all the windows as he went. Presently he stopped outside a shop called simply HEALTH. In the window were two pictures. One was of a miserable-looking woman with a great many wrinkles, bags under her eyes and hair like string. The other showed the same woman, but this time smiling, with a smooth skin and shining hair. In her hand she held a box of globules to which she was pointing. Under the picture were the words, "Magical transformation. I grew ten years younger in a single night."

"That is something like magic!" the wolf thought admiringly, and he pushed open the shop door and went straight in.

"I see you have boxes of magic pills. What I want is a spell..." he began saying to the anxious-looking woman behind the counter.

"A smell? Ah, yes. Can I suggest these charming little lavender bags... so delicious. You can just sprinkle them about your linen cupboard..." she began.

"No, you don't understand. I want a magic potion. Something you drink. Or eat. I'll have a couple of those boxes of globules the lady in the window has in her hand," the wolf said. Making Polly younger when he caught her would also make her tenderer and possibly stupider. While the worried woman was finding the pills, the wolf wandered round the shop. The more he looked, the more sure he became that this was the right place for spells. So many bottles full of different-coloured fluids! So many small packages done up with gold string, with pictures of herbs outside. When the wolf caught sight of a black cat stalking through the shop, and then saw an old-fashioned twig broom leaning in a corner, he knew he had at last found a witch's lair.

"That's her broom, I suppose," he said to the worried woman.

"The besom, yes. We like the old customs here," she said, making a neat parcel out of the two boxes of pills.

"Do you use it too? I suppose it's strong enough," the wolf said. The woman looked as if she'd be quite a load.

"I find it far better than any of the modern brooms," the woman said. "Can I interest you in anything else?" she asked.

"I'd be very much interested in anything that could make a young girl behave kindly to wol...to animals," the wolf said.

"Do you mean she isn't kind to our dumb friends?" the woman asked, shocked.

"She certainly isn't."

"Treats them badly? Pulls the wings off flies? Doesn't look after her pets?"

"Starves them," the wolf said sadly.

"But that's terrible!"

"Haven't you got something which would change her? A bottle of medicine? Some more pills?"

The anxious woman shook her head. "Nothing will change a bad nature like that except education. Someone must take her in hand and teach her. What a terrible story! Perhaps you could give her little lessons and tell her how wickedly she's behaving?"

"I've been trying for years. But it's a very difficult case," the wolf said sadly. He picked up his parcel and left the shop.

A day or two later, Polly was upstairs in her bedroom when she heard a loud knock on the front door. She thought of going down to see who it was, but she had learned to be careful, so she opened the window and looked cautiously out to see who was below. There was nothing and no one to be seen.

She went downstairs and saw a small parcel lying on the doormat inside the front door. A label tied on it said simply TO POLLY.

"A present. But it isn't my birthday," Polly thought. She sat down on the mat and tore off the paper.

Inside was a round pill-box. The piece of paper stuck to the lid had writing on it, which read:

MAGIC!
UNTIL YOU TRY THIS MAGIC REMEDY
YOU WILL NEVER BELIEVE HOW
THE WRINKLES WILL FADE AWAY
THE SKIN BECOMES CLEAR AND YOUTHFUL
YOUR STEP REGAINS ITS SPRING
LIFE LOOKS PROMISING
MAKES YOU TEN YEARS YOUNGER.

TAKE THREE GLOBULES AFTER EACH MEAL

The pill-box was full of large green globules.

As Polly was looking at them, she heard the letter box rattle and the end of a long black nose pushed itself a short way through.

"Am oom om em?" a muffled voice asked.

"I don't understand," Polly said.

"Bother. Can't talk with that trap thing round my mouth. I said, 'Have you got them?'" the wolf's ordinary voice said from the other side of the door.

"The green globules?" Polly asked.

"From a friend," said the voice.

"What am I supposed to do with them?"

"Swallow them, of course. How can anyone be quite so stupid?" the voice said, impatient.

"But it says on the box that they will take away my wrinkles, and I haven't got any," Polly said.

"Perhaps the globules will prevent your getting any."

"And they are supposed to make my skin clear and my step springy."

"Well? You don't want to have muddy skin and to plod around like a camel, do you?" the wolf asked.

"And, Wolf! It says the globules will make me ten years younger," Polly called out.

"And that much tenderer. A delicate morsel. Like one of those very small sucking pigs you see sometimes in butchers' shops. A very small Polly..." The wolf's voice died away into happy dreams of guzzling greed.

"But..."

"Don't let's have any of this endless talk, girl. Eat up your nice globules and don't argue," the wolf said.

"But, Wolf, you haven't counted. The globules will make me ten years younger."

"Hurry up and swallow them, then. I'm hungry."

"Wolf, I am seven years old," Polly said.

"Seven. Eight. Six. What does it matter now?"

"You aren't very good at numbers, Wolf. I am seven. If I eat these globules, and they make me ten years younger, how old do you think I shall be?"

"Two? One and a half? Six months? All good ages. Delicious ages. Just what I enjoy most," the wolf said.

"You can't count, Wolf. If you take ten away from seven, it leaves minus three."

"What is minus?" the wolf's voice asked suspiciously.

"It would mean that I wouldn't get born for another three years."

"Say that again. Slowly," the voice said.

"If...I...eat...these globules and they make me...ten... years...younger...I shan't get born again as a baby for another...three...years."

There was a short silence.

"Are you sure of that?" the voice asked.

"Numbers is my best subject at school," Polly said.

"Another three years, you said. You mean that there wouldn't be any Polly for that long? I'd have to wait for three whole years?"

"That's right," Polly said.

"And then you would get born? A small, fat, juicy Polly? Who wouldn't have learned to talk? No, it's no good. I can't wait that long," the wolf's voice said from the other side of the door. Polly heard a disappointed groan.

"Do you want me to start straight away?" Polly called out. There was no answer. Polly peeped through the letter box and saw a dejected-looking tail disappearing towards the garden gate. A second box of green globules flew off to one side of the owner of the tail. On the other side went a small bottle of tenderizer. "Spells. You can't trust them now like you could in the good old days," the wolf muttered angrily as, once more disappointed, he trotted towards his own home.

4.

Songs My Mother Taught Me

IT WAS early evening and just beginning to get dark. A huge yellow moon was hanging about behind the trees, three times as large as necessary. Polly was sitting on the window-seat, practising the recorder. She hadn't been learning very long, and she could only play easy tunes. "Baa, Baa, Black Sheep" wasn't too bad. "I Had a Little Nut Tree" was better.

By the time she'd played it through six times, her mouth and her fingers were tired. She put the recorder down and looked out of the window. It didn't really surprise her to see the wolf standing beyond the hedge, making signs at her.

Polly opened the window a little. She was on the first floor and she felt safe up there.

"Hi, Wolf!" she said.

"Did you hear that?" the wolf asked.

"Did I hear what?" Polly said.

"That horrible noise. That caterwauling. As if a grasshopper were trying to sing with his hind legs…"

"That was me practising my recorder," Polly said, offended.

"You mean you meant to make that noise? Did it on purpose?"

"I didn't think I was that bad. 'I Had a Little Nut Tree' was all right."

"Do you really think so? I've always thought it a very disappointing song," the wolf said.

"Disappointing? Because it didn't have any nuts? I'd rather have the silver nutmeg and the golden pear."

The wolf looked astonished. "I don't know what you're talking about," he said.

Polly recited:

> "I had a little nut tree
> Nothing would it bear,
> But a silver nutmeg
> And a golden pear.
> The King of Spain's daughter..."

"Nonsense! You've got it entirely wrong.It's not at all like that," the wolf said, testily.

"No, I haven't. I learned it at school," Polly said.

"I learned it from my mother. This is what she taught me:

> "I had a little nut tree
> That wasn't any good.
> I really wanted meat, but
> It had only wood,"

said the wolf.

"Trees never do have meat," Polly said.

"Then why sing about them?"

"I don't, much. It's just that it's not so difficult to play," Polly said.

"You call that playing? What other songs do you know?"

"Humpty Dumpty," Polly said.

"Go on, then. No, not on that revolting penny whistle..."

"It's not a penny whistle. It's my new recorder," Polly protested.

"Whatever it is, leave it alone. Just tell me the words," the wolf said.

Polly began:

> "Humpty Dumpty sat on a wall,
> Humpty Dumpty had a great fall.
> All the King's horses and all the King's men
> Couldn't put Humpty Dumpty together again."

"Wrong," the wolf sighed.

"What do you mean, wrong?" Polly asked.

"You've never learned the right words. Listen:

> "Humpty Dumpty sat on a wall,
> Humpty Dumpty had a great fall.
> I licked up the yolk and the white as well,
> But I couldn't be bothered with the shell,"

said the wolf.

"You ate him!" Polly said, shocked.

The wolf looked slightly ashamed. Then he said, "Well, if the King's men couldn't help the poor old fat thing, there wasn't much I could do, was there?"

Polly thought about this.

"You eat eggs, don't you? He was only a great big egg," the wolf said.

"Ye...es. Only not raw," Polly said.

"Raw eggs are very good for the voice," the wolf said. He opened his jaws widely and yodelled. Then he sang:

"*Mary had a little lamb*..."

"I know that. And it's not about eating," Polly said, pleased.

"What do you mean it's not about eating? It's not about anything else," the wolf said.

"*Mary had a little lamb,*
Its fleece was white as snow,
And everywhere that Mary went
The lamb was sure to go,"

Polly said.

"No," the wolf cried, outraged.

"Yes. That's what it says," Polly said.

"Of course it doesn't. Who wants to know about the colour of its fleece? What my mother taught me is far more interesting," the wolf said, and raising a paw in the air, he declaimed:

"*Mary had a little lamb,*
And then, not feeling full,
She had some more, and more, until
All that was left was wool."

And who cares what colour that was?" he asked.

"I think that's horrible," Polly said.

"Not at all. If she was so anxious to have the lamb going everywhere she did, the best thing she could do was to make sure it was inside her," the wolf replied.

"Are all your songs about eating?" Polly asked.

"What else is there to make a song about?" the wolf asked, simply.

Polly considered the songs she knew. It did seem true that a great many of them were about eating. "Little Jack Horner." The Queen in "Sing a Song of Sixpence." "Jack Sprat." "Goldilocks," with all those strawberries and cream. Even the pussycat who went to London to see the Queen had certainly eaten the little mouse she found there.

"The song about you is all about eating, too," the wolf said.

"You mean, 'Polly put the kettle on'?" Polly asked. She had always felt a little embarrassed by that song.

"Of course."

"But it only says 'tea'. And I don't think it means a real sit-down tea you eat, with bread and butter and cake. I think it's only the sort of tea that comes out of a teapot," Polly said.

"Nonsense. It's about quite a solid meal," the wolf said.

Polly repeated:

> "Polly put the kettle on,
> Polly put the kettle on,
> Polly put the kettle on,
> We'll all have tea.

If they'd been going to eat, it would say, butter the bread, or get out the cake tin."

"What a miserable meal to ask your friends in to enjoy! Now, mine would really be quite something," the wolf said.

"What does yours say?" Polly asked.

> "Polly make the water hot,
> Polly make the water hot,
> Put it in a great big pot
> And then jump in . . ."

"I wouldn't," Polly said. The wolf took no notice. He went on:

> "Clever wolf knows what to do,
> Leaves it for an hour or two,
> Gobbles up the Polly stew,
> It's all gone away."

"I wouldn't jump in. That would be stupid," Polly said again.

"Exactly. That's what my mother said. I mean, she said you were stupid."

"I haven't jumped into a pot of boiling water, have I?"

"Not yet," the wolf said.

There was a short pause.

"She used to sing me a lullaby," the wolf said, dreamily.

"Who did?"

"My mother. It was very soothing. Beautiful words, it had.

> "Bye, baby bunting,
> Your father's gone a-hunting,
> He's gone to find a Polly in her
> Home to make your lovely dinner."

"He never did, though," Polly said.

"He knew he could leave it to me," the wolf said.

Polly picked up her recorder. She was finding this conversation either frightening or boring, she couldn't quite decide which.

"Are you going to play again?" the wolf asked, apprehensive.

Polly played the tune of "Oranges and Lemons." It was difficult and the notes did not always come out just as she meant them to.

"What's that tune?" the wolf asked, stretching his neck over the hedge.

"It's meant to be 'Oranges and Lemons'."

"It sounds to me more like 'Onions and Kidneys'," said the wolf.

"There isn't a tune called 'Onions and Kidneys'," Polly said.

"Of course there is. It's a bit like what you were trying to play just then."

"All right. Sing your song, then," Polly said.

Not untunefully, the wolf sang:

> "Onions and Kidneys
> Say the bells of St Sydney's.
> I'd like something sweeter,
> Says the bell of St Peter.
> Try our jam tarts,
> Say the bells of St Bart's.
> A well-roasted boy,
> Say the bells of St Foy.
> Poached girl on toast,
> Is what we'd like most,
> We'll have her for tea,
> The bells all agree ..."

"I don't agree," Polly said quickly.

"That doesn't matter. If everyone else agrees, you get eaten. That's the law," the wolf said. He bounded over the hedge and stood in the garden, immediately underneath Polly's window, his long red tongue lolling out of his mouth, his teeth wickedly agape.

"Lean further out of the window, Polly," he said.

"I'm not allowed to. Mother says not to," Polly said, primly.

"A pity. Never mind. Everyone agrees that you are there for me to eat. I shall wait until it is a little darker, and then I shall jump up and get you," the wolf said, lying down, prepared to wait.

Polly thought quickly.

"I shouldn't advise you to wait too long, Wolf," she said.

"What do you mean?"

"Only that it might be dangerous," Polly said.

"Dangerous for you. Not for me," the wolf said, in a self-satisfied voice.

"Wolf! Don't you know the song about 'Boys and girls come out to play'?" Polly asked.

"Of course I know it. A stupid song. Something about a ha'penny loaf. Cubs' play," the wolf snorted.

"I don't think your mother can have taught you the right words," Polly said.

"My mother was a good wom... a good wolf. Don't say a word against her," the wolf said.

"What words did she teach you for that song?" Polly asked.

The wolf closed his eyes and recited in a sing-song voice:

"Girls and boys come out to play,
The moon doth shine as bright as day.
Leave your supper and leave your sleep
And come with your playfellows in the street.
Come with a whoop and come with a call,
Come with a good will or come not at all.
Up the ladder and down the wall,
A ha'penny loaf will serve us all . . .

"I never cared for that," the wolf said, shaking his shaggy head.

"And anyway, you've got it wrong," Polly said.

"You mean there's more than a ha'penny loaf?" the wolf asked, interested.

"Something much better.

"... *Come with a whoop and come with a call,*
A well-cooked wolf will serve us all.
We'll roast his ribs and curry his tail,
And pickle his head in the salting pail,"

Polly finished.

There was a short silence. Then the wolf asked, "What did you say was to be well cooked?"

"A wolf," Polly said.

"Do boys and girls often eat wolf?"

"If it's well cooked. Especially at midnight feasts," Polly said. She put the recorder to her mouth and thoughtfully played the first few bars of the tune.

The wolf jumped.

"Don't do that!" he said.

"Why not, Wolf? I'm just trying the tune over."

"But suppose someone heard you? Suppose those boys and girls you mentioned...What would they think if they heard?"

"I suppose they might think there was something amusing going on in the street. After all, the moon is nearly as bright as day now. They might come with a whoop and a call," Polly said.

"And if they did, they'd expect...? They might think that I was waiting for...? No! It's too horrible to imagine. Polly! May I ask a favour?" the wolf said, imploring.

"As long as you don't ask me to jump into a pot of boiling water," Polly said.

"What a barbarous idea! Of course not. No. All I want is

that you should refrain from trying out that dreadful tin trumpet...I mean, would you be kind enough to do anything else but play those melodious tunes on your splendid instrument for the present? I...I seem to have a headache. I require perfect silence. If you would just sit quietly there while I return home to take a couple of aspirins and go to bed with a hot-water bottle, I should be infinitely obliged," the wolf said. He leapt over the hedge and started trotting fast down the road. As he went Polly heard him mutter to himself. "Curry my tail! The idea! Pickle my head! I don't know what boys and girls are coming to."

Polly shut the window. The evening was becoming chilly. She put the recorder away in its case and went down to supper. Baked beans and toast.

"Did you have a good practice?" her mother asked.

"Very good," Polly said.

"Can you play 'Begone Dull Care' for the school concert next week?"

"I expect so," Polly said. And she thought to herself, "Anyway, I can play 'Begone Stupid Wolf' and make him go, too."

5.

Outside the Pet Shop

POLLY was standing outside the pet shop near her home and looking at the animals in cages in the windows. She liked the slant-eyed kittens, playing with each other, and the hamsters, sharing an apple. She was watching a tortoise, and wondering whether it was asleep or just feeling tired, when the person standing at her side suddenly spoke.

"Very boring," the person said.

"What? What's boring?" Polly asked.

"All these creatures. Dull, boring, stupid," the person said.

"The kittens aren't boring. Look at that stripy one trying to bite its own tail."

"Kittens always do that. It's not amusing."

"I think it's funny," Polly said. The stripy kitten had managed to put a paw on the end of the tail it was chasing, and now tried to pounce on it and take it by surprise. As the kitten jumped, so did its tail, right out of reach. The kitten looked hurt and surprised.

"Silly little animals. Imagine not knowing where your own tail is. I would never want a kitten as a pet," the person said.

204

"What would you want as a pet?" Polly asked. She was beginning to suspect that she knew who this person was, and she was quite interested to find out what sort of pet the wolf would choose for himself. She had a nasty suspicion that he might choose a juicy little girl, and that he wouldn't keep her as a pet for very long. He would probably turn her into his dinner.

"I certainly would not have a tortoise. They are boring, too. Asleep most of the time, and probably taste as uninteresting as they look," the wolf said.

"The budgies aren't asleep. I wouldn't mind having a budgie," Polly said.

"Hardly a mouthful...I mean, their conversation is so limited. Imagine having to listen to nothing but Tweet, tweet all day long."

"I'd rather like a white mouse," Polly said, pointing to a cage in which several mice were running over a wheel.

"Your ideas are so small. Why don't you go for something nearer your own size?"

"You mean, like a monkey?" Polly asked. She had once seen a monkey in the pet shop. It had sat in a too small cage, looking at all the passers-by with sad, hopeless eyes.

"Aha! It wasn't me that said you were like a monkey. It was you," the wolf said, triumphant.

"I didn't! I just said that a monkey was larger than a white mouse."

"I would not advise a monkey. Nasty, spiteful things. You never know when they'll turn and bite you. Not because they are hungry, in the ordinary way, but just to be horrible. Or pull your hair," the wolf said.

"I've always thought I'd like a pony," Polly said.

"How can you be so...ordinary? Girls always want ponies."

"I wouldn't mind a cat, even. Or a dog."

"That's more ordinary still. Everyone has cats and dogs. Why don't you find a pet who is more interesting than a wretched cat or dog? Someone that no one else has thought of?"

"You mean, like a snake?"

"Of course not a snake. I wouldn't want a snake. Is that the best you can think of?" the wolf asked crossly.

"I'd rather like to have a baby crocodile. He could swim in my bath. Only I suppose when he grew up I wouldn't be able to keep him," Polly said.

"You certainly wouldn't. If he was in the bath with you, there wouldn't be much left of you by the time you got out. I'm thinking of something quite different. Can't you guess what it is?"

"A dolphin? They are supposed to be very clever."

"Not a dolphin. Why anybody should be interested in keeping a fish, I don't know. The animal I am thinking of is not a crocodile nor a budgie nor a dolphin. He is large. He has four legs. He has a tail and he is very, very clever. Much cleverer than any other animal you can think of," the wolf said.

"Can he talk?"

"Of course he can talk. You ought to know that."

"It's a parrot," Polly said, forgetting about the four legs.

"It is not a parrot. Stupid, they are. All they can say is 'Clever Polly'. And that means nothing," the wolf said quickly.

"A large animal. Very clever, with four legs. With big ears?" Polly asked.

"Big enough for him to hear everything worth listening to," the wolf said, his own ears pricking up.

"A donkey," Polly said.

"Grrr. Mind your manners. Donkeys are not clever. They are slow and obstinate. This creature is intelligent..."

"I know! It never forgets anything," Polly cried.

"Right!" the wolf said.

"Has it got a long nose?"

"Long? It is not one of those snubby, useless little noses that you humans have. It is an elegant and very acute nose."

"It's an elephant," Polly said, sure that this time she had guessed right.

"It is not an elephant. Really, I can't remember when I met anyone with so little brain," the wolf declared.

"Not a dolphin. Not a donkey. Not a snake. Not an elephant. Tell me something else about him," Polly asked.

"This creature is remarkably sharp," the wolf said.

"A hedgehog. Their prickles are very sharp."

"Hedgehogs do not have fur."

"You didn't say fur."

"Didn't I? I must have forgotten. The animal I am thinking of has a thick coat of very elegant fur," the wolf said.

"What colour?" Polly asked.

"Black. Black as ebony."

"He's a mole. Moles have black velvet coats and long snouts."

The wolf stamped with impatience. "You can't really be so stupid. Moles are blind, or very nearly blind. They spend their time living underground. I...I mean, the animal I am thinking of, lives entirely above ground, in a very distinguished way..."

"Is he gentle?" Polly asked.

"As a lamb," the wolf replied, showing his sharp yellow teeth in what he hoped was a pleasing smile.

"Does he know any tricks?"

"Tricks?" the wolf repeated, astonished.

"Does he catch lumps of sugar? Can he balance them on his nose? Does he beg for food?" Polly asked. She was enjoying this conversation.

"Certainly not. He has no need for such foolish games. Tricks, indeed! He is not a clown. And as for begging, of

course not. Why should an upright and self-respecting Wo...
animal be forced to beg?"

"Well, what does he do? Why do you think he would make
a good pet?" Polly asked.

"He is well brought up. Most people want their pets to be
well brought up. He is large. Can take care of himself. He is
faithful. He has been after...I mean, he has been following
the same person for years. Never looks at anyone else."

Polly thought about this.

"I see. This pet you are recommending is a large some-
body, in a black fur coat. He has a long nose and large ears.
He doesn't do any tricks, and he has been faithfully following
the same someone for years. Is that right?"

"About right," the wolf said.

"But if he has been after this someone for years and hasn't
ever caught up with her, I don't see that he can be so very
clever."

"Ah! But if only she would take him into her house as a pet,
she would soon discover just how much cleverer...and more
lovable, of course, he is than she has ever realized," the wolf
said.

"It's no good, Wolf. I don't want a large black hairy pet,
especially not one with long ears and nose and a lot of very
sharp teeth. And my mother and father don't want me to have
a big pet who talks. They don't even like my having a very
small white mouse, or a hamster. So, not today, thank you
very much," Polly said, and she walked away towards her
home, leaving the wolf outside the pet shop, grinning in at
the window and terrifying a harmless guinea-pig, who didn't
at all care for that display of long yellow teeth, even if they
were the other side of a plate-glass window.

6.

The Trap

"WHAT DO you think it's there for?" Polly said to her sister Jane. They were looking over the gate at an unusual object lying in the lane that ran along the side of their garden.

"Looks like a packing crate on its side," Jane said.

"Why do you suppose its lid is tied back with that piece of string?"

"Don't know. Anyhow, it's very boring. And there's a horrible smell," Jane said. She left Polly at the gate and went back into the house.

"I see you are admiring my tr...my latest piece of work," the wolf said, appearing suddenly on the other side of the crate.

"I didn't realize it was yours, Wolf. What is it?" Polly asked.

"I can't tell you that, you stupid little girl. If I told you what it was for, it wouldn't take you by surprise, would it?" the wolf said crossly.

"Is it a present?" Polly asked. Surprises were sometimes presents, she knew.

"Certainly not. Why should I give you a present?" the wolf said.

Polly couldn't think of a good reason why he should. She asked, "Why is the lid tied back with that bit of string?"

"Aha! That's what is so extremely clever. When someone goes into that tr...into that box to get the delicious lump of meat which I have placed at the further end, the string is loosened and the lid slams shut, and, hey presto! I have caught my prey."

"And then what happens?" Polly asked.

"I go in and gobble her up. With the delicious piece of meat for afters," the wolf said. He closed his eyes and licked his lips.

"Like a mousetrap?" Polly said.

"That's right. Like a mousetrap. But I am not trying to catch a mouse. I don't care much for mice. Too many whiskers and bones to be worth bothering with."

"If it isn't for a mouse, who is it for?" Polly asked, though she had already guessed what sort of animal the wolf meant to catch in his trap.

"You ask too many questions. Why do you want to know?"

"I just wondered whether the animal you want to catch is interested in raw meat," Polly said.

"Everyone is interested in raw meat," the wolf said.

"I'm not."

There was a short, appalled silence.

"Say that again," the wolf said, presently.

"Say what?"

"You said...I thought that you said...Perhaps my ears deceived me. I distinctly thought I heard you say that you were not interested in raw meat," the wolf said.

"That's right. I don't like raw meat," Polly said.

"You mean that if you saw a delicious hunk of raw meat at the further end of what looked like a perfectly ordinary tr... wooden box, you wouldn't go in and get it?" the wolf asked. He could hardly believe what he heard.

"No. I wouldn't. Especially if it smelled like what you've got in there," Polly said.

There was a short silence.

"Ah well! One lives and learns. I must be getting along, now. Nice to have seen you, Polly. No doubt we shall be meeting again," the wolf said sadly, as he turned away along the lane, dragging the unsuccessful trap behind him.

"He'll be back," Polly thought. She had had experience with the wolf before. She knew how difficult it was for him to give up an idea that had once seemed a good one.

"Road's up again," Polly's father said, coming in, cross, after a long drive home, to find a large hole in the road just outside his own garage.

"What is it this time? Gas? Electricity? Drains?" Polly's mother asked, ladling out hot soup into bowls for the family.

"Didn't ask. Wasn't anyone there. No lights, no signs. Disgrace," Polly's father said.

"I'll have a look tomorrow. Take care. Soup's hot," Polly's mother said, a little too late. Polly's father had already burned his tongue.

The next morning, after breakfast, Polly looked out from her garden and saw the hole in the road. As her father had said, there were no protective barriers and no lamps. There was only one workman, a large person in blue dungarees, hacking away at the road surface with an old-fashioned pickaxe.

"Why are you digging that hole?" Polly called from the gate.

The person stopped his digging and looked towards her. He shook his head without speaking and lifted the pickaxe for another stroke.

"Is it for the electricity? Or the gas? Or the water?" Polly asked.

"Never you mind what it's for. Ask no questions and you won't hear any lies," the person said, a little out of breath with the effort he had been making.

Polly considered this. Some people, she thought, told lies without being asked questions.

"Is it going to be a much larger hole?" she asked presently, as the workman drove smaller holes in the road surrounding the first one.

"It will be enormous," the workman said. He jumped on a crumbling edge and said, "Ow!" as he disappeared. The edge had given way under his feet. A moment later the top of his head appeared on a level with the road surface.

"Did you see that?" he asked, scrambling up out of the hole.

"I wish you'd tell me what the hole is for," Polly said.

"Can't tell you that," the workman said, raising his pickaxe for another stroke.

"Is it a secret?" Polly asked. She loved secrets.

"It's a secret," the workman agreed. He raised his pickaxe again and brought it down with an immense thump into the hole in the road.

There was a hiss, a rush, a roar. Polly took several steps back into her garden, as a column of water, perhaps ten feet high, shot up from the water-mains pipe which the pickaxe had hit. The workman stood under a shower-bath of falling water, while the road at his feet rapidly turned to a flowing river of mud.

"Waugh! Whoosh! Atishoo!" the person said, trying to

struggle free of the cascade of water. "Why don't you *do* something? Hoosh!" he said, angrily, to the dry and interested Polly on the further side of the garden hedge.

"Engineers! Police! Fire Brigade!" the person spluttered. He reached for his pickaxe and aimed a furious blow at the point where the water was spurting. There was a deafening explosion. Blue flames crackled across the waterfall. The person had managed to hit not only the water mains, but also the electric cable.

An angry woman appeared on the doorstep of a neighbouring house.

"My electric has gone out! You've cut off my electric!" she said, pointing at the wet and bedraggled workman.

"I never touched your electric," the workman said.

"It's gone off! And there was my nice chicken, only half cooked," the woman said.

"Did you say a half-cooked chicken?" the person said, eagerly. He was drenched, he was singed, but he was also hungry. Water was still gushing up under his feet, but he seemed hardly to notice this.

"I'll telephone 999," Polly said. But when she reached the telephone in her house, she found that it was dead. The person digging a hole in the road had cut through the telephone wires as well as everything else. After this the road was barricaded off for several days while men from the Metropolitan Water Board, from the London Electricity Board and from the Post Office came and mended all the different bits and put the surface of the road back again.

"That wasn't very clever, Wolf," Polly said, looking out of a first-floor window and seeing the wolf sadly gazing at the large knobbly patch in the road where, not so long ago, he had dug his ill-fated hole.

"How could I know there were all those pipes and wires

and things just there?" he grumbled, kicking a loose stone crossly into the gutter.

"Haven't you ever seen men digging up the road? Or sometimes it's the pavement. There are always lots of pipes and wires, all muddled up together."

"No one told me," the wolf said sulkily.

"Anyway, why were you digging that hole? Were you trying to get down to Australia?" Polly asked.

"My dear Polly! Don't you know that Australia is on the other side of the world? Twenty thousand miles away, or something like that?"

"I just thought perhaps you thought you could get there by digging straight through," Polly said.

"Straight through all those tangled-up wires and things? No, thank you. Anyhow, if Australia is twenty thousand miles away, how could it be at the bottom of a hole that I'm digging here?"

"Because the world is round. Australia is directly underneath us," Polly said.

The wolf sighed loudly.

"I don't know whether you are really as stupid as you pretend, or if you make these things up to annoy me. Of course the world isn't round. Anyone can see it's flat. If it was round," the wolf went on, thinking hard, "some of the people would be falling off all the time. They'd be upside down. Stop talking nonsense. If you can," he added grimly.

"Well, what were you digging that hole for?" Polly asked.

"That's a secret."

"Is it a secret now, when it isn't there any longer?" Polly asked.

"It certainly is. It was part of a very clever plan, which I shall carry out successfuly at another time and in another place," the wolf said.

"If you want to dig a big hole, why don't you try something easier than the road? Why don't you dig in the earth? On the Heath, for instance?" Polly asked.

The wolf considered this suggestion. Then he asked, "Do you often go for walks on the Heath?"

"Nearly every day."

"Goodbye, Polly. I have just remembered some urgent business. I hope we shall meet again soon," the wolf said, and Polly saw him hurry away down the road in the direction of the Heath. She had a very good idea of what his urgent business was going to be.

Sure enough, a few days later, when she was coming home with her sisters from walking across the Heath, she heard loud puffing sounds, and saw someone working hard on a small patch of grass surrounded by low bushes.

"Hi!" the someone called as the three girls came near.

"What do you want?" Polly called back, prudently keeping the bushes between herself and the working person.

"Come here and see what I'm doing. No. That isn't what I mean. Come here and see what I'm not doing. No. That's not right, either. Come here and don't see what I'm doing," the wolf said, leaning on his spade.

"You mean come right up to you and don't look?"

"That's right," the wolf said, pleased.

"You want me to walk towards you but to look somewhere else?" Polly said.

"You could shut your eyes. In fact, that would be the best way to do it," the wolf said.

"I don't think I'm clever enough to walk straight through between the bushes with my eyes shut," Polly said.

"How terrible it must be for you to be so very, very stupid," the wolf said, showing his teeth in a large smile.

"Could you do it?" Polly asked.

"Of course."

"Perhaps if you showed me how, I would be able to copy you," Polly suggested.

"Dead easy," the wolf said.

"Show me, then," Polly said.

The wolf went to the far side of the patch of grass inside the ring of bushes. He shut his eyes.

"Like this," he said.

"And then what happens?" Polly asked.

"You just step boldly forward and walk across this fine grassy space. Like so," the wolf said, and he stepped forward.

"I think it's time we went back to tea," Polly said to her sisters. As they turned towards home, they heard behind them a sudden loud cry.

"What's that?" Lucy asked, stopping short.

"Perhaps someone has fallen down," said Jane.

"Into a large hole," Polly said.

"Why should anyone dig a very large hole and then fall into it?" Lucy asked.

"Because," Polly answered, "he is not a very clever wolf."

7.

The Wolf Goes Wooing (1)

"At last I see where I've been mistaken," the wolf said. He was reading one of his favourite books, a collection of stories about clever animals, princes and princesses, wicked witches and terrible dragons. His old mother had given it to him when he was nothing more than a young cub and had told him that everything he needed to know would be found in this excellent book.

"The mistake I've made has been to try to catch Polly by tricks. I've tried to take her by surprise. To pounce. Of course she has always run away. Now I understand the right way of going about it, I shall try a quite different method," the wolf said to himself.

A few days later, Polly was sitting on the swing in the front garden when she saw the wolf walking carefully down the road. On his head he wore a small crown of gold-coloured paper. In one hand he carried a short stick. When he reached the garden gate he stopped and leaned over it.

"Good afternoon, Polly," he said.

"Good afternoon, Wolf," Polly replied.

"I hope you are well," the wolf said.

"I'm very well, thank you, Wolf."

"I wonder..." the wolf said, looking round. His eye fell on a flower-bed of tulips which had been carefully planted there several months before, by Polly's mother.

"I wonder if you would be kind enough to get me a glass of water? I've come a long way in the heat and dust," he said.

Polly was a kind girl. When the wolf put out a long red tongue, turned his eyes upwards and panted thirstily, she didn't like to refuse. She went into the house and came out in two or three minutes' time, carrying a tumbler of cold water. To her surprise, when she offered it to the wolf, he didn't immediately take it. Instead he handed her a large bunch of bright yellow tulips.

"For the fairest in the land," he said, bowing. His paper crown fell off. He quickly picked it up and put it back, tipped crazily over one ear.

Polly looked round the garden.

"Wolf! They're our tulips. You've picked them all. They're Mother's best flowers. She'll be furious," she said.

"Nothing is too good for a beautiful princess like you," the wolf said, not seeming to care about Polly's mother.

"And I'm not a princess," Polly said.

"To me you will always be a princess. And I'm a prince. Can't you see my crown? And my sceptre?" the wolf asked. He pointed to the lop-sided paper crown and flourished the small stick in his left paw.

"I don't understand..." Polly began.

"You can't help being stupid," the wolf agreed. Then, remembering his new idea, he added quickly, "Not stupid. Just a little slow to understand the new situation, perhaps."

"What am I supposed to do with these?" Polly asked, looking at the bunch of tulips in dismay.

"Put them in water, of course," the wolf said, taking the flowers from her and plunging them into the tumbler of water which Polly had brought from the house.

"I thought you were so hot and thirsty," Polly said.

"That was a cunning trick so that you would go into the house and I could pick these beautiful flowers for you," the wolf said, very much pleased with himself.

"Why do you want to give me flowers?"

"Aha!" the wolf said.

"Aha what?" Polly asked.

"Aha! I have a new plan. I see now, Polly, that I have been wrong in trying to catch you unawares. I shouldn't have tried to take you by surprise. The right thing to do with beautiful young girls is not to pounce, but to approach them gently. To woo them. That is why I have come here today to give you flowers. And the usual three gifts, of course," the wolf said.

"The usual three gifts? What are they?" Polly asked.

"According to my book, always things that are very difficult to find. For instance, the smallest dog in the world. Or the most beautiful princess. But of course, I don't have to go looking for her, because that's you," the wolf said in a hurry.

"What else?" Polly asked, interested.

"You might ask me to build a superb palace outside your gates in a single night."

"Would you be able to do that?"

"I should have a very good try," the wolf said modestly.

"Are there any other gifts to choose from?"

"You might want a golden bird. Or the water of life. Or a dress made of moonshine," the wolf said.

"You mean you could find any of those things?"

"Of course. A prince can always accomplish the task that has been set for him," the wolf replied.

"Like killing a dragon?" Polly asked.

The wolf hesitated. Then he said, "Are there any dragons around here nowadays? As far as you know?"

"I don't think there are many. But it's one of the things brave princes often have to do before they get the princess."

"Does your father have any special dragon in mind? A reasonably mild dragon, who wouldn't object to putting up some sort of fight, just for the look of it? And who would then pretend to be defeated and to die? Just for a short time, you understand. Something like that?" the wolf asked.

"No, I don't think my father knows any dragons," Polly said.

"Any of the neighbours been complaining about having dragons in the garden lately? Or in the house?" the wolf inquired.

"Not that I've heard," Polly said.

"Then let's forget about dragons, shall we? If nobody round here is being bothered by dragons at present, there doesn't seem much point in going out and looking for them. Let sleeping dragons lie, is what my old aunt always said. Or, indeed, die. Let sleeping dragons die. Peacefully, in their lairs. We don't want to cause any disturbances, do we?"

Polly remembered some of the earlier attempts the wolf had made to catch her. She didn't feel sure that he had always tried to avoid disturbing people. There had been the time when he had meant to blow up her house, which wasn't exactly a peaceful occupation.

"Well? Which is it to be? The palace? The golden bird? The smallest dog in the world? Which do you want first?" the wolf asked.

"I think I'd like the smallest dog, please," Polly said. She had not forgotten that she would never be allowed to keep a large pet. A very small dog might perhaps be hidden in her toy cupboard. Or, if he was small enough, even in the box where she kept her special treasures.

"I shall be back tomorrow," the wolf said. And went.

It was late in the afternoon of the next day that the wolf arrived at Polly's garden gate. He was again wearing the paper crown, but this time he had left the stick behind and instead, in his paw, he was carrying a brown paper bag.

He leaned over the gate.

"Polly!"

"Yes, Wolf?"

"I have brought you what I promised. The smallest dog in the world."

He handed Polly the brown paper bag. She looked eagerly inside.

"There isn't any tiny dog. Just a lot of nuts," she said.

"Of course. Who ever heard of keeping tiny dogs loose in paper bags? They'd get terribly tangled up in each other's legs. Don't you know that the smallest dog in the world always comes out of a nut?" the wolf said.

"I don't know that I'll be allowed to keep so many dogs," Polly said, looking into the bag again. There were at least forty hazelnuts there.

"I daresay there won't be a dog inside every single nut. You know what they say. Don't count your nuts until they are cracked," the wolf said.

"Do you know which nuts have dogs and which haven't?" Polly asked.

"Not exactly. They look rather alike. We'd better open a few..."

"I'll go and fetch the nut-crackers," Polly said, starting for the house.

"Oh no, you don't. I know what you mean to do. You'll go into the house and never come out again. I can crack nuts with my teeth," the wolf said.

"I've always been told not to try," Polly said.

"You have such small teeth. Feeble. Now, choose your nut, and I'll crack it open for you," the wolf said.

Polly took a nut from the bag and handed it to the wolf. The wolf cracked it between his teeth and held out the two halves of the shell to Polly. But inside was no tiny dog, only an ordinary nut kernel.

"You picked the wrong one," the wolf accused Polly.

"You said they all looked alike," Polly reminded him.

"Let's try another," the wolf said.

The second nut also had nothing but a kernel inside. The wolf quickly ate it. He pointed to the paper bag, and Polly brought out a third. But this one contained nothing at all.

"Perhaps they're the wrong sort of nut," Polly suggested.

"Nonsense. The book says quite clearly that the smallest dog in the world came out of a hazelnut. The trouble is that you haven't found the right one. Get on with it. He must be in there, somewhere," the wolf said.

As fast as he could crack them, the wolf opened nut after nut. But each one proved disappointingly to be nothing but a perfectly ordinary hazelnut. Most of them had kernels, which the wolf quickly swallowed. He did not offer Polly any. Faster and faster the shells fell around him, and he had hardly eaten one kernel before he was cracking the next nut. The supply in the bag dwindled until there was only one nut left. Polly was just taking it out of the bag, when suddenly the wolf spluttered and choked.

"Hauch! Hawk! Haroosh! Ahaugh! A-haugh! A-choo! Hauch! Hack! Harrock!" the wolf exclaimed.

"Did it go down the wrong way?" Polly asked.

The wolf coughed and nodded his head. He still couldn't speak.

Polly waited till he had recovered. Then she said, "Wolf! There's only one nut left."

"Splendid. Then this is THE nut. Prepare to meet the smallest dog in the world."

The wolf cracked the last nut with great care. He spat out the shell and held out his paw with the contents of the nut on it for Polly to see.

"It's not a tiny dog," Polly said.

"Are you quite sure?" the wolf asked.

"Quite. It's just an ordinary nut kernel. Like in all the other nuts," Polly said.

"There must be another nut left," the wolf said.

Polly looked in the paper bag.

"No. That was the very last one."

The wolf scratched his head.

"Extraordinary! Out of all those nuts, not one containing the smallest dog in the world! Not one of them, in fact, containing a dog of any sort or size."

He thought about this.

"I suggest that we forget about the dog. Or, better still, we do a deal. After all, I did bring you a great many nuts. Suppose we say that twenty nuts count the same as one very small dog? That would be generous. Considering the size of the dog."

"No. It has to be the smallest dog in the world, or it doesn't count at all," Polly said.

"Of course! I was forgetting. One of those nuts did contain the smallest dog in the world," the wolf cried.

"I didn't see it," Polly said.

"No. Most unfortunately, you didn't. Why? Because, entirely by mistake, I swallowed him. He was in that last nut but one. The nut that went down the wrong way. You remember?"

"I remember. But . . ." Polly said.

"That was the smallest dog in the world."

"How do I know that?" Polly asked.

"If it wasn't, why was that the only nut that made me choke? All the others went down the way they should have gone. But the dog inside that nut didn't just follow down the long red lane like an ordinary kernel. He chose a different path. I remember now the feeling on my tongue. As if a very small animal was trotting across it. In the wrong direction," the wolf said.

"I don't believe it," Polly said.

"I also heard him bark. Before he'd got right down. You must have heard him too."

"I didn't..."

"But you must agree that that nut was quite different from all the others," the wolf urged.

"Because you were in too much of a hurry."

"He was in too much of a hurry. That's the trouble about these very small dogs. They don't wait to find out what would be best for them."

"Anyway, you haven't given me any sort of dog," Polly said.

"I brought him here," the wolf protested.

"And then you ate him."

"It was a mistake. I didn't mean to," the wolf cried. But it was no good. Polly had gone into the house and shut the door.

"I shall be back. Tomorrow I shall be here with the second gift," the wolf promised. "I'll probably be building you a palace tomorrow," he said to the firmly shut door.

But Polly did not come out again, and the wolf went sadly home.

8.

The Wolf Goes Wooing (2)

"POLLY! I have come with the second gift," the wolf said, from his usual place outside the garden gate.

"That's very kind of you, Wolf," Polly said.

"Come a little nearer and I will lay it at your feet."

"I'll come this near. That's enough," Polly said, standing a little distance from the gate. The day before, when she had gone right up to the gate to hand the wolf a glass of water, and again to look into a paper bag, hoping to see the smallest dog in the world, she had forgotten how little he was to be trusted.

"It's sad that you should be so young and so suspicious," the wolf said.

"It would be sadder still if I weren't suspicious and never lived to be not so young," Polly said.

"Ah well. Let's talk about something else. I have brought you the second of the three gifts with which I am going to win you."

"What is it?" Polly asked.

The wolf held up a string bag.

"It was quite extraordinary. I thought that this task might

be the most difficult. I wondered if it might not prove impossible. But I'm delighted to be able to tell you that one can buy them anywhere. They are not even very expensive."

"What are they?" Polly asked. She was impatient to know what the second gift could be.

The wolf put a paw into the bag and took out a large yellow apple.

"Golden apples." He rolled one under the gate towards Polly. She picked it up.

"I don't think this apple is made of gold, Wolf," she said.

"Excuse me. I have the shopkeeper's word for it. 'What are those apples?' I asked, and he said, 'They are Golden.'"

Polly took a large bite out of the apple. "I wouldn't be able to do that if they were really made of solid gold," she said.

"There must be some mistake. Perhaps the next one..." the wolf said, rummaging in the bag. He took out a second apple. It looked exactly like the first.

"That one isn't gold either. Bite it and see," Polly said.

"Oh no! You don't catch me that way! You want me to be stupid enough to try to bite an apple made of real gold, so that I blunt my teeth. Then I shouldn't ever be able to eat you up like a piece of crisp bacon. Oh, no!"

"Just as you like. Don't eat it then. But it's a waste, because even if these apples aren't really golden, they are delicious."

"That's what the shopkeeper said. He said they were golden *and* delicious," the wolf said. He smelled the apple in his paw and cautiously scraped it against his teeth. A moment later the second apple had disappeared.

"The third apple must be the golden one. The man very kindly gave me two delicious apples, and one, this last one, is golden. You couldn't expect more than that for thirty pence," the wolf said as soon as his mouth was empty enough to speak.

"That apple isn't golden either," Polly said, looking at it as the wolf drew it from the string bag.

"But the shopkeeper assured me..." the wolf began. Polly interrupted him.

"Wolf! This sort of apple is called Golden Delicious. That's its name. Like I'm called Polly. Like other apples are called Coxes, or Granny Smiths. This yellow sort of apple is called Golden Delicious. It doesn't mean that they are really made of gold," Polly said.

"Why didn't he explain properly? I told him distinctly that I wanted golden apples, and he sells me these stupid things," the wolf said, angry. He threw the third apple over the gate. It rolled across the grass to the sandpit, where small fat Lucy was sitting, burying a doll she didn't care for. Without looking up, Lucy picked up the apple and began to eat it.

"Now that horrible child is eating my last apple. I am leaving you. Grieved. Hurt. Disappointed. But I shall be back soon with the third and last gift," the wolf said, turning away from the gate. He took off the gilt paper crown. He obviously thought it was no longer necessary to pretend to be a prince come a-wooing on this occasion. He threw the string bag over his shoulder and trotted away down the road.

Polly wondered what the third and last gift would be. In the stories she had read there were certainly three gifts, but she couldn't guess which the wolf would choose to bring. A magic ring would be useful. So would a cloak that made the wearer invisible. Best of all would be Fortunatus's purse, which always had a gold coin in it, however much you spent from it. "But I hope he doesn't bring me a beautiful princess. I wouldn't know what to do with her," Polly thought.

It was nearly a week later, on a fine and sunny afternoon, when Polly, sitting on the grass in the front garden, and colouring a large picture of a hungry dragon and a beautiful princess, heard a curious sound from the other side of the hedge.

She went up and peered through the leaves and twigs.

Outside in the road the wolf was standing. He seemed to be speaking to someone, but who the someone was, Polly couldn't see.

"Why not?" the wolf asked.

There was no answer.

"Just this one more, and I'll never ask for another," the wolf said.

No reply.

"You owe it to me. I bought you. I paid good money for you. You belong to me. It's your duty to do what I tell you," the wolf scolded.

Polly edged closer to the privet hedge. The wolf seemed to be speaking to someone below him, right down on the road level. Perhaps, Polly thought, he had at last discovered the smallest dog in the world.

But she didn't see a dog of any size. Instead she saw, lying on the road, a little piece of material. It was about the size of a small sheet of newspaper. It was torn at the edges and not very clean. But as Polly looked carefully, she saw that it was a ragged fragment of a very old, very worn Persian carpet. She could just make out a pattern of something like little trees and, round one frayed corner, a border of zigzag lines.

"I could easily bite you and tear you up into shreds," the wolf said angrily to the carpet.

The carpet shrugged. If you have never seen a carpet shrug, I can tell you that it is a very expressive gesture.

"It was only a very short journey this morning. You can't be that tired," the wolf pleaded.

The carpet gave an irritated shake, as much as to say, "Stop bothering me."

Polly went to the garden gate and leaned over so that she could see both the wolf and the carpet, and the wolf, if not the carpet, could see her.

"What's the trouble, Wolf?" she asked.

The wolf picked up the fragment of carpet, came to the further side of the gate, and slapped the carpet down on the white, dusty road in front of it.

"It's extremely annoying. I managed to find the third and last gift I promised you. This flying carpet. Or rather, this part of the original flying carpet."

"It's not very large," Polly said, looking at the small square of carpet.

"That's the trouble. It claims that because it is only a small piece of the whole carpet, it can no longer fly as often or as quickly as it used to," the wolf said.

"But it does fly?" Polly asked.

"Only when it feels like it."

The carpet wrinkled itself.

"Don't laugh at me!" the wolf cried, stamping an angry paw.

The carpet's wrinkles became deeper and it quivered with silent laughter.

"Maddening! You...you ordinary rug!" the wolf shouted. Instantly the carpet flew off the ground and slapped the wolf smartly on the nose, covering him at the same time with a good deal of white dust and small pebbles which it had managed to pick up from the road.

The wolf coughed and then sneezed. The carpet, back on the ground, gave a wriggle. It was clearly saying, "Mind your manners, you!"

The wolf tried again.

"I beg your pardon. Of course I meant to say, this beautiful, elegant, clever carpet can fly anywhere and at any time, but being old...I mean to say, being a carpet of great experience and wisdom, sometimes needs to rest quietly. In order to preserve its magic power. You understand?"

The carpet spread itself out on the road and preened itself.

"Has it flown anywhere with you?" Polly asked.

"Of course. I couldn't bring you a flying carpet without first trying it out. I suggested that it should lift me from the ground. It was a mistake, though, to try the experiment in my kitchen, where the ceiling is rather low," the wolf said, rubbing the top of his head.

The carpet wrinkled again. It was clearly amused at the memory. The wolf wisely pretended not to have seen.

"Since then, things haven't been too easy. This miser... this beautiful carpet does not feel able to take me to any place and at any time, as it could have done in the olden days, when it was all there. I mean, when more than this precious fragment was at hand. As you probably remember from reading your 'Arabian Nights', the whole carpet could transport any number of people as far as they chose to ask. And at any time. This...this treasured remnant is apparently too old and too tired to answer to the command in the same way. It needs to rest very often. In fact, it seems to be resting, doing nothing, most of the time," the wolf said, showing his teeth in a threatening manner.

The carpet hunched itself, ready to spring for the wolf's nose.

"Of course I understand this. Real magic is very tiring. We don't want to strain it," the wolf said hastily.

The carpet flattened itself out again.

"But there it is, Polly. A truly magic flying carpet. You can't say I haven't done what I promised. I said I would bring you three gifts, and I have. I have won you, Polly. By all the rules in the book, you are now mine," the wolf said. He leaned over the garden gate and put a large black paw on Polly's shoulder.

"Wait a moment, Wolf. Those three gifts. I never even saw the smallest dog in the world," Polly said.

"He was extremely small. You weren't wearing your spectacles, so you missed him," the wolf said.

"I don't need spectacles. I didn't see him because he wasn't there."

"But you heard him. He barked loudly when I swallowed him. Quite by accident. He came out of his nut too quickly. It was entirely his own fault."

"I heard you spluttering," Polly said.

"That wasn't me. That was the noise he made as he went down," the wolf said.

"And the apples weren't real gold," Polly said.

"The best gold is always soft. I think you didn't keep them long enough. You and your horrible sister were so anxious to eat them up directly you saw them, you didn't give them a chance to harden up. Greed is very unattractive," the wolf said virtuously.

"Anyway, I don't believe that carpet can really fly," Polly said.

"You saw it come up and hit me on the nose just now."

"That could have been a trick."

Two corners of the square of carpet lifted a little, looking like two ears pricked up on a dog's head.

"Come out here and stand on it. Say, 'I wish you to take me to the wolf's kitchen' and you'll see," the wolf said.

"That's hardly any way. I could walk there, easily…"

"Do!" the wolf said eagerly, but Polly took no notice.

"If it's really a magic flying carpet it ought to be able to take me to the other side of the world," she said.

"It can."

"How do I know it can?" Polly asked. The carpet wriggled. It knew it was being talked about.

"Try it. Ask it nicely, and I am sure it will oblige. So long as it isn't still too tired."

"If I do, and it does take me to the other side of the world, I think I'll stay there for a bit and look around," Polly said.

"That wouldn't do at all. I need you here," the wolf said.

"Then why don't you ask it to take you somewhere? Then I'd see that it really is a magic carpet," Polly suggested.

The wolf moved towards the carpet. He sat carefully on its middle, legs crossed. It was a tight fit. He had to hold his tail very close, in order to tuck himself neatly on to the very small piece of carpet, with no bits hanging over the edges.

"Take me to my kitchen," he said.

The carpet did not stir.

"Oh, all right! *Please*," the wolf said.

The carpet wriggled.

"Don't do that. You're tickling me underneath," the wolf said.

Polly waited.

"I don't believe it can fly at all," she said.

"Don't say that. You might hurt its feelings and goodness knows what it might do. You have to be polite. Like this. Please, beautiful, clever, kind carpet, take me to...to Brighton," the wolf said.

The carpet shuddered.

"I don't think it likes the idea of going to Brighton. Perhaps it doesn't like all those pebbles on the beach. Or it's frightened of getting wet in the sea. Why don't you suggest that it takes you somewhere it would like to go to? Like its own home?" Polly suggested.

The wolf looked hard at her.

"Sometimes, Polly, I think you have the glimmerings of intelligence. That is not a bad suggestion," he said. He patted the carpet gently. "Elegant, superb, gifted, wonderful carpet,

grant me this one wish and I'll never ask you for anything again. Fly with me to your native land, to Persia, to your home."

There was a rush of air, a column of white dust, a short yelp of surprise, and then silence. The road beyond Polly's garden gate was empty. Only a small clean square on the dusty ground remained to show where the flying carpet had once lain.

"I wonder," thought clever Polly, "how the wolf is going to get home from Persia? Because I'm quite sure the carpet won't ever agree to bring him back."

Last Stories of Polly and the Wolf

Illustrated by Jill Bennett

I.

The Wolf at School

POLLY was on her way to school one morning, when she found the wolf trotting beside her. There were a great many other people around, so she was not particularly frightened, but she was curious.

"Where are you going, Wolf?" she asked.

"I'm going to school," the wolf replied.

"My school?" Polly said.

"Of course, your school. Isn't it the best round here?" the wolf asked.

"Much the best. But Wolf...if you're thinking you'll be able to get to eat me in school, you'll be disappointed. There are always crowds of us all together. If you tried to eat me, you'd get caught and probably shot. Or something."

The wolf wasn't listening. "Crowds? Of plump little girls? Of good, juicy little boys? Like this lot here?" he asked, looking round at the pavement covered with children hurrying towards the school gates.

"You won't have a chance to eat any of them," Polly said, answering what she knew was in the wolf's mind.

"Hm. Pity. But I don't know why you are always thinking about food. That's not what I am going to school for. My mind is on higher things," the wolf said virtuously.

"Higher than what?"

"Higher than my stomach. Brains, you stupid little girl. I am going to school to develop my brains. I am going to school so that I can become clever. Even cleverer than I am already," the wolf added hastily.

"Who told you school would make you clever?" Polly asked.

"Read it in the paper. There was an advertisement. DO YOU WANT YOUR CHILD TO BE SMARTER THAN ANYONE ELSE'S? START EARLY LEARNING LESSONS NOW. I know you have lessons at school, and as I haven't got a child it seemed meant for me. I shall stay in your school until I can outsmart you, Miss Polly. Then, when I've eaten you up, and perhaps a dozen or so of these other children, I shan't need to learn any more and I shall leave."

By now they had reached the school gates, and the other children were squeezing their way through. "I don't think you can just walk in and join in the lessons without asking," Polly said to the wolf, as they stood outside, left to the last.

"You must introduce me. Go on! If you're so clever, you can think of some way of getting me in. If you don't... Grrrrrr," the wolf said, showing his teeth.

Polly looked round and saw that they were alone. "All right. I'll try," she said, and they went together across the playground to the cloakroom door.

"Good morning, Polly," said Miss Wright, but when she saw Polly's companion, she said quickly, "You know we don't allow pets in the classroom. Your dog must go home. Immediately!"

"He's not a dog. He's a friend who's come to stay with us from abroad. To learn English," Polly said quickly, while she

whispered to the wolf, "Get up on your hind legs and try to
look like a friend from abroad." Beside her she could hear the
wolf growling. "Dog! Pet! Never been so insulted in my life!"

"He's very large. Isn't he too old for this class?" Miss Wright
asked.

"He's big for his age," Polly said.

"He's very dark. And hairy."

"He's foreign. He doesn't speak the language very well yet.
If he could sit next to me, I could help him," Polly said, thinking it would be better not to let the wolf sit next to Susie, who
was the plumpest girl in the room, or next to Freddie, who
might tease him into behaviour unbecoming to a pupil in
Miss Wright's class.

"Foreign? How interesting. What country does he come
from? What are you, dear?" Miss Wright asked the wolf. Polly
wondered if he had ever been addressed as "dear" before. His
answer was indistinct, and Miss Wright looked puzzled for a

moment, then she said, "Hungary! Well now! I don't think we've ever had a child from Hungary in our school before. We must all do our best to make you feel at home."

"I'd feel at home quicker if I could have something to eat," the wolf muttered.

"What's that, dear? I didn't quite catch what you said."

"He says he's feeling the heat," Polly said.

"Really? You could take off your coat, if you're feeling too warm, dear. Now let's all get out our exercise books, shall we, for our first lesson? Numbers!"

"Take off my coat? Doesn't she know it's my skin?" the wolf said, a little too loud.

"What was that you said?" Miss Wright enquired.

"He said his coat is quite thin," Polly said out loud.

"And what is your friend's name?" Miss Wright asked.

"Wol– Wolly," Polly said, having had no time to think up anything better.

"We don't like nicknames in this class. I shall call him by his proper name, Walter. When you speak to me, Walter, you must call me Miss Wright. Do you understand?"

"I will not be called by a stupid name like Walter!" the wolf said, very loudly indeed.

"What did you say?" Miss Wright asked.

"He says he wants a drink of water," Polly said.

"Then he'll have to wait until the lesson is finished. I can't have you all running in and out whenever you feel like it. Now, we really must get on with the lesson. Let's see who can add up quickly, shall we? Who can tell me what ten and ten make?" Miss Wright began. Sally put her hand up, ready with the answer, but before she could speak, the wolf said, "Ten what?"

"Do you know the answer, Walter? Good...good boy. What is it then?"

"Ten what?" the wolf repeated.

"It doesn't matter what. It's just a number, dear. Ten any-thing," Miss Wright said.

"Of course it matters what. Ten buns would be good. Ten little pigs would be better. Ten fat little girls like that one would be better still. Only I haven't got a freezer, they'd be difficult to store. I'll settle for the pigs," the wolf said.

"I don't know what you're talking about, dear. Perhaps they do numbers differently in your country. So we won't worry about buns or pigs, will we? So what do ten and ten make?" Miss Wright repeated.

"Twenty," Polly said quickly. Numbers was one of her best subjects.

"She didn't put her hand up! I was going to say twenty!" Sally complained.

"I'll give you another question, then. What is twenty-four divided by eight?"

Sally took a little time to think about this. But the wolf had heard one of his favourite words. "Who ate it? What did they eat?" he asked.

"Walter, didn't you hear me tell you that you must say 'Miss Wright' when you speak to me? And I didn't see your hand go up, either," Miss Wright said.

"Five," Sally said.

"No, that's not right. Very well, Walter, you tell us. Twenty-four divided by eight."

"Was it the ten little pigs?" the wolf said.

"I wasn't talking about pigs."

"Did they eat the buns?" the wolf went on.

"Three," Polly said, loudly, hoping that Miss Wright would not hear this remark.

"What is three supposed to mean? Oh! Yes. Eight into twenty-four. Quite right, Polly. Now, who can tell me what seven and six make?"

By the end of the numbers lesson, the wolf was confused, Miss Wright was cross and Polly was exhausted. "I don't think that can have made you any cleverer," she said as they put away their books and got ready for the play they were rehearsing for the end of term.

"I've never heard such nonsense! What use are numbers if they aren't fastened to something? You don't see five or three or a hundred just floating about in the air. If she'd said five sausages, or three apples or a hundred beans, I'd have understood what she was getting at. It could even have been interesting. Now what do we do? Isn't it time for school dinner yet?"

"Not nearly. Miss Wright's going to give us our parts for the school play."

"What's the play about? If it's about little Red Riding Hood, I could act the wolf. I bet I'd do it much better than any of these silly little creatures," the wolf said hopefully.

"It isn't Red Riding Hood. It's Hansel and Gretel. There isn't a wolf in it, so I don't know if Miss Wright will let you have a part."

"I know that story! They get lost in a wood, don't they? I'm sure there must have been a wolf in that wood. Woods in fairy stories always have wolves in them."

"This one didn't. It had a witch who lived in a gingerbread house."

"Why gingerbread? Nasty stuff. It makes my throat tickle."

"To catch children who liked it. Then she cooked them and ate them."

"That sounds like a good part. I shall be the witch."

Polly thought this was unlikely. But when Miss Wright was distributing the parts, no one else, except a very small boy called Eric, wanted to act as a witch, and at last Miss Wright was forced to notice the large black paw which had been waved every time she offered the part to another child, who turned it down. "You want to be the witch, Walter? Are you sure you can manage it? She doesn't have much to say, but..."

"She catches children to eat," the wolf said.

"Don't worry, dear. You can be sure that our story has a happy ending, though of course I don't know how you may have heard it in Hungary."

"Well, Wolf? Now you've had a whole day in my school, do you feel clever? Cleverer?" Polly asked as they came out of the gates at the end of the afternoon.

"Much cleverer. That story we were acting was an inspiration to me. In fact, I think I'll skip school tomorrow. I have some urgent business to attend to in another direction," the wolf said, and, rather to Polly's relief, he hurried away.

It was a few days later, that, on her way home from school, Polly saw a curious construction standing shakily in the road near to her own home. It looked like a badly put together garden shed, made out of brown paper. Windows and doors were drawn on the paper. Some sticky tape fastened a candy bar on one wall. On another was written a message:

THIS HUSE IS MAD OF G JINJEBRED

Polly stood still to examine it. She had an idea that she knew who had put it there and who was likely to be inside it. While she was looking, the building shook violently, there was a tearing noise, and the paper of one of the windows burst open.

"Who's there?" said a voice.

"Me. Polly," said Polly.

"A little girl? Lost in the wood?"

"I'm not lost and this isn't a wood. But I am a girl."

"That's the important part. Have a candy bar," said the voice.

"There's only one," Polly said.

"It's for you."

"I'm not sure..." Polly began, but before she could finish, the door of the house had been wrenched apart, and the wolf stood there, grinning at her horribly.

"Got you! I knew you'd never be able to resist a candy bar," the wolf said.

"I haven't had it yet," Polly pointed out.

"Hurry up, then. You eat that first, then I'll take you home with me and put you in my oven, like the witch did to Gretel. At last!" the wolf said, happily.

"I thought you didn't like gingerbread," Polly said.

"Hate it. The gingerbread was for you, not me. What I'm looking forward to is a good roast dinner. Roast girl."

"You haven't read your fairy stories carefully enough. Don't you know what happened to all those children the witch roasted in her oven? They didn't turn into roast child, they turned into gingerbread," Polly said.

"I don't believe you!" the wolf cried.

"Have a look at the play. I've got it here, because I'm learning my part," Polly said, offering the book to the wolf, who looked quickly at the end, snarling with disappointment.

"It's a cheat! It can't be true! Do you mean to say, Polly, that if I roast you now, you're going to become a gingerbread girl? Like these pictures in the book?" the wolf asked.

"I should think so. It seems to be the rule when you catch someone with a house made of gingerbread and sweets," Polly said.

"But I don't like gingerbread!" the wolf cried.

"I'm afraid that's all you're going to get," Polly said.

"It isn't fair! That woman who taught us said the story ended happily! This isn't a happy ending!" the wolf moaned.

"I don't think she meant it would be happy for a wolf. Too bad. You'll have to think of something else, won't you? See you at school on Monday?" Polly called as she quickly made her escape. But somehow she didn't think the wolf would be coming back to school to make him clever enough to catch even cleverer Polly.

2.

Thinking in Threes

"HOW DID they do it? Goldilocks just walks in at the front door, without being asked, and if they'd remembered to bolt the bedroom window, they'd have got her. And I can't get Polly to my house without all the trouble in the world, and then I've never managed to keep her there," the wolf said to himself, closing the book of fairy tales in which he had just read, for the twentieth time, the story of the Three Bears.

He thought deeply. Was it because they were bears, and not wolves? No. Goldilocks didn't know who lived in the house when she found it. She must have been hungry, that was why she'd gone into an empty house to eat their porridge. "Easy-peasy. All I've got to do is to get some porridge," the wolf thought. No sooner thought than done. He fetched his basket and set out for the shops.

"A pound of porridge," he said to the man behind the counter.

"Sorry, sir, we don't sell porridge. Oats, sir," the man said.

"Oats? I'm not a horse."

"No, sir. I can see that you're not a horse. I didn't mean to be rude, sir. Oats is what porridge is made of. Very easy, it is. You just boil oats in water."

"And that makes porridge?"

"Yes, sir. Instructions on the packet."

The wolf took the packet and read the instructions. Making porridge did indeed seem easy. He bought two packets in case his efforts with the first did not prove successful, and went home very much pleased with himself. "Aha, Miss Polly! I'll have you eating in my house very soon—and eaten soon, too," he said to himself.

A day or two later, Polly was passing the end of the street where the wolf lived, when she smelled a really horrible smell. She looked along the road and saw a trickle of smoke coming out from under his front door. She ran as quickly as she could towards it, and arrived just as the door was thrown open, and a gush of smoke and a slightly singed wolf leapt out.

"Wolf! What's the matter? Is your house on fire?" Polly panted.

"What? Who? No, no. No cause for alarm. I just left something to cook for a little too long. Why, it's Polly!" the wolf said, wiping black paws on a black apron.

"Smells terrible. What were you cooking, Wolf?" Polly asked.

"Nothing particular. Porridge, that's all. Porridge," the wolf said.

"I thought you didn't like porridge?"

"Hate it. Looks like putty, tastes like mud and feels...Ugh!" the wolf said.

"Then why...?"

"For a visitor. Which reminds me. I suppose you wouldn't care to come in and have a bite to eat, Polly?" the wolf asked, very sweetly.

"No, thank you, Wolf."

"I could make the other packet."

"Is that going to be porridge too?"

"How did you guess? I probably wouldn't burn it this time."

"I'm really not hungry, thank you, Wolf."

"Pity. Never mind. Another time," the wolf said and watched Polly disappear up the road.

"I'm not going to make that disgusting stuff again. Chairs, that's what I need. Polly will come past my house, feeling very tired, and when she looks in and sees three chairs all empty and ready for her to sit on, she won't be able to resist coming in to try them out. I'll see what I can arrange to tempt her tomorrow," the wolf said to himself.

It was not the next day, but a week later, that Polly was near the wolf's house again. She looked down the road and saw, not smoke this time, but a group of boys apparently reading something on his front door.

When she reached them, Polly saw a large sheet of paper fastened to the knocker, on which was written:

NOTICE
THERE ARE THREE CHAIRS IN THIS HOUSE

The boys were busy writing a message underneath.

So what? We've got four chairs and a put-U-up

The door opened suddenly, and the wolf bounced out. "How dare you write on my door?" he shouted at the boys. "Someone's been writing on it already," one of the boys said.

"That doesn't mean you have any right to. Who wants to know that you've got a put-U-up?"

"Who wants to know you've got three chairs?" the boy answered.

"She does," the wolf said, pointing with his head towards Polly.

"No, I don't."

"Yes, you do. And one's too high, and one's too low, but the other's just right. Come in and try them," the wolf said.

"I don't think I'd better," Polly said.

"Yes, you'd better. It would be fun."

"Not much. Not for me."

"I'd enjoy having you," the wolf said, and his long red tongue flicked out of his mouth for a minute. He laid a large black paw on Polly's shoulder and began to steer her in through the doorway.

"Why don't we all come in? Come on, boys," Polly said, holding on to an arm she found near her.

"I asked you. I don't want all of them," the wolf said, disgusted. But it was too late, the boys were already through the doorway and looking about the wolf's living room. There were indeed three chairs. The wolf had decided not to spend good money on buying anything new, but to adapt what he'd already got, to fit the story.

"Why is that chair on the table?" the smallest boy asked.

"To make it too high, of course. Stoopid!" the wolf replied.

"Stoopid yourself. Now no one can sit in it," the boy said.

"Is this supposed to be a chair?" another boy asked. He was looking at what appeared to be a seat almost on the ground.

"That's the one that's too low. I chopped its legs off," the wolf said, complacently.

"That's cruel. How would you like it if someone chopped your legs off?" the boy said.

"I'm not a chair. I'm a wo– I mean, I don't need to be made any lower. I'm the proper height for a . . . for the sort of person I am," the wolf said.

"This one's all right," a third boy said, sitting in the only other chair.

"You shouldn't be sitting in it. Polly's supposed to do that," the wolf complained.

"That's all right. I'm not tired. Thank you very much for showing us your interesting furniture, but I think it's time we went home to our teas," Polly said, moving towards the door.

"No, wait! You haven't tried all the chairs yet and said this one's too high and this one's too low and this one's all right and then you break it," the wolf said.

"If she doesn't want to break it, I will," the third boy said,

and before the wolf could stop him, he had got out of the chair, picked it up by one leg and brought it down on the corner of the table with a crash which sent splinters of wood flying round the room. The little chair lay sadly on the floor; it had lost three of its legs and its back was broken. "Like that?" the boy asked.

"You wicked boy! You've broken my only good chair! Go away and don't ever come back!" the wolf cried out. "Not you, Polly. You stay here and I'll... I'll make some more porridge," he said quickly.

"No, thank you, Wolf. I don't like porridge any more than you do."

"But you haven't tried the beds!"

"You have three beds?" Polly asked. She knew now which story the wolf had been reading lately.

"Well, nearly three," the wolf said.

"And one's too soft and one's too hard, but the other one is just right? And I'm supposed to try them all and then go to sleep in the little one?"

"That's right! You'd make a good detective, Polly."

"Thank you, Wolf. Would you tell me how you've managed about the beds? To make one too hard and the next too soft?"

The wolf smirked. It was not a pretty sight. "It wasn't easy, I can tell you. First of all, I put a lot of stones and some firewood into the big bed, under the bottom sheet. That'll be hard enough, I thought, and I tried it, and it certainly was. Then for the middling-sized bed that's too soft, I thought there isn't anything softer than feathers, so I ripped open my pillows and I've covered my settee with feathers. It's so soft you can't hardly breathe. You'll see, Polly, when you come upstairs to try."

"So now you haven't any pillows?" Polly asked.

"I sacrificed them for a good cause," the wolf said.

"What about the last bed? The really comfortable one?"

The wolf looked embarrassed. "I've had some trouble with that. To start with, I haven't got any more beds, and it didn't seem worth buying a brand new one just for such a short time. I tried putting two chairs together, but that wasn't a great success. I kept on falling down between them whenever I tried to stretch out. Then I made a sort of nest on the floor, but it was distinctly draughty. I thought perhaps you'd be able to advise me, Polly. After all, you're the person who's going to find it so comfortable. I did wonder if you could go to sleep in the dirty linen basket..."

"Certainly not! I'm not dirty linen."

"Perhaps in the bath? It's quite dry, I don't use it very often."

"Not the bath. Even if it hasn't been used for months."

"You're being very difficult," the wolf sighed.

"And, Wolf, it's all very well to try to have three of everything, but there's one thing you haven't thought of that you can't have three of," Polly said.

"No, there isn't. I had three bowls for the porridge, and three chairs—until that nasty child destroyed one. And I've nearly got three beds. There's the bottom drawer of my kitchen dresser, I could make that very cosy with a couple of dishcloths and an old towel. That would make three beds, wouldn't it?"

"But there's only one of you," Polly said.

"Of course. I am unique!" the wolf said, proudly.

"There were three bears."

The wolf looked at Polly. He hated to admit it, but it seemed to him that she was winning the argument again, just as she had always won all the arguments they'd ever had. At last he said, in a small voice, "You mean, it doesn't work if there's only one of me?"

"That's right. Now if you had a wife to be Mother Wolf..."

"But I don't want a wife! I want a meal!" the wolf cried.

"...or a baby to be Little Wolf..."

"I've never liked cubs much. Noisy, rough little creatures. A baby would disturb my elegant bachelor life," the wolf said.

"Then you can't expect me to be like Goldilocks and come in and eat your disgusting porridge and sit on your chairs and sleep in your dirty linen basket or your bath. Or even in a drawer," Polly said.

"Is that your last word?" the wolf asked.

"Not quite. Don't read so many fairy stories, Wolf. Face real life instead. Whatever cunning plans you make to catch me and eat me, you are never going to succeed, because what you don't realize is that I'm Clever Polly and you are the..." But the wolf was looking so disappointed that Polly hadn't quite the heart to say what she really thought of his brains, so she ended her sentence, "...you are just a Unique Wolf."

3.

At the Doctor's

WHEN THE wolf came into the doctor's waiting room, he saw that it was crowded. There were several old ladies and old gentlemen, who didn't interest him much.

"Too tough and stringy," he thought. But there were other patients who looked much more promising. One mother had two toddling twins, another had a succulent looking baby, and a fat little boy who was running round and round the table made the wolf's mouth water and his eyes glisten. He hoped that all the older people would get in to see the doctor first. Then, when he was left alone with the children, he would have a chance to seize one of them and leave quickly before anyone noticed.

"I don't have to go in to see the doctor today. I can always come back next week for what I need," he thought.

The mother with the juicy baby was called next, but to the wolf's disappointment she took the baby with her. Next, one of the old gentlemen left. The two old ladies went together. Then another old gentleman disappeared. Meanwhile, one of the twins had fallen asleep on a chair and, to the wolf's delight, its mother was the next to go into the surgery. She took the wakeful twin with her, but after a quick glance at the other, she left it sleeping.

The wolf got up and went over to the table. He pretended to be studying the books and magazines that covered it, picking them up one after another and turning the pages. Then he tucked one under his front leg and, as if by mistake, crossed the room so that he was sitting on the chair next to the sleeping twin.

The fat little boy who had been running round the room and falling over people's feet now stopped in front of the wolf.

"That's not your chair!" he said.

"It's not yours either," the wolf said.

"You were sitting over there," the fat little boy said, pointing.

"Yes, and now I'm sitting here," the wolf said.

"Why?"

"So that I can look after this baby who's asleep," the wolf said, seeing his chance.

"You aren't looking after it. Its mum told my mum to do that," the little boy said.

"We can both look after it," the wolf said.

"You don't look like someone who looks after babies."

"Oh, but I am! I often look after babies. I'm very good at it. I look at them and wonder whether they'd be good to fry or...I mean, whether they're going to be good or if they're likely to cry. Things like that."

"I don't believe..." the little boy had begun to say, when his mother called him. "Bill! Come over here! It's our turn to go and see the doctor. Hurry, now, or we'll miss our turn."

"Aha! My chance has come," the wolf thought as he saw Bill and his mother leave the waiting room. He put out a paw towards the still sleeping twin, when its mother's arm came between them.

"It's all right, I'm back. Thank you so much for looking after her. It's difficult when you've got two at once, isn't it?" the twins' mother said, scooping up the spare twin, decanting it into a twin buggy which appeared from nowhere, and wheeling both babies briskly out of the waiting room.

Ten minutes later, the doctor's voice called, "Mr Wolfe?" and the wolf reluctantly followed the white-coated figure along a passage to the surgery.

"Do sit down. New patient, I think. What seems to be the trouble?" the doctor asked, scribbling on a long white form in front of him.

"Trouble?" the wolf asked.

"WHAT DO YOU NOTICE WRONG?" the doctor said, very loudly and clearly.

"I'm not deaf!" the wolf said indignantly.

"I beg your pardon. I was asking you what seemed to be the trouble?" the doctor asked again.

The wolf did not know what to answer. Could he explain

to this sympathetic doctor that the trouble was that he wanted to catch Polly and eat her? Or might this be misunderstood? He said, doubtfully, "I have trouble with a girl. Quite a small one, but I can't seem to catch her when I want to."

"A hyperactive child, perhaps?" the doctor asked.

"Uh?"

"She is too active for you? Never sits still? Talks too quickly and too much?"

"Much too much," the wolf agreed, glad to be understood at last.

"Sleeps badly?"

"I'm not sure about that."

"Is she aggressive?"

"Uh?"

"Aggressive. Fights with her mates. Won't do as she's told."

"I don't know about her mates. She certainly never does what I tell her," the wolf said.

"Argues a lot?"

"Never stops arguing. I can't tell you. Whatever I say or whatever I do, it's always talk, talk, argue, argue, till I don't know whether I'm standing on my head or my tail...my feet," the wolf said.

"Is she in the waiting room? Let's have her in and I'll take a look at her," the doctor said.

"No. You can't. She's not there. Anyway, what good would just looking at her do?" the wolf asked.

"Bring her in tomorrow, then. Anything else bothering you?" the doctor asked, in the sort of voice that means, "I haven't got time to listen to you any more, you'd better leave."

"I'm bothered about not getting enough to eat. I'm hungry!" the wolf said, hoping that this would make the doctor more sympathetic.

The doctor looked more interested. "Unnatural appetite?" he suggested.

"Depends on what you mean by unnatural. It's quite natural for a wo– for the sort of person I am."

"Three hearty meals a day, is that it?"

"When I get them," the wolf said sadly.

"Good mixed diet? Plenty of veggies and fibre?"

"Veggies? Fibre?" The wolf shuddered.

"What, then? Convenience foods? Ready-made frozen stuff?"

"Meat," the wolf said.

"Just meat? Nothing else at all? That's not what I call a healthy diet. Not to mention the expense."

"I can eat cake. Polly once cooked a delicious cake," the wolf remembered.

"Who is Polly? Never mind. What you need is an appetite depressant," the doctor said, drawing his prescription pad towards him and beginning to scribble rapidly.

"A what?" the wolf asked, alarmed.

"Appetite depressant. Something to take the edge off your appetite so that you don't get these terrible feelings of hunger. And try to eat some fibre, there's nothing like it for filling the stomach. Good for the bowels too," the doctor said.

"There's nothing wrong with my stomach. Or my bowels," the wolf said, indignant.

"I'm surprised. Have this made up at the chemist, and come back and see me in a couple of weeks. And do, for goodness' sake, try to get down some bran or wholemeal bread for breakfast. And, by the way, if you'd like to bring your little girl, I might be able to suggest a diet which will quieten her down a bit. Next please!" the doctor said briskly, opening his door and bustling the wolf out.

"Bran! What does he think I am, a rabbit? Whoever heard of

a wolf eating bran?" the wolf asked himself as he walked down the street towards the chemist. While he was waiting for his prescription to be made up, he passed a tempting-looking butcher's and nipped in just in time to secure a large piece of steak for his supper. He hadn't much faith in the doctor's advice for himself, but he decided that it would be worthwhile finding out what he might suggest to make Polly easier to catch.

It was nearly three weeks later that Polly saw the wolf waiting at the school gate at the end of the afternoon's lessons.

"Hi!" the wolf said as she came down the path.

"Hi, Wolf! What are you doing here?"

"Waiting for you," the wolf said.

"I'm not going to walk home with you," Polly said, remembering that there might not be many people about in the road where she lived.

"No, no. Of course not. That's not what I wanted to ask you."

"What did you want to ask?"

"I wanted to tell you that I have consulted a very clever doctor."

"Have you been ill? Poor Wolf!" Polly said, kindly.

"I have not been ill. I was consulting him about you."

"But I haven't been ill either."

"He says you are hyperactive."

"No, I'm not! What's that mean anyway?" Polly asked.

"Means you can't keep still and that you talk too much and argue too much and run about too fast, and it isn't good for you."

Polly began to understand what the wolf meant. She said, "You mean I can run faster than you?"

"Only when I've just had dinner. Not now, this minute..."

"I'm not running. I'm staying here till my friends are ready to go home."

"Ah. In that case... But no. I want to advise you about your diet."

"You mean what I eat?"

"That's what diet means."

"Go on, then. You can tell me, but I don't promise to do it."

"This very clever doctor says you should cut out dairy foods."

"What's that?"

"Milk. Cheese. Butter. Anything made with milk or cheese or butter. He says it will make you feel much better."

"What about you, Wolf? Did he tell you what you should eat, too?"

"He was wrong," the wolf said.

"What did he say?"

"He said . . . And I don't like bran and I hate vegetables."

"What for? Why bran? Why vegetables?"

"To fill me up when I get hungry. Instead of . . ." The wolf stopped in the middle of his sentence. He did not mean to let Polly know that the doctor thought he ate too much meat. After all, what was Polly herself? Not bran. Certainly not a vegetable.

"Why didn't he tell you not to eat cheese and milk and all that?"

"I am not hyperactive," the wolf said smugly.

"When he says hyper-whatever it is, he means clever," Polly said.

"That's not what he said."

"But he did say that talking and arguing a lot was hyper-something?"

"Ye-es."

"Wouldn't you like to be clever, Wolf?"

"I am clever," the wolf said.

"Clever-er, then? Cleverer than me?"

The wolf considered this. "It might be an advantage, yes."

"Then you ought to be eating all the things he said I shouldn't. Lots of butter and milk and cheese and cream. Then you'd always be able to run faster than me and you'd be cleverer than everyone else. That's sense, isn't it?"

The wolf thought about this for some time. It did seem sense. If those foods made Polly as quick and clever as she was, they ought to have the same effect on him.

"Why do you think the doctor told me to eat bran and vegetables, then?" he asked.

"Perhaps he guessed that you wanted to catch me to eat and he didn't like the idea," Polly said.

"But that's unfair! It was me went to see him and asked for his advice! He ought to have been on my side!" the wolf cried.

"People are unfair," Polly said, with feeling.

"He cheated me!"

"But anyway, now you know what to do," Polly said.

"I'm going straight off to the dairy. I'm going to drink a pint of double cream and eat as much cheese as I can swallow. And next time we meet, stupid little Polly, you'll see, I shall run like the wind and my brain will be working so well it will dazzle you. As for you, you'd better go on my diet. Cabbages and bran. We shall meet again," the wolf cried as he left the school gate and walked sedately down the road.

Polly looked after him. "Oh, Wolf! You certainly aren't dazzling me with your cleverness yet," she thought.

4.

In Sheep's Clothing

THE WOLF stood in the school playground, waiting for the children to come out at the end of the afternoon. The parents, mostly mothers, who were waiting there too, looked at him suspiciously and none of them came over to speak to him. He was so very dark, so very hairy. None of them could remember noticing him there before.

Boys and girls began straggling out of the building. Some clutched large sheets of paper on which they had painted portraits of their families. Others carried egg-boxes, cardboard

cylinders from used toilet rolls, empty cotton reels, shells, nuts, melon seeds and corks, from which they had made pretty and possibly useful gifts. For Christmas was coming, and the children in this school were encouraged to be generous with their time and ingenuity.

The wolf had to wait for what seemed a long time before he saw Polly in a group of children, talking excitedly. This lot carried something different. One child had a pair of large wings in her hand, two more had long, striped robes over their arms, and Polly was carrying a baby doll wrapped in a long white shawl.

"Hi, Wolf!" Polly called out when she saw him.

"Hi, Polly! What's that doll for? I thought you didn't play with dolls."

"I don't. Not much. Anyway this doll isn't mine, she's Lucy's. I just borrowed her for the nativity play."

"What sort of play?" the wolf asked.

"A nativity play."

"What's that?"

"It's about the first Christmas. You know. Jesus being born in a stable and all that. We're acting it the day after tomorrow, and I'm going to be Mary. She's Jesus' mother. It's the best part."

"A play! Couldn't I be in it too?" he said. Surely acting in a play with Polly and several other deliciously small children would give him a chance to get one of them.

"It's only for my class to act in. And there aren't any more parts to go round."

"Who else is there besides Mary and that doll?"

"There's Joseph. Benjie is being Joseph. And there're some angels. Sophie over there is an angel. You can see her wings."

"Why isn't she wearing them on her back if she's an angel?"

"She will when we act our play. There's an innkeeper, that's Michael. He has to say, 'No room, no room.' And then we go into the stable and I have the baby."

"Anyone else?" the wolf asked.

"Three kings…"

"Couldn't I be a king? I'd be very good as a king," the wolf suggested, rather fancying himself in a crown.

"No, you couldn't. Derek's one of them and the twins are being the other two. And Marmaduke's being King Herod, who's horrible and wants to kill all the babies."

"To eat?" the wolf asked.

"I don't think so. And there are a lot of shepherds. They don't have much to say, so they're the children in my class who can't remember long speeches."

The wolf had brightened at the sound of shepherds. "Shepherds? With sheep?"

"I suppose so. But no one wants to act a sheep."

"I would," the wolf said.

"You? Be a sheep? But you're nothing like a sheep."

"I could act like a sheep."

Polly wasn't sure that he could. "How?" she asked.

"Baaa. Baaa...aa. Baa...a...baa...a. Baa!" the wolf said loudly. Several of the parents standing in the playground turned round to look and one or two of them laughed.

"How was that?" the wolf said, pleased with the effect.

"It wasn't bad. But you don't look like a sheep."

"I haven't dressed for the part yet. After all, when I came out this afternoon, I had no idea I might be asked to be in a play."

"No one has asked you," Polly said.

"So when is the performance, Polly?" the wolf went on, taking no notice of this remark.

"The day after tomorrow. Wolf...!" Polly began, but before she could finish the sentence, the wolf had gone.

"Benjie. Sophie. Marmaduke. Not to mention Polly. And a lot of shepherds who are too stupid to say anything. I ought to get one of them," he thought as he trotted home.

When he got there, he went straight to his larder; this was something he always did, sometimes hoping that though he had left it nearly empty when he went out, it might miraculously have filled up in his absence. But the shelves were as bare as before. The wolf sighed, shut the larder door and walked into his sitting room where, on the floor, lay a not very clean, whitish-grey fur rug. It had belonged to the wolf's grandfather, and how he had got it it is probably better not to know. It was, in fact, a whole sheepskin, and it was the thought of this priceless possession that had made the wolf so confident that he could take part in Polly's nativity play.

For the rest of that day and for most of the next, the wolf practised. He practised with pieces of string and with safety pins and elastic bands. He even tried to sew with a needle and thread. For most of the time, he practised in front of his long mirror, and at last, on the very morning of the performance,

he was satisfied. He not only sounded like a sheep, he now looked like one. After a light midday meal, he carefully dressed himself in his disguise and made his way to Polly's school, using side streets so as to avoid notice.

He managed to slink in at a back door. He heard a gabble of excited voices coming from a classroom further along the passage and, looking cautiously through a glass door, he saw a great many children dressed for the play. He saw a couple of angels in long white nightgowns and gauzy wings. He saw two kings, exactly like each other, wearing golden crowns. He saw several boys and girls in striped robes, with pieces of material wound round their heads. One of them carried a small stuffed lamb under his arm. So these were the shepherds, the wolf guessed. On the further side of the classroom, he saw Polly in a blue dress, with a blue veil on her head, holding the doll baby by one leg, upside down.

The wolf pushed the door open and joined the actors.

"Hey! Who're you pushing?" angrily asked a small stout king in a red robe edged with gold tinsel.

The wolf swallowed a snarl and the temptation to take a

mouthful out of a plump leg very near to him, and said, "I just want to get over to the shepherds." He knew he would have to be careful until everyone was off their guard and thinking about nothing but the play. He did not want to make a disturbance, and he was particularly anxious that Polly should not see him yet.

"Timmy! here's one of your sheep!" the red king shouted.

"We haven't got any sheep," a shepherd called back.

"There's one here. Don't know who. Miss Wright must've got someone in extra."

Lucky, thought the wolf, that no one seemed surprised at this, and no one took any particular interest in him. He lay down under one of the tables pushed against the wall and amused himself by remarking which children were fatter or slower (or both) and so would be the easiest prey. After a short time he noticed that the teacher was looking over each child's costume, hitching up the wings on one angel, tying up Joseph's shoelaces (they came undone again a moment later) and taking the doll baby away from Polly-Mary. "You don't have the baby in the first scene, that's when the angel comes to tell you you're going to have it," she said, and put it on a chair.

"Now, we're all going into the hall. Very, very quiet, please. Sophie and Polly, are you ready for Scene One? The others can stand at the side and watch, but no talking and no fighting. Understand?" She gave the three kings a special glare, and led the way out of the classroom.

The wolf trotted quietly behind the children. Along one long passage, turn a corner, another passage, and then a swing door into the hall. People were singing. The wolf caught one or two words: "...midwinter...snow...snow...long ago." It sounded cold and disagreeable. Why not sing about something pleasant, like hot soup, a roast joint? Chips? He found himself jostled among the children and crowded into a small space at the side of the stage, with one of the kings leaning against his shoulder and a shepherd treading on a hind paw.

"I wish..." So many juicy little arms and legs all round him. "But I must wait. If I gave myself away now, I'd never get out of here alive," he thought, and licked his chops silently.

The singing had stopped. The curtain was drawn back from the front of the stage, and the wolf heard, "Hi, Mary. You're going to have a baby and it's called Jesus."

"But I'm not even married!" Polly's voice answered.

"That doesn't matter, because it's God's baby," the angel said, and walked off. Then Joseph walked on and told Mary they had got to go on a long journey. "But I'm going to have a baby!" Mary said, and Joseph said, never mind that, she could have the baby in a hotel somewhere on the way.

"When do we get to the shepherds?" the wolf asked a child next to him in a loud whisper. He was bored with all this talk about the baby.

"Not till after the baby's got born, silly," the child whispered back.

"No talking!" Miss Wright's voice hissed behind them, and the wolf had to wait while Mary and Joseph were told that there was no room in the inn. "But you can use the stable, if you like," the innkeeper said kindly.

There was some more singing. The wolf was by now not only squashed, but also terribly hot. The children round him were all warm and excited and he was wearing an extra skin. An elastic band round one of his ankles was too tight, and a shepherd behind him was apt to tread on the fleshy part of his tail. It was a relief when Miss Thompson whispered, "Go on, Timmy, it's the shepherds now," and the group round the wolf moved out on to the stage.

The lights were bright here, and for a minute the wolf's

eyes were dazzled. Then he saw Polly, in her blue veil, sitting
on a stool, surrounded by bales of straw, with the doll baby
on her lap. Joseph stood behind her. The shepherds moved
towards her and the wolf followed them.

"Hullo, Mary. We heard about your baby, so we've come to
have a look at him," the largest shepherd said.

"You're welcome," Polly said. She still hadn't seen the wolf.

"We've brought him some presents. Here's an apple," one
of the younger shepherds said, holding out the apple.

"Thank you. I'm sure he likes apples," Polly said.

"And I've brought a lamb," another shepherd said.

The wolf thought this was a good moment to give a loud
Baa...a...a. Everyone jumped, and the child carrying the
stuffed toy lamb said, "You aren't supposed to say that."

"Why not? I'm a sheep, aren't I? 'Baa' is sheep language,"
the wolf said.

"You didn't say that when we rehearsed yesterday," the first
shepherd said.

"I wasn't here yesterday. But I am today. Baa...aa," the wolf said, annoyed.

"He's made me forget what I was supposed to say," the smallest shepherd said, and burst into tears.

"It doesn't matter, just go on. Thank you for the lamb, it will be nice for Jesus to play with when he's older," Polly said, quickly.

"You're not the lamb I'm giving Jesus, this is," said Timmy, showing the toy lamb.

"I don't think he's a lamb at all. He's got black paws," another shepherd said.

"Some sheep do have black feet. And black noses," the wolf said.

"He's got a long black tail that sticks out behind, too," the second shepherd said.

"I haven't! Have I?" The wolf tried to look over his shoulder. There was a tearing sound and the wolf was aware that the fleece was slipping badly and a large safety pin at the back of his neck had come open.

"I don't think he's a sheep either," Joseph said, interested, and coming round to look.

"I'm not! I'm a wo–" the wolf began, but Polly interrupted. "Of course he's a sheep. He came in with the shepherds, didn't he? And he's wearing a sheep's coat."

"Polly, you know who I am. Tell them," the wolf complained.

"Children, get on with the play, it's time you made room for the kings," Miss Wright hissed from the side of the stage.

"I expect you want to get back to watch your flocks by night," Polly said politely to the shepherds, who began to shuffle towards the way out. To the wolf she whispered, "You stay here. And don't forget, you chose to be a sheep in this play, now you've got to act like one."

"You mean I've got to go on saying 'Baa'?"

"That's right. Just 'Baa' and nothing else."

"Don't I get anything to eat?"

"Sheep eat grass. I don't think there is any grass round here. There's a little straw if you'd like that."

"Don't sheep eat meat ever? Not a mouthful of leg?" the wolf asked, gazing at the fat little leg of one of the three kings who were now preparing to offer their gifts to the baby Jesus.

"Certainly not! Thank you very much, that'll make a nice smell in this stable," Polly said to the third king, who had just given her a box supposed to contain myrrh.

"But I'm not an ordinary sheep. And I'm hungry!" the wolf said, rather too loud. The fat-legged king turned round and said, "Shh! It's my turn to talk now. We're going home without seeing Harold again because we know he means to try to kill your baby. That's all. Bye-bye."

"Who's Harold?" the wolf asked, wondering whether this was someone who shared his taste in food.

"Herod, not Harold. Don't talk, Wolf. You're not supposed to say anything but 'Baa'."

"But that's silly."

"Sheep are silly. If you wanted to do something clever, Wolf, you ought to have acted a different part."

"So I've got to go on being a silly sheep and I can't catch anyone? Not even you?"

"I'm afraid so. I'm sorry, Wolf. Joseph and I have got to go now. But you can stay for a bit and go on being a sheep, if you want to. Until we've all gone home, then you can go back to being a stup— to being a wolf again. Come on Joseph, it's time we went to Egypt," said Clever Polly, and left.

5.

You Have to Suffer in Order
to Be Beautiful

THE WOLF stood in front of his long mirror and looked at himself all over.

"Nothing wrong there. Long legs, lean, healthy body, kind, intelligent face. No two ways about it, I'm a good-looking fellow," he thought. He pulled in his stomach and bent a front leg to make the muscles stand out. "And I'm not really overweight. I've got big bones, that's all.

"I've been making a mistake. I shouldn't have told Polly that what I really want is to eat her. I should have pretended that I admired her. In stories, the girl always falls for the man who says he wants to marry her...Ugh!" The wolf shook his head. "Why are they always so keen on marriage? But if I pretended to want to marry Polly, then when I'd got her home with me...Yes, that's it! I shall woo her. After all, it wasn't always handsome young princes those girls fell for. Look at Beauty and the Bea—. Well, Polly isn't exactly Beauty, so she can't expect to get a Prince."

"Yes, Mr Woolf. And may I ask how you came to hear of me?" the immensely smooth, pink-cheeked doctor asked the wolf, who was sitting on the opposite side of an elegant desk in a consulting room in a private health clinic.

"I saw your advertisement..."

"I never advertise. It is not allowed in medical practice," the doctor said, displeased.

"I read something in the newspaper that said you could work miracles. Make people look different."

"Perhaps miracles is a slight exaggeration. But certainly many of my clients tell me that they are very happy with what I am able to do for them. So what can I do for you?" the doctor asked.

"It's a very delicate matter," the wolf said.

"Ah! Perhaps you have some special reason for coming to see me at this moment in time?" the doctor suggested.

"Yes, I have. A very special reason." Because if I look quite different, and Polly doesn't recognize me, I'll have a better chance of catching her, had been the wolf's clever idea.

"An affair of the heart, perhaps? There is some girl you wish to approach? But so far, you have not dared?"

"I can dare, all right. But she won't listen to me."

"You wanted to make some changes to your appearance?" the doctor asked.

"What sort of thing do you suggest?" the wolf asked.

"Well, for instance, noses. Not everyone is satisfied with the nose they have. I can alter a nose to almost anything you might require. Roman? Snub? Classical? Short and appealing? Long and learned? Now in your case, Mr Woolf, I should suggest a certain curtailing..."

"Doing what? My tail's all right," the wolf exclaimed in alarm.

"Curtailing. Shortening. It has no effect on the olfactory function, I assure you."

"Olfactory?" the wolf asked.

"You'll be able to smell with it as well as before."

"So I should hope! If I couldn't smell, I might just as well not have a nose," the wolf said.

"Then there are teeth. I work in conjunction with a first-class dental surgeon. Now it seems to me that your teeth leave quite a lot to be desired. If you'll forgive my saying so, they are on the large side and a little discoloured. It happens in later life, you know."

"Later life! I'm in my prime!" the wolf said, angrily.

"Of course. I did not mean to imply... But you might like to consider a really good set of dentures. Something smaller and whiter. I assure you, it would have a really dramatic effect on your general appearance."

"Dentures? What are dentures?" the wolf asked.

"New teeth. Fitting perfectly so that there would never be any danger of them slipping and so causing you unnecessary embarrassment," the doctor said.

"You mean false teeth?"

"Exactly. Dentures."

"Would they be able to gnaw bones?"

"Certainly."

"And chew up a juicy little gir—, a juicy little Pol—, juicy little anything?"

"They would function perfectly," the doctor said.

"He's awfully difficult to understand. It must be being so clever makes him use all these long words," the wolf thought. Aloud he said, "I'm not sure about false teeth. I'll think about it."

The doctor looked him over carefully. "Then, if you don't mind my suggesting it, we might tackle the problem of super-fluous hair."

"What's that?" the wolf asked, puzzled again.

"Superfluous hair. You are more bountifully endowed with hair than most of us." The doctor himself, indeed, was almost completely bald. "We could tackle that with electroly-sis, though I must warn you that it would take time."

"What do you want to do with my hair?" the wolf asked, not having understood a word of this last sentence.

"Remove it. Not all of it, of course. Just some around the upper part of the face, to give you a more open, friendly ex-pression."

"I've got a friendly expression," the wolf said.

"Of course, Mr Woolf. Delightful expression. But a *leetle* dif-ficult to see with that very luxuriant growth of hair over the forehead and cheeks. I can't help feeling that this young woman you are interested in might respond to—shall we say, a less hirsute approach."

"Her suit? Or my suit? But I haven't got one!" the wolf cried, thoroughly confused by all this language.

"She might like you better without so much hair," the doc-tor said, annoyed at having to use ordinary words.

"What was that word you used about my hair?" the wolf asked.

"Superfluous. Means you have too much of it," the doctor said.

"Not that one. Electro something."

"Electrolysis. It is a means of eliminating super-unwanted hair, by the insertion of an electric needle into each hair root..."

"Sounds uncomfortable. Does it hurt?" the wolf asked.

"Only for a moment," the doctor assured him.

"And that gets rid of the lot? All in a moment?"

"No, no, Mr Woolf. Each individual hair has to be dealt with separately."

"Wow! And these extra teeth? I suppose it doesn't hurt to have another set to put in when you need them?"

"Having first extracted the original dentition."

"Uh?" said the wolf.

"First of all, we take out everything you've got there."

The wolf shuddered.

"What about the nose job?"

"That necessitates a few days in hospital while we break down the bones of your face and construct a totally new form. Sometimes we have to take a little skin from a leg or arm in order to cover the new nasal apparatus."

"Take skin from whose leg or arm?"

"Yours, of course, Mr Woolf. It is a perfectly simple procedure."

"I'll think about it," the wolf said. He did not mean to think about it at all. He saw that all these operations were going to hurt a lot, and he did not mean to suffer that much even in order to catch stupid little Polly.

"My secretary will see you on your way out," the doctor

said, rising from his chair and shaking the wolf's paw rather coolly. He did not believe that this client was likely to come back to ask for a complete reconstruction of his appearance, however much he wanted to get his girl.

"That will be one hundred and fifty pounds, Mr Woolf," the charming secretary said, as the wolf passed through her office.

"A hundred and fifty? Pounds? You must be joking!" the wolf snorted.

"Will it be cash or a cheque?" the charming secretary asked.

"I haven't got my cheque book on me just now," the wolf said. This was not surprising, as he did not have a cheque book anywhere.

"Perhaps you could drop a cheque in the post this afternoon?" the secretary said.

"Perhaps," the wolf said, and left. "A hundred and fifty pounds, for threatening to break the bones in my face, skin my leg, take out all my teeth and electrocute my fur? The man's a monster!" the wolf thought as he hurried down the street.

"Polly," the wolf said, looking over the fence into Polly's front garden, where she was lazily swinging herself in the sun.

"Yes, Wolf?"

"Would you like me better if I didn't have so much hair... fur?"

"Bald all over, d'you mean? No, I wouldn't. I think you'd look terrible," Polly said.

"Suppose I had an extra lot of teeth? False ones?"

"What for? You've got enough, haven't you?"

"Or if I had my nose shaped differently?"

"But you wouldn't look like a wolf if you had a different nose," Polly said.

"But would you like me any better?"

"No. I like you just as you are," Polly said, quite affectionately.

"Wonderful! Then come with me, Polly. Now! To my home. Make me the happiest of...wolves."

Polly laughed. "No, thank you, Wolf. I like you a lot, but I don't trust you for a minute. I like you where you are now—

on the other side of the garden fence. And like a wolf, not with your long nose made short or with all your teeth pulled out. Just go on being yourself, and I'll stay like I am. Safe," said Clever Polly.

6.

Kind Polly and the Wolf in Danger

THIS STORY is different from all the other stories about Polly and the wolf, because it doesn't start with the wolf planning how he can have Polly to eat.

One day, Polly went out to do some shopping for her mother in the village. She had bought a cauliflower and some potatoes at the vegetable shop, and a pound of sugar and half a pound of biscuits at the grocer's, and she was thinking of going home again, when she heard a loud noise coming from a side street. She ran to the corner and looked along the street and saw a crowd of people all very angry about something. The people were shouting and someone was howling. Polly thought that she knew that howl, and she hurried up the street.

As she got nearer the crowd, she could hear more distinctly what the people were saying.

"Ought not to be allowed!"

"Would worry the sheep!"

"Cause a dog fight!"

"Steal a hen!"

"These beasts are dangerous. Should be behind bars!"

"Might bite a baby!"

"Could easily kill a child!"

"Someone muzzle it!"

"Someone shoot it!"

Polly began to believe that she knew whom the voices were talking about, but she still hadn't managed to get through the crowd to see if she had guessed right. Now she heard other voices saying other things.

"Interesting shape. Don't know if I've ever seen one exactly like that before. A new breed, perhaps?"

"Look it up in the *Gazette*."

"Like to have a look at its bones. Preserve the skeleton in formaldehyde..."

"Curious sound it makes. Don't know if I've ever heard a dog howl exactly like that..."

Polly pushed through the inner ring of trousers and skirts and saw a wooden tea chest set up on end. Out of the top of the tea chest stuck the head of the wolf, and over this head, someone had thrown a net, which was held down by the edges of the chest. The wolf was in a bad way. His fur was draggled, he was trembling and he was looking this way and that with huge, terrified eyes.

"It'd make a splendid exhibit for the local museum. Stuffed, of course," a large man in a tweed jacket was saying. Polly saw a glimmer of hope cross the wolf's face, and she realized that he was thinking of being stuffed as an agreeable sensation after a large meal. But the hope disappeared the next moment, as a woman added, "You have to be careful how you kill an animal you want to stuff. A bullet through the heart is fine, but whoever shoots must know how to be accurate."

"I'm against killing. This animal should be in a zoo," another woman said.

"Doesn't look in very good shape to me. Death might be a mercy," a man said.

"Shouldn't be shot, though. Call in the local vet."

"Spoilsport! Why not have a chase? We could get the hounds. Creature would enjoy a good run for its money," said another voice.

"Cruel! I object! No blood sports here!" said someone else.

"In any case its body should be preserved for expert examination."

"Call the police!"

"Send for the Master of the Hunt!"

"Fetch my gun!"

The voices grew louder and more quarrelsome. Everyone seemed to be shouting at everyone else. Polly managed to edge closer. "Wolf!" she said.

The wolf turned his miserable eyes towards her.

"You here?" he said.

"What happened? Why are they all so angry? What did you do?"

"I didn't do anything," the wolf said sullenly.

"I don't believe that. Tell me the truth."

"I didn't do anything out of the ordinary. I've seen plenty of people do it."

"Go on."

"I've often seen people go round sniffing at other people's babies."

"Sniffing at them?" Polly asked, surprised.

"Bending right over their prams, with their noses in the children's faces. And you can hear them smacking their lips."

"Probably kissing them."

"Nonsense! Sniffing to see if they're ready to eat. Smacking their lips when they know what a good meal they're going to have."

"Is that what you did?" Polly asked.

"Only one or two. The first was a scrawny little thing, not worth its salt. The second wasn't any good, either. It hit me. I did not hit back. Naturally I didn't want a struggle."

"And then?"

"Then I saw exactly what I needed. Small, plump, juicy-looking. Not unlike you, a few years ago. I was just unwrapping it, to make sure it was perfectly fresh, when this woman came dashing out of the shop and started screeching and calling me all sorts of names, and then a couple of men came up and got hold of my legs, and they held my jaws so that I couldn't speak, and they pushed me into this revolting box and covered me with a net."

"Oh Wolf! What did you expect? Had you forgotten that people don't eat babies?"

"I can't think why not. There seems to be a very good supply," the wolf said.

"Would you eat wolf cubs?"

"Certainly. If I was hungry."

"Well, most people don't eat babies. So when they saw you sniffing into prams, they realized that you weren't a human. They knew you were a wolf."

"No, they don't. They don't know what I am. Didn't you hear what they said? They think I'm very unusual," the wolf said, with a little pride.

"Don't be too pleased about that. It's because you're so unusual that they want to dissect you."

"What's dissect?" the wolf asked.

"Cut you up to find out how you work."

"Cut me up alive!" the wolf cried.

"Not alive. Dead."

"Cut me up, dead?"

"Or shoot you and stuff you. Not with food. With cotton wool, or whatever you stuff dead creatures with," Polly explained.

The wolf shuddered.

"Or they might want to hunt you. With dogs."

"What am I going to do?" the wolf said, and at his howl, several people in the crowd turned round to see what was happening.

"Don't stand so close, little girl. That animal is dangerous," a man in spectacles said.

"I've met him before," Polly said.

"Then you know that he is a threat to our community," Spectacles said.

Polly thought quickly. "I'll tell you what I do know. He's a very strange animal. There's never been anything quite like him here before." (*That's true enough*, she said to herself.) "In fact he's Unique."

"I am NOT," she heard the wolf mutter behind the net, but she took no notice and went on.

"You know what a fuss everyone makes about not letting rare kinds of plants and animals disappear. I can tell you, if you hurt this animal, there's going to be a terrible fuss. You'll get blamed by everyone important. The Queen will be angry, and the Prime Minister will be furious, and I wouldn't wonder if the whole village didn't get punished."

There were murmurs among the crowd. They were obviously impressed. She heard, "Seems to know what she's talking about." "Don't want the place to get a bad name." "Remember

what the Green Party said on television the other night, about preserving the balance of Nature."

"I expect one of the television stars would tell everyone what a terrible thing had happened here," Polly said, reminded of the power of TV.

"She's right. We don't want to be held up to scorn as vandals," the tweedy man said.

"Animal Rights," said a thin woman who hadn't spoken before.

"I still think it should be put behind bars. In a zoo," said a fat man.

"Polly! I won't go into a zoo," the wolf said in an undertone.

"Can't I have it to keep in my room?" a small boy asked his mum, who said, "Sorry, sweetie, I don't think Dad would like it."

"That wouldn't be too bad," the wolf said, looking over the small boy hungrily.

"He shouldn't be in a zoo. He should be allowed to roam free," Polly said.

"Not around our village!" someone said quickly.

"Where he belongs. In forests, or on hills. Wherever he came from," the thin woman said.

"Where did you come from, Wolf?" Polly asked, wondering why she had never asked this question before.

"Can't remember. I didn't come out of a box, I do know that."

"In fact, he's almost certainly one of an endangered species," Polly said.

"I don't! I wouldn't, anyway, if you let me go!" the wolf cried.

"Wouldn't what?" Polly asked.

"Make dangerous speeches. It's not the sort of thing I do."

"I didn't say speeches, I said...what that means is that you're very special and we ought to take great care nothing terrible happens to you."

"Now that makes sense...Why don't all the other..." the wolf began, but he was interrupted by the man in spectacles, who had raised his hand and said, "Ahem! Ahem! It seems to me that we should take a vote on the question of what to do with this...this...unusual animal. I for one am not prepared to take the responsibility of advising its destruction..."

"What's that?" the wolf whispered to Polly.

"Killing you," Polly whispered back.

"...by whatever means. The choice therefore lies between sending it to one of the many zoological institutions in this

country, or, as my friend here has suggested, letting it go free
to its natural habitat..."

"Natural what?" the wolf wanted to know.

"Where you live, Wolf."

"...wherever that may be. Could we have a show of hands,
please? Those wishing the animal to go to a zoo put up their
hands."

He counted. "Four... six... Are you holding up your hand,
Madam, or adjusting a hatpin?... Seven..."

"Wolf! If I loosened the net here, could you creep out?"
Polly whispered. She had discovered that she could pull the
edge of the net a little away from the bottom of the tea chest.

"If I make myself very thin."

"And if I do, will you promise...?" But Spectacles had now
finished the first count and there were too many people looking round. Polly waited till she heard the second counting
begin. Then she finished the sentence. "Will you promise not
to try to catch me to eat ever again?"

"Of course. I promise. Now let me out," the Wolf said, far
too quickly.

"You didn't mean that. Think about it."

The wolf thought. "You mean really, truly, never?"

"Really, truly, never."

"But it's been fun! Hasn't it?"

"Sometimes. Frightening, too."

"Being frightened is fun. And anyway, you're so clever,
Polly. You've always managed to escape up till now."

"You've never said I was clever before," Polly said.

"I didn't realize how clever you are till I heard you say that
about dangerous speeches," the wolf said.

Polly was pleased. She began to say, "Well, just promise..."
But the sentence never got said, for at that moment the wolf,
seeing that she wasn't thinking about holding the net as tightly

as before, pushed his head up and pulled it out of her hands. There was a bump, a crash, and a moment later, the wolf was out of the tea chest, free of the net, and was streaking down the High Street, terrifying passers-by and only just avoiding cars and bicycles.

Luckily no one blamed Polly.

"But I wonder what he thinks his natural habitat is? I'm sure it's not forests or hills, it's much more likely to be this village where he knows his way around," she thought and wondered if she would ever see him again. Probably. He wasn't likely to give up now that on this occasion it had been the wolf who had flattered and fooled her. Clever Polly had for once met a not-so-stupid wolf.

CATHERINE STORR (1913–2001) was born Catherine Cole and brought up in Kensington, London. A talented organist, she studied with Gustav Holst at St Paul's Girls' School. She graduated from Newnham College, Cambridge, with a degree in English literature and went on to study medicine. She began practicing as a psychiatrist in 1944 and worked at Middlesex Hospital in the 1950s and '60s before becoming an editor at Penguin in 1966. She published her first book, *Ingeborg and Ruthy*, in 1940, and married Anthony Storr, a fellow psychiatrist, in 1942. They had three daughters: Sophia, Emma, and Polly—for whom she wrote *Clever Polly and the Stupid Wolf* and its sequels. In addition to her stories about Polly and the Wolf, she went on to write some one hundred books for young readers and adults, including *Marianne Dreams*, *Marianne and Mark*, *Lucy*, and *Tales from a Psychiatrist's Couch*. About her work, she once remarked, "I don't write with a child readership in mind, I write for the childish side of myself."

MARJORIE ANN WATTS is the daughter of *Punch* cartoonist Arthur Watts. After training as a painter and illustrator in the 1940s, she worked for a time as an art editor and typographer before embarking on a career writing and illustrating books for children. In addition to her stories for young people, she has also published a novel, a story collection, a memoir of her childhood in wartime London, and a children's guide to European painting.

JILL BENNETT was born in South Africa and spent part of her childhood in Jamaica before moving to England. She studied theater design at the Wimbledon School of Art and did a postgraduate year at the Slade School of Art. She has illustrated more than fifty children's books, including Roald Dahl's *Fantastic Mr. Fox* and *Danny the Champion of the World*, and books by Helen Cresswell and Dick King-Smith.

RHODA LEVINE and EDWARD GOREY
He Was There from the Day We Moved In
Three Ladies Beside the Sea

RHODA LEVINE and KARLA KUSKIN
Harrison Loved His Umbrella

BETTY JEAN LIFTON and EIKOH HOSOE
Taka-chan and I

ASTRID LINDGREN
Mio, My Son
Seacrow Island

NORMAN LINDSAY
The Magic Pudding

ERIC LINKLATER
The Wind on the Moon

J. P. MARTIN
Uncle
Uncle Cleans Up

JOHN MASEFIELD
The Box of Delights
The Midnight Folk

WILLIAM McCLEERY and WARREN CHAPPELL
Wolf Story

JEAN MERRILL and RONNI SOLBERT
The Elephant Who Liked to Smash Small Cars
The Pushcart War

E. NESBIT
The House of Arden

ALFRED OLLIVANT'S
Bob, Son of Battle: The Last Gray Dog of Kenmuir
A New Version by LYDIA DAVIS

DANIEL PINKWATER
Lizard Music